GEORGIA COFFMAN

Stuck with the Movie Star
by Georgia Coffman

Olive Branch Bakery © Mae Harden
Editing by Amanda Cuff, Word of Advice Editing
Cover Design by Kari March
Paperback Formatting by Jill Sava, Love Affair with Fiction

To Kelly.
Thank you for all of your support and
encouragement while I wrote this book!

ONE

Madison

"Oh my God. Oh my God." I plop into the seat next to my friend Tessa, then sling my purse onto the table, rattling the silverware and margarita glasses on top of it. Our other two friends, Bree and Erin, stare at me from the other side of the half-eaten chips and salsa as I repeat, "Oh my *God*."

This is an *oh my God* times three moment, and it's the perfect news for margarita night, which has become our weekly tradition over the last two years. Same restaurant, same friends. Same familiar faces behind the bar too. The only thing we switch up is the margarita flavor. Sometimes we choose classic lime, but others, we go with strawberry or mango.

Tonight is a classic kind of night, evidently.

"What's going on?" Tessa asks at the same time Bree says, "If you're not going to follow that up with the fact that you finally got laid, don't bother continuing."

1

Erin sets her glass down as her innocent gaze bounces between us.

I stick my tongue out at my crude friend. "Is sex the only thing you think about?"

"It's all that matters outside of this table." Bree waves around us and shrugs, a mischievous twinkle in her expression.

Shaking my head, I grab a pitcher and fill my glass to the brim, then take a few gulps of the frozen drink. As I power through my brain freeze, I manage to say, "I met a guy."

Bree claps and sits up straighter. "Yes!"

Erin cracks a smile, and Tessa grips my forearm as she demands in the supportive yet enthusiastic tone I've come to know well, "Tell us everything."

"We met last week on one of those dating apps Bree set up for me."

"You're welcome." She takes a minibow from where she sits.

I toss my long red locks over my shoulder and lean forward to give them the scoop. "We've talked every day, and it's been so nice to have someone wish me good night, you know?"

"Hey," Erin cuts in. "I text you goodnight hugs all the time."

I move a crumpled napkin out of the way and place my hand on hers. "While that means a lot, it's nice for it to come from a guy I want to fork."

"No, no. Don't start that again." Bree wags her finger at me. "I thought we'd moved past *The Good Place's* Disney version of curse words."

"You're the reason I even got hooked on the show," I remind her, and Tessa and Erin agree.

"That might be true, but I thought we loved cussing too much to give it up just because a good show—*wait*." Bree narrows her eyes at me. "Did you say you *want* to fuck him? Like you haven't already?"

I almost choke on my margarita as I hold in my laughter. Damn. Bree loves juicy gossip more than a hair stylist and her hairspray. "I hate to disappoint you, but no, we haven't slept together yet."

"You came in here with promise!" Bree slumps back in her chair and crosses both arms over her chest like we're teenagers.

We pause when the bartender approaches our table to ask if we want refills. Our chorus of "yes" isn't even complete before she pulls a full pitcher of the deliciously sweet and tangy drink from behind her back like she's revealing gold.

Which, in a way, she is.

Since we frequent this restaurant and bar every Thursday, the staff know we're here more for the drinks than the chips and salsa—although we don't turn those down, either.

Shonda smiles as we exchange pleasantries. She's tending bar tonight instead of our usual "host," Harvey. He's the tattooed magician who serves the perfect margarita every week like he invented the drink, but Shonda's blend is good too.

After we thank her for the new round, Erin turns to me, a relaxed grin spreading as she toys with the rope bracelet around her wrist. "You were saying?" she asks evenly.

"We went on our first date earlier tonight, which is why I'm late." I smile around the salted rim of my glass.

Tessa scoots her chair closer to me. "Tonight? And it ended so soon?"

"You didn't leave early because of us, did you?" Erin frowns. "You should've just called. We wouldn't have held it against you."

"She's right," Bree chimes in.

"It wasn't because of you. He had to work early tomorrow, so we called it a night." I shrug, but internally, I scream in celebration.

I refuse to let Tessa's and Bree's remaining frowns change that.

Erin at least transforms hers and offers me a warm and positive smile, which puts me at ease.

But it only lasts for a second.

Erin's judgment of guys and dates is the worst of us all. If she's the only optimistic one, what does that mean for my case?

Bree lifts a perfectly waxed brow, thanks to yours truly. "Where did he take you—the mall?" She grimaces, her arms still crossed over her ample chest.

"No." I huff. "Chaz and I went to Central Park, drank coffee, and talked. It was refreshing not to worry about shopping for the right fancy outfit and spending hours getting ready, especially since I've been swamped at the salon this week." I toy with the stem of my margarita glass, getting lost in the recap of my evening with Chaz. He was polite and easy to talk to.

When the back of his hand brushed against mine, I felt giddy.

And when he kissed my cheek before we parted ways, it made me weak in the knees.

"But I did splurge on this pair of Lululemon leggings just for tonight. I probably should've spent the money on groceries, but I'm not sorry about my choice." I laugh, but it comes out squeaky.

I'm trying to save face, and it's not working—*damn it*.

"The only thing I like about this story is that you bought yourself some magnificent leggings. Seriously, your ass is rounder than a peach in those things," Bree praises.

"I don't know about his name. I knew a Chaz, and all he did was make jokes, even at my grandmother's funeral." Erin scrunches her nose up.

Tessa shushes them. "What this sounds like to me is the start of a nice and meaningful relationship. Jumping right into bed with a guy is not a good sign for your joint future." She stares pointedly at Bree in particular.

Bree holds her hands up in surrender. "I jump into bed with guys because I'm *not* interested in sharing a future. With anyone. Period."

We roll our eyes in sync. For as long as we've known Bree, she's been the perpetual one-night stand enthusiast. In the two years we've been friends, I don't think she's had a relationship for longer than a couple orgasms.

"Besides"—Bree scowls at Tessa—"you're only encouraging us to find long-lasting love because you're so damn happy with a billionaire hottie. Which is not fair, and I'm still mad at you, by the way. I'm mad at him too because he will no longer take my calls or answer my texts."

"That's because you keep asking him to send pictures of your ass to his friends," Tessa tsks.

Bree gasps, clutching her chest. "How dare you. I insist on him sending pictures of my *rack* to his friends. You know my ass is my least attractive feature."

"You did *not* just say that." I tilt my head in doubt. The woman has a figure that's worthy of a Times Square billboard—an hourglass shape with a perky ass that makes men do a double take every time she walks by.

Erin smacks Bree's shoulder. "You say a lot of ridiculous things, but that may be at the top of the list."

Bree wipes her lips with a napkin, leaving light pink lipstick smudges on the white cloth. "All right, all right. We're not getting into the top favorite things about myself when we have more important things to discuss." She straightens in her chair and scoots the wicker basket of remaining crushed-up chips to the side. *Here we go.* "Mads, can I be blunt with you?"

She doesn't give me a chance to respond, not that I was planning to. Bree Finley is going to tell me what she thinks no matter what, which is why I love her and our entire girl gang so much.

We tell each other the truth—always.

"It's not a romantic first date if he takes you to the same place that middle-aged men play weekend football and pigeons breed." I open my mouth to object, but she holds her finger up. "He took you on a free date, which obviously means he's not interested since he didn't invest in tonight."

"He bought the coffees…" I try to defend him, but then I recall that they were only a couple of dollars total since we ordered the small ones from a truck. Even a McDonald's burger costs more than that.

"Let me guess—he kissed you on the cheek at the end of the so-called *date*?"

"The air quotes are just rude." I glare at her. "But yes, he did."

"Oh, my sweet, sweet Madison." She gives me a tight-lipped smile that might seem sarcastic on anyone else, but Bree means it. Believe it or not, the tough love she's quick to give out is only meant to help us live our best lives.

But the truth stings.

"Fucking hell." I groan, then swipe my margarita glass from in front of me, nearly spilling the contents on myself. What would it have mattered, anyway? I'm a naïve and self-destructively positive woman. So what if I add "slob" to my resume?

I down the rest of my drink, giving myself another brain freeze.

"Normally, I'd say Bree is wrong. That Chaz is totally into you—he'd be crazy not to be." Erin bites her lip and glances at Bree before her eyes settle back on me. "But I made excuses for the guy who kept his own hair in the freezer, so what do I know?"

Bree holds her arms wide in an all-knowing gesture as Tessa and I shake our heads.

"It's true. I'm so rattled by my poor judgment that I've relinquished all control to Bree. She vets each of my dates now and consults on outfits, lipstick color, and even my toothpaste."

"Toothpaste?" I ask.

"I tried getting into a new brand after vegetarian guy suggested it, but it just turned my teeth green for two days. I couldn't leave my house." Erin shudders.

Bree rubs her arm sympathetically as I raise my full glass toward the center of the table. "To being single forever because it's better than settling for creeps and non-interested assholes." Tessa grabs her glass to clink with us, but I stop her. "You're happily engaged and not allowed to toast with us bitter single ladies."

"Bitter? Speak for yourself. But I do love a good toast." Bree clinks her glass to mine and Erin's as the three of us agree not to let Tessa join.

She's one of the lucky ones.

Although I'm thrilled Tessa found Carter and that they're engaged now, part of me is also insanely jealous. Their love story makes me hold on to hope that my initial instinct about Chaz was right.

That he'll call to ask me out again, and sparks will fly.

I've dated bad boys. Funny and silly guys. Spontaneous and chill guys too. They were exciting—for the most part, anyway—but they were all temporary stops along the way.

Since Tessa's engagement, I've realized I'm ready for something serious. I *want* to be in love.

And I want my search for it to be over already.

"No way!" Bree swipes her lit-up phone from in front of her. "They're filming *Ghost Predators* right here in the city," she says, her attention glued to whatever's on the screen.

"What's *Ghost Predators*?" Erin eyes us.

"The question isn't what it is, but *who* is starring in it." Bree grins coyly as she finally turns the phone screen around. "Ian Brock, ladies."

Instantly, I freeze, my tongue halfway out of my mouth to wipe the grain of salt from my bottom lip.

Bree reveals an image of a guy with short dark hair and a gorgeous grin, but it quickly blurs. The chatter from the restaurant becomes muffled as blood roars in my ears and flushes my cheeks.

Did I hear her correctly?

Did I see…

"Ian Brock!" my friend repeats.

Yep, I heard her and saw *him* right.

Tessa snaps her fingers. "Oh! Isn't he the guy from that Netflix movie—the romantic comedy? What's it called?" She waves for us to finish her thought.

It's on the tip of my tongue to cut in and put them out of their deep-thought misery, but thankfully, Bree's at our table. Her knowledge of Hollywood happenings expands across mountain ranges, so she promptly answers Tessa's question. "*Happily Ever Swingers*. The one where the couple thinks their new neighbors are swingers. Ian plays the hot neighbor husband, and I watch the scene where he takes his shirt off by the pool at least once a day now."

"You are so bad." Erin giggles as she applies Chapstick across her bottom lip.

I gulp, rubbing my suddenly sweaty palms over my spandex leggings.

I know the scene she's referring to—in fact, I know it too well.

It's clear in my mind, even though I watched the movie with Bree and Tessa almost a year ago. Erin would've joined us, but she had too many papers to grade and couldn't afford a distraction.

When the shirtless scene came on, my jaw came unhinged, and I hid my lusty reaction behind the enormous bowl of popcorn we were sharing.

"There's an open call for extras. Who's calling into work sick and joining me?" Bree's eyes land on every one of us for a few solid seconds each.

I pick up a chip with shaking fingers and answer, "No. Not a chance. Even if I wasn't already booked for the next few weeks, I still wouldn't go. You're insane as it is just by gawking at pictures of celebrities on the internet. I can't imagine what you'd be like seeing one in person."

"We do know, given how you still don't act normally around Carter, and he's been in our lives for over a year," Tessa teases.

"I'm with them." Erin shrugs toward Bree apologetically.

"I'll go alone, then." Bree juts her chin up.

"We'll be on standby to bail you out of jail." Tessa snorts.

"Cheers to bailing me out of jail." Bree raises her glass for another toast.

We clink, and I'm thankful when Erin switches topics to the meeting she just had with the principal at her school. She criticizes him about his coffee breath and constant use of "check it" in an attempt to be hip and cool.

My mind races as nostalgia takes over for the rest of the night.

I get lost in a time when Ian Brock was just Ian Bowman—our class clown.

And my first love.

When I knew him, he never watched movies much, preferring to make out during them, instead. But he's starring in films now. I've seen him in small roles here and there, but the last couple of years have been big for him, as he's played alongside headliners and household names.

No matter how many times I see his name in the media or floating across the screen, though, it's hard for me to wrap my head around the fact that it's the same person. That we went on to live such different lives after graduation.

And I often hate how unfair the universe is to have given him such a glamorous lifestyle—and smirk—when he deserves worse.

Karma really snoozed on that front.

I'm drained by the time we settle the bill, call out our goodbyes as we duck into cabs, and head home, the lights around the city blurring as I remain in this fog of memories.

When I finally reach my apartment and crawl into bed, I sigh. It was another successful girls' night out.

Until they mentioned my first heartbreak.

Ian and I haven't been in the same time zone since our breakup over ten years ago, and now, he's going to be in New York.

In *my* city.

The chances of running into him are slim to none—I'm more likely to meet Big Foot—but the fact that he'll be this close still puts me on edge.

Instead of falling straight to sleep like I'd hoped, I'm wired.

When my phone buzzes on the nightstand, I'm thankful for the distraction. I'm surprised to find Carter's name on my screen, though. He never calls me out of the blue, especially not at this hour—we're creeping up to midnight.

"Hello?" I ask warily. "Is everything okay?"

"You're going to love me more than you already do," he gloats. "And then, Tessa will love me even more than she already does, so really, this opportunity benefits us both. It's such a good one that I had to call right away, even though I know it's late."

"Don't leave me guessing." I laugh and put the phone on speaker, then grab the bottle of lotion from my nightstand.

"Tessa just got home from margarita night. Are you at your apartment too? And are you sitting down for this? You need to be sitting." The man is giddy and ridiculous right now. I can't imagine what he's going to say next. What is so important that it couldn't wait until the sun came up?

"Now you're just making me nervous," I say as I rub lotion down my shin and back up.

"A makeup artist for a movie has quit, and they're desperate to fill the position since they start filming in two days. I was on my way out of the office today and overheard the frantic woman charged with finding a replacement freaking out to my assistant. Evidently, they're friends from a different lifetime. Because I'm such a nice guy, I gave her your name. You'll be getting a call first thing in the morning, unless they're still on LA time and call any second." He sounds so thrilled and proud of himself.

But I'm panicking.

A movie? *Me* do makeup for actors for a freaking *movie*?

There's a long pause while I try to process what he's saying, and then he asks, "Are you getting a call yet?"

"No." I pinch my brows together.

"Damn. I thought for sure I'd say 'any second,' and you'd get a call."

I blink rapidly, bringing my bedroom in and out of focus as I rest my moisturized hands on my knees. "Carter, hang on."

I take a deep breath, and the lavender aroma infiltrates my senses.

But it does nothing to soothe my nerves.

"What are you talking about?" I ask. "Why would they agree to let me come on? I've never done film makeup before."

"But you're Madison Taylor." His tone grows serious, and the confidence in it makes my spine straighten like each syllable holds a string, tightly pulling it upward. "You are the best stylist I know, and I've used the best of the best—in the States and elsewhere. No one compares to your attention to detail and pride in your work. I didn't recommend you because you're friends with my fiancée. I did it because I have absolutely zero doubt you can and will exceed expectations."

My mouth falls open, and my chest expands. I was wired before, but his pep talk gives me a whole new rush.

"When they call, please do yourself a favor and accept their offer," Carter says. "Then knock them on their asses."

That's the last thing I get from him before he clicks off, and I stare at the phone like it's going to start ringing again with the proposition of a lifetime.

When it doesn't ring, I stand and pace by my bed, too amped up to lie down.

Can I really do this?

My mind racing, I head to the kitchen for a water but stop on the way and stare at my desk of nightmares, as the girls call it. They have a point. Four mannequin heads sit on top of my rustic desk, each with different makeup on both sides of their faces. A few wigs are strewn between them, and too many eye shadow palettes to count litter the rest of the surface.

I run my fingers over the dingy wooden desk I bought at a thrift store and study the pictures I've hung up on the wall as I dust the powder residue from my fingers. It's why I bought a cheap table to begin with—I knew it would get dirty and possibly ruined.

This is where I spend many nights. I lose sleep in order to practice the latest beauty trends to keep my skills sharp for when I expand into new territory.

The day I bought the first chair for my salon felt like the beginning of the rest of my life.

And it was. But I've never felt like that was the end of the line for me.

This movie gig could be just the exciting new thing I was looking for.

TWO

Ian

As I emerge onto the sidewalk after a subway ride from Hell, a blast of cold air from my left slaps my cheek.

And it's much better than a slap from my co-star.

When my agent called with news that I got the part in *Ghost Predators* and would be playing opposite Annalisa Hughes, I put my hand over the mic on my phone and squealed like a beauty pageant queen. I was excited for the lead role in a big-screen film, sure, but also because I'd be working with a Hollywood icon.

Just as I imagined it would be, it's been fun and games between table reads and interviews until Annalisa surprised me last night.

And not in a good way.

Annalisa Hughes might be a respected actress, but last night, she became my ex-girlfriend after she snuck into my hotel room to grill me over some of my Instagram messages from women I've never met.

I tried to reason with her that they were just fans. After all, she has three times as many herself, so I figured she would understand. But she wouldn't listen, and when I told her we should see other people, I don't think she heard that, either, given that she texted me first thing this morning to meet her.

Instead of accepting her invite, I'm currently sneaking into our final table read to avoid her and am damn proud of myself as I disappear into an alley undetected.

Until I slip on what appears to be melted ice cream on the asphalt, although it looks more like vomit.

Don't go there, Bowman.

Placing my palm on the wall next to me, I steady myself and check up and down the alley to make sure I'm still alone. Once I confirm that I am, I stand upright, only to realize I just leaned on the side of a dumpster instead of the brick wall, and now my hand is grimy.

"Fucking hell," I grumble as I pull my leather jacket tight with my clean hand to fight against the late winter chill. Hoisting my backpack higher onto my shoulder, I keep my head down and continue toward the front of the apartment building.

Luckily, the sidewalks are busy, and people are more preoccupied with staying safe from the chaotic cars winding through traffic to notice a naïve actor.

Over the last couple of years, I got caught up in the thrill of this industry and wanted a slice of the fantasy for myself. For a while, it worked too. It seemed like the Second Worlders from *Ghost Predators* had dropped me into the spiritual realm. Because while most of my life lately has been as glamorous as I expected Hollywood to be, the last couple of weeks have not, this particular moment included.

A cab driver honks at the U-Haul truck in front of him, and no matter how ridiculous I looked a moment ago as I slid through the alley like I'm about to rob a building, I give thanks that I'm not either of them. How the hell do they get those monsters down the narrow streets of this city? I'd take down signs and fire hydrants faster than a line of dominos falls.

At the corner of the building, I politely nod to a few women walking on the sidewalk, then search for Annalisa's dark hair. When I confirm there's no sight of her, I rush to the revolving door and duck inside.

Not even paparazzi have made me work this hard to hide.

"Hello, and welcome, Mr. Brock," the doorman greets me. He's "welcomed" me all week, each time like it's my very first visit.

Smiling, I continue toward the elevator at twice my normal walking speed and repeatedly push the button until I hear the ding of its arrival.

I let out a relieved exhale once the doors open on our director's floor. Richard is using the corner apartment during production, and while my suite at a five-star hotel in the heart of Manhattan is luxurious living, Richard's place is far beyond that.

I'd be worried we were imposing by using it for our table reads, but there are four separate rooms, each of which feels like it's in another part of the building with their different styles.

"My big star!" Richard exclaims as he ushers me inside.

I grab a coffee from the counter by the door and lift it between us. "Thanks for that, and this."

At one point in my life, I was accustomed to living and

working on a Texas ranch, where I spent summers helping my uncle herd cattle and sheep. Now, I'm more used to things like nice beaches, extravagant cast parties and movie premiers, and endless streams of coffee.

It's fucking nuts how fast life can change.

I set my coffee down and run to the bathroom to wash my hands of the goop from the alley. When I return, I take a seat at the table, where everyone else is already settled.

Empty cups and trash from a deli are herded to the middle of the rectangular wooden surface. The screenwriters, a producer, a few members from Richard's team, and the other actors greet me with variations of "good afternoon" and head nods.

"Howdy." I tip an imaginary ten-gallon hat, and they continue their conversation about the Met.

Even though most of them gush over it, it's not on my list of places to see while I'm in town. I much prefer the outdoors.

When the chatter lulls, I notice Annalisa is still missing. "Where's our Melinoe?" I ask the group cautiously.

One of the writers checks her phone. "We haven't heard from her yet."

I open my mouth to speak, but we're interrupted right as Annalisa storms into the room like the celebrity she is. Ripping her sunglasses off her nose, she shoots daggers at me, and I swear even her irises are red.

She's fuming, but she plasters on a smile and greets everyone, nonetheless, offering apologies and excuses for being late.

And we dive right in to reading lines, pausing less frequently than our first read-through for feedback and changes. We start filming tomorrow, so this is it.

For the next hour and a half, we bounce between dialogue, during which I'm simply Justin, an average guy from Mississippi who's tossed into the supernatural world after a mysterious and manipulative evil spirit knocks on his door.

Annalisa is just Melinoe, or Mel, the goddess of ghosts, who comes to help a confused Justin escape danger.

She and I fall in love and embark on a taboo affair.

It's an epic tale of true love and the greater good.

From what my agent says, *Ghost Predators* will be my "in" for more and bigger projects, and it'll help me branch out into other genres.

So far, I've mostly acted in teen movies and a few adult rom-coms. Although they were fun in their own way, it's not exactly the brand and reputation I was hoping for when I started out over ten years ago.

Of course, back then, I didn't even think a movie career was in the cards for me. After all, the closest I'd ever gotten to the movie industry was the year I worked at a video store back in Texas.

But here I am. I'm still trying to find my way, but this role makes me feel like I'm on the verge.

I just need to make sure I contain things between Annalisa and me.

She cut her eyes at me a few times, even when she and I were supposed to be happy.

What if her hostility seeps into her character while filming? *Fuck.*

"That's a wrap, folks!" Richard throws his script onto the table as I finish scribbling down the last of my notes.

We all cheer and clap as if this has been the hardest part of the whole process. Never mind we haven't begun filming yet.

"Ian, walk with me." Richard nods toward the other room, and I follow while the others linger around the table and coffeemaker.

Once we're out of earshot, I open my mouth to compliment his instruction, his fucking shoes—anything to wipe the stern look from his face—but he cuts me off.

"Whatever dispute you and Annalisa have ends now," the director warns, placing a hand on his hip. "There's no room for personal drama on the set, so leave it in your trailer tomorrow."

"Got it, and done."

He gives me a tight-lipped smile and turns his back to me as he puts his phone to his ear.

Guess I'm dismissed.

Out in the main room, I stuff the tattered notebook into my backpack and stand. I sling it over my shoulder as Patrick, one of the supporting leads, approaches me. "Nice job today, Ian."

"Right back at you." I fist-bump him and smile. "Takes a whole team to stop those ghosts."

"Right on. I love that you're always in character, man." He nods and falls into step with me.

I briefly glance over my shoulder for Annalisa but don't see her anywhere—thank God—and Patrick starts up again. "I've been meaning to ask. Who is your dialect coach? Your southern twang is so spot-on most of the time."

"Excuse me?" I tilt my head toward him as we exit Richard's place.

Patrick waves his arms and frantically says, "No, no. I'm so sorry. I didn't mean it in a bad way. I've just noticed that you fall into more of a Texas accent than a Mississippi drawl on occasion, but it's barely noticeable to the common ear. I've spent years training with various dialect coaches, so my ability to differentiate between accents is a bit superior, you could say."

I work my jaw back and forth as we step onto the elevator to take us down to the lobby. Since we're crammed in with some of the others from the team, I wait to address Patrick's question once the elevator spits us out.

Crossing the lobby, I explain, "I'm originally from Texas, so I didn't use a coach this time around. If I need one in the future, though, I know just the guy to come to for recommendations." I wink, then pick up speed to get ahead of Annalisa.

It's not the first time I've been asked about my accent. I've even had some casting directors and talent agencies turn me away because of it, but it's part of who I am. I'm not ashamed of it. Quite the opposite—I like it. It reminds me of home, which is comforting.

What I don't tell many people is that I lived in San Diego for the first eight years of my life. It's why I jumped at the chance to move back to California after high school to finish college and start my acting career.

Part of the reason, anyway.

My brother wasn't in southern California, so it seemed like the right place to go.

By the time I emerge onto the street, I'm itching for a beer.

Except I don't make it very far.

Annalisa stands outside the revolving door, her jean-clad hip jutting out and arms crossed over her chest. Her eyes hold a venomous color not even found in snakes, and the moment I halt, chills rack my body.

"Annalisa, hey." I rock on my heels, then lunge to the right to avoid the embrace she's trying to pull me into. "Great job today. You've really leaned into your character and—"

"What the hell is that supposed to mean?" She spins to face me as I sidestep a pedestrian. "Are you saying I'm a witch of some kind?"

"No…" I search around us to make sure I have witnesses if she decides to castrate me on the sidewalk. "Not a witch. You're a goddess in the movie. So, definitely not what I was referring to."

"I know what I am in the movie," she snaps.

"Right. Great. Glad we're on the same page. So I'll be going now." I hook a thumb over my shoulder and take a few steps backward.

But she just follows me, step for step. "Where the hell were you earlier? I waited for you for thirty minutes."

I tread carefully like I'm on the edge of a mountain. "I told you I want to see other people."

"So, we won't be hooking up anymore—is that what you're saying?" She purses her red lips.

"That's exactly what I'm saying, just like I did last night too."

"You didn't mean it."

"I did, though."

"You *didn't*," she insists through gritted teeth.

I don't realize I'm still walking backward until I bump into someone. They throw me a nasty snarl and carry on, leaving me alone with Annalisa and her murderous glare.

"Look, I'm sorry it didn't work out." I stop moving and hold a finger up. "But this is the end of the line for us. We're not together anymore, so you can feel free to go meet someone else. Someone who's into giant sunglasses like you are. Someone other than me." I mutter the last part under my breath as I catch Sarah coming out of the building, waving one arm in the air while the other clutches her phone to her ear.

"Bye," I say as I do dance moves that have never been popular in order to dodge Annalisa's attempts to hold me in place.

It's not that I'm the kind of douchebag who sleeps with women, then breaks their hearts, no matter how some media outlets portray me. Most of them call me a player. They say I have a hypnotizing smirk and enough exes to fill a stadium, but in reality, my ex-girlfriends couldn't even fill an elevator.

I'm just not great at confrontation or sharing bad news. Rather, making light of every situation is my strong suit.

As I near, Sarah jabs a finger at her phone screen, huffing.

"Everything okay?" I ask.

She jumps, snapping her gaze up to mine. "Oh, hey, Ian. Everything's fine now." She checks her phone and takes a deep breath. "Our makeup artist fucking quit because she decided at the last possible minute to move to Ohio to raise her newborn baby, and we start shooting tomorrow. But thanks to a dear friend of mine, I filled her position already and am free to deal with the rest of the headaches of movie prep."

"That sounds… great," I offer.

I'd say something more reassuring and positive, but I can't discern her mood. Sarah's robotic and determined tone regarding the original makeup artist makes it sound like she quit to lie on the couch and eat Doritos.

But she shared the good news in the same tone, so who can tell?

No matter how long I've been part of Hollywood, that's one thing in a long list that often catches me off guard in this industry. How straightforward and focused—sometimes even detached—people are. They keep their focus on the end goal and never turn sideways to check out the view. I've noticed people like Sarah are creatures of habit, much like my uncle's chickens with their coop. It's hard for her to break the sacred routine of crossing the next item off a list.

But I'm more like a goat with too much curiosity and desire to explore the adventure from point A to B.

"Jesus Christ," she grumbles, then strings along a few curse words before answering her ringing phone.

I nod to her, but she turns her back as she chews out whomever is on the other end of the line.

When I turn around, Annalisa is nowhere to be found. I take one long breath and cough as the cold wind hits my lungs.

Doesn't matter, though, because I'm a free man.

My conversation with Annalisa was successful, I knocked Patrick down a peg with my charm, and I'm in New York City.

"Time to explore," I say to myself and stand out of the way as a stream of people float by. I study each of their faces in search of a friendly one, which is harder to do than in LA.

These people don't get enough sunlight.

The streetlight changes color, letting the crowd cross, which decongests the sidewalk. A couple of women stroll by, relaxed and nonchalant like they have nowhere to go. *Bingo.* "Howdy," I greet them. "Do you know of a good place to get a drink around here?"

One of the women taps her chin, rocking sideways until

she stops to point across the street, where a yellow awning covers the entrance to a bar. "They have a ton of lagers, IPAs, and other stuff to choose from."

"Thank you kindly." I smile and set my sunglasses in place over my eyes. I'm about to step off the curb to cross the street but stop when I hear one of the women again.

"Wait." She places her hand on my shoulder. "You look so familiar."

The friend snaps her fingers. "Do you go to spinning class with Kirk?"

"No." The other one shakes her head, then squints at me. "You're that guy…"

"Ian Brock." I stick my hand out and give them my brightest smile. "Nice to meet you, ladies."

"Oh my God," they simultaneously whisper in awe, each carefully shaking my hand like it's made of thin glass. The blonde one even places a second hand over my knuckles and rubs the top of my hand like she's trying to conjure a genie in a bottle.

"I watched your Netflix movie while I was on my Peloton last week," she says. "I laughed so hard and almost fell off."

"I need to add *lethally funny* to my resume," I joke.

Giggling, they ask for a picture, and I oblige. When the signal turns again for us to cross, I wink and wave over my shoulder, a strange inkling settling in my stomach. How surreal is it to be recognized on the damn street? It happens every now and then in LA, but I didn't know what to expect on this coast.

I rub my chin, laughing under my breath.

I've been getting more and more attention lately, especially since I started dating Annalisa. This movie is generating a lot of buzz too, and many people have seen me on social media, the original catalyst for my budding acting career—one that's taken me to new places where I've met interesting people.

Life is fucking crazy, indeed.

As I enter the bar, my phone vibrates with a new message from my agent, who's more like my big brother than the one I actually have.

At least Keith and I are friends.

> **Keith:** Don't get too comfortable over on the other side of the country. You need to get back here as soon as possible to save me from endless tea parties and dance recitals!

I chuckle as I recall all the times he's shown up for a beer on the beach with glitter nail polish on his toes, courtesy of his toddler twin daughters. He loves them more than anything, but as the only testosterone in the household, he needs an outlet.

> **Me:** You know I love the beach and warm weather too much. I'm actually surprised my balls haven't frozen yet.

I run my gaze over the different beers available on tap. As I order one, I settle onto a stool, letting the chatter and music fill my ears and calm my nerves. I might be alone here tonight, but it's better than going back to my empty hotel and pacing the floor of my suite, which was my alternative.

In any case, I need a minute to myself to celebrate.

I start filming a fucking movie tomorrow.

No matter how many I've been a part of or what I'll do in the future, I make it a point to celebrate each one.

Because I'm living the dream, and I won't let anything stand in my way of holding onto it.

THREE

Ian

Ghosts.

There are so many of them roaming the base and scarfing down breakfast burritos from the food truck.

I've arrived at the set with plenty of time to spare, call sheet rolled and wrinkled in my crushing grip as I take in the trailers and trucks, crew members scrolling their iPads, and of course, the extras dressed as ghosts.

I blink around to take it all in and smile, growing more enamored by the buzzing atmosphere.

Creativity floats around us like magic fairy dust, and it's all more intoxicating than the five beers I had last night with a guy named Willis while we played Jenga.

I check the time and note I still have ten minutes before I need to be in costume, so I move to the side and out of the way, where I unroll my call sheet and skim down to my name. When I first held one of these sheets, I got so overwhelmed with the long list of crew members, scene descriptions, production team, and other relevant people that I needed a shot of whiskey.

It felt like we were teaming up to solve world hunger or something.

Then, I quickly figured out that not every box on the call sheet applies to me, so I zero in on my parts alone. Makes it much easier to focus.

Once I scan the scenes we're filming today and refresh my memory, I glance up to the makeup slot to check if I recognize the name of the new person, but it just says *TBD*. Humming, I put the pieces of paper in my backpack and stuff my hand into my pocket as I make my way to the wardrobe trailer, a gust of cold wind biting at my cheeks.

I hope whomever Sarah got for makeup can cover my red nose, or else this movie's turning into a holiday film starring Rudolph.

As I walk, I check my phone for any new messages from Annalisa. She texted me a few times last night like nothing's changed, but I didn't respond.

How many other ways can I tell her it's over?

Would telling her about Richard's warning help? She cares about this movie and her career as much as I do, so it could work to tell her the director will be pissed if we don't get our personal shit together.

Then again, it would probably fuel her advances, instead. After I saw the darker side of her the night she snuck into my hotel room, I wouldn't put it past her to use this pressure as leverage over me.

This is a damn nightmare.

Patrick exits the trailer, decked in a dark suit. It's his

costume for his role as the evil spirit who comes to manipulate my character. He looks nothing like the guy in a bright salmon shirt and khakis from our table read yesterday.

"Good morning." I nod, standing to the side to let him by.

"Brock." He gives me a tight-lipped smile, then dips his head back down to the script in his hands, his eyebrows furrowed.

I watch him as he continues reading and walking, almost bumping into a pair from the camera crew moving equipment into position. Without glancing up, Patrick moves out of the way at the last second like he has a third eye.

I'd think the whole thing odd, especially his short interaction with me, but I've come to know that's how he is. Focused and driven, whether we're discussing dialect coaches or preparing for the first day of filming.

I disappear into the trailer and welcome the instant heat that warms my cheeks. "Morning, Dola."

The short woman shuffles some hangers of clothes around, then locks gazes with me. "You and your smirk. No wonder Annalisa's obsessed with you."

"Now you're just being too kind," I joke, but inwardly, I cringe.

Dola giggles and shoves a T-shirt at my chest, and I wrap my hand around it. She chews on her bottom lip as she reaches for my pants, and I thank her before disappearing behind a curtain to change.

Once I'm fully dressed, she doesn't do much else since I'm supposed to be as plain as they come. Finished with me, she sends me on my way, but not before she kindly teases, "Don't break too many hearts today. We have ghosts to deal with."

Winking, I check my phone and confirm I'm still on time. I also check a new message from my mother, who wishes me good luck on my big day. I text her back and receive an immediate response that she's so proud of my brother and me both.

It's as if he's standing over her shoulder and wanting to make sure he doesn't go unnoticed.

I scoff under my breath and tuck my phone away as I reach the trailer for hair and makeup. I'm just about to climb the few steps up to the door when a flash of red catches my eye. Turning to fully face the familiar mane of thick and wavy hair, I note a unique shade of bright red with almost blonde streaks.

The morning rays cast a glow around her in a brilliant aura. When she tosses her long strands over one shoulder and glances in my direction, my knees almost give out. Like I'm suddenly too heavy to stand on them.

I know her.

Wait. How is she here?

It can't be.

"What are you doing here?" she asks, stopping a foot away from me and blinking faster than flashing disco lights.

My body comes alive, even though she asks the question with a mix of shock and disgust—emphasis on the latter.

But that's not what I focus on.

I continue staring at her like she'll vanish if I blink. I haven't seen or talked to her in years, and yet, it's unmistakably her.

Madison Taylor.

Once upon a time, I spent night after night contemplating what I'd say to her if I ever saw her again. And now's my chance.

Except my mind is blank.

Her gaze darts around us, bouncing to the trailer, to Sarah who whizzes by as she rambles on the phone, then to the asphalt.

Until she finally peers up at me.

"This is *your* movie." She says it as if understanding just dawned. Like some piece of an unknown puzzle finally landed in place.

"That's right, gorgeous," I manage, then clear my throat. "Madison Taylor," I say in awe, sweeping my gaze over her.

She was tall in high school, but she's even taller now, with long, slim legs to boot. Her breasts grew two cup sizes, and her eyes are a deeper green than they were at seventeen.

She's every bit a woman and every man's wet dream.

"Ian Brock," she says, and I instinctively wince. Why does it bother me that she didn't use my real name?

Her expression brightens the longer she stares at me, and a slow grin spreads as she says, "How cool is it that you're an actor now?" She reaches out and squeezes my bicep, nodding her approval.

Instantly, I wish I wasn't wearing this thick coat so that I could feel more of her. Would her touch be warm and familiar?

"And you're so fit. Then again, you always were—star football player and all."

I shrug, easing into my stance as I try to reacquaint myself with this spitfire I once knew. "You remember how athletic I was on the football field?" I wink, using my signature charming tone.

"I do," she says and drops her voice to a seductive whisper. "Will you be doing any stunts during production? Any flips? Hanging by a rope, perhaps?"

I lean in, cupping my hand around one side of my mouth like I'm telling her a secret. "I have a stunt double, but I will be briefly suspended in the air for one shot. I'm—"

"Great. I hope you fall on your ass," she snaps, losing every bit of amused mischief she just held.

"What?" I frown, extremely confused.

She brushes past me, bumping my shoulder with hers with extra force like she wants to hurt me herself instead of waiting.

I jump when she slams the door, and surprisingly, it jostles my memory. "Oh, right," I mutter as more than one incident pops into my brain.

There's a slew of reasons she'd be pissed at me, and I wouldn't blame her for any of them.

Madison Taylor would be considered *the one who got away* by anyone from a Hollywood screenwriter to a Nashville country singer, but there's so much more to the story.

I skip to catch up to her and fling the door of the trailer open, then skim over the line of chairs and lights across the top of the mirrors. The counters are white, as are the walls, but the chairs are black, giving the room a modern minimalist appearance.

But I don't think it was on purpose. Just practical and reasonable.

Neither of which I would use to describe Madison right now.

She jerks a swiveling chair to face a mirror as I enter, and the space seems more cramped with the three of us—me, Madison, and her rage.

"Remember IBS?" I start, easing into a self-deprecating memory to lighten the mood as I near her like I would a dicey science experiment. "That Collin Johnson was a real clever thinker in high school."

"Oh, he wasn't the only one to figure out that *Ian Bowman Sucks* is also a bowel movement acronym," she says, her tone sarcastically sweet. "Oh, wait. It's Ian *Brock* now."

"Shit. You're still mad about junior bio."

"Mad that you flung a *worm* at Joey Tanner but missed, and it landed in my hair, and then I had to wash it repeatedly and eventually ended up chopping off six inches because I could still smell the formaldehyde?" She clutches her chest dramatically and deadpans, "Now why would such a thing piss me off? Really, I'm just glad you weren't our quarterback, because that arm of yours wouldn't have done us any favors."

"Wow." I blink. "You remembered the word *formaldehyde*—you're beyond pissed."

She twists her lips, and her eye twitches. "What's that supposed to mean? I'm too dumb to remember the name of a chemical?"

Frowning, I lurch forward. "No! That's not at all what I'm saying."

"It sure sounds like it is."

"Biology just wasn't your best subject. You were better at English and history."

"Gee, it's mighty gracious of you to give such a compliment." Her Texas drawl grows deeper as the red in her neck spreads up to her nose like she's cold.

"Lord, you're just as stubborn as I remember," I muse, recalling the whole scene of the worm incident like it happened yesterday. Then more memories of Madison and me flood my mind. It all feels like it just occurred, especially now that the shock has worn off.

I mean, I never expected to see her again, let alone run into her on a movie set.

But damn, here she is, sharp tongue, sass, and all. She's the slice of home I needed, even though the only thing she's done so far is insult me and wish me harm.

Again, as I mentally take note of the long list of things she could be mad about, I don't blame her.

"Sit." Arching an angry brow, she points to the seat. "This is my first time doing makeup for this sort of thing, but I was given strict and detailed instructions on the tight schedule—although nowhere in the middle of all that was I told I'd be working with *you*. Nonetheless, we need to get moving." She checks her watch, then grabs a bag and unzips it to reveal brushes, glass bottles of foundation, and other items.

I do as I'm told and sit, but I can't stop myself from squirming. Since when did makeup trailer seats become so uncomfortable? "I didn't know this is the line of work you're in."

"There are a lot of things you don't know about me," she clips, holding on to her grudge like I once did a football.

But as she leans close to stuff napkins inside the collar of my shirt to keep it from getting dirty, the fire in her green eyes engulfs me.

And not all of it is from anger toward me.

It's like the dark whiskey-colored flecks in her irises are speaking to me—to say they're not mad, but sad.

When she applies the first of a lightweight foundation to my skin, her nostrils flare, and I tense as her warm breath hits my lips, reminding me of the way she used to kiss me.

She was so passionate, and it wasn't because we were teenagers in wild lust. She was insatiable in every sense of the word—spontaneous, strong-willed, sexy.

After that worm landed in her hair, she leapt over the

table toward me, claws out and vengeance in her soul before she pulled out the slimy—and very dead—creature from her head.

All she wanted was to make me pay, which she kept repeating under her breath during the rest of class.

I paid too.

It happened after football practice when I was tired, and my guard was down. I reached my car and opened the door without peering inside first, and wouldn't I know it? Madi had put a cake in the driver's seat, and I sat on it.

To further humiliate me, the entire football team saw, and Collin Johnson recorded the whole thing. The bastard lived to embarrass me.

I had to hand it to Madi, though—it was hilarious.

And one of the many reasons I fell for her.

"Stop smiling," she cuts into my thoughts. "The crinkles around your lips are leaving creases in the makeup."

"Your wish is my command."

But my attempt at a joke does nothing to penetrate her cool expression as she smooths in the areas above my cheeks, then grabs a brush.

"What about the time I crashed my dirt bike into your garage door? Is that why you're mad?"

She sighs. "That would be why my father still hates you. It didn't help that you drank half his whiskey afterward." A ghost of a smile plays across her pink lips, and I lean forward for a better view of it.

It takes me back.

Back to the fun we used to have—damn, the good ole days, indeed.

Madi quickly drops any sign of a grin like it was an

accident to begin with and straightens her posture as she rips the napkins from my collar. "You're all set," she says, and she might as well have told me to eat shit.

Grabbing her wrist, I stop her and stand, rising to my full height, which is only a couple inches taller than her. I rake my gaze over her face, searching for the girl I used to know, and she's there. In every subtle freckle sprinkled across her nose and cheeks.

In the curve of her lips.

The wide eyes that constantly look like they're amazed by the world.

Her sweet perfume wraps around all my senses, and I inhale my fill like it's calling to me—I'm mesmerized.

I open my mouth to ask her to meet me for dinner later so that I can start to make everything up to her, but the door to the trailer swings open, making us both jump.

"Hi." A young woman enters, waving and slinging her bag onto the minisofa along the opposite wall. "I'm Searcy, the makeup artist's assistant," she says, digging into the bag.

"Right." Madison pulls her arm from my grasp to shake Searcy's hand, and she introduces herself as well. She glances back at me, checking me over, then points to the chair. "Wait. This side looks darker. Sit."

As we get back to work, I eye Madison while she and Searcy exchange tips and instructions, as well as war stories of their industry.

I don't get a word in as more people file in and take the seats lining the wall of the trailer, bright bulbs illuminating us all, but it's like I'm invisible.

"Okay." Madison drops the brush onto the counter and stands upright.

As I rise from the chair, Searcy goes to the other side to keep working like she's playing duck, duck, goose with the actors.

"So, listen…" I wipe my suddenly clammy palms down my pants.

Madi's nostrils flare as she stares at me in the mirror, and I spin around, grasping her wrist again.

But I don't have a chance to finish what I want to say this time, either.

The door to the trailer opens again, and my last chance to ask Madi to dinner floats out into the breeze.

Annalisa steps inside, takes one look at my hand on Madi's wrist, and scrunches her face, anger etched into every moisturized feature. "What the hell is going on here, Ian? Is *she* why you don't want to date me anymore?"

I grind my jaw.

She pins her stare on Madi. "I'm Annalisa Hughes. But I'm sure you already know that. And you are?" Her deep and sudden inhale is loud, and the trailer grows tense. "You know what? Never mind. It doesn't matter."

She continues rambling, but I don't make out what she says. Madison's cheeks are red, and she purses her lips like they're zipped closed.

We might not have seen each other in over ten years, but I can still read her. And she obviously wants to tell Annalisa off but is afraid of the consequences.

"Ian, are you trying to make me jealous? Because you know I hate games, but this one might be working. I'm super—"

"Listen, Ian and I are n—"

"We're together!" I blurt, holding our joined hands up like that's all the proof Annalisa needs.

The other four people in the trailer snap their attention to us.

Annalisa gasps, and Madi turns her narrow glare toward me, mouthing, "What the fuck?"

I force a smile and tighten my grip on her hand, silently begging her to go along with this. I turn back to my co-star-slash-stalker and take a leap. "We're old friends"—*not a lie, actually*—"and we reconnected now that I'm in New York, which is where she lives." *Also not a lie.* "One thing led to another, and we're dating again." I shrug, still holding Madison's warm hand in mine.

Annalisa crosses her arms, studying both of us like she's looking for any tiny flaw in my story.

After a brief pause, I lean over and kiss Madi's cheek, inhaling her sexy scent one more time and whispering in her ear for good measure, "Please. I'll explain later."

She schools her grimace and turns toward Annalisa. "It's so great to meet you," she bites out, her face even redder than before. "Ian, *sweetie*," she says, turning to me. "I'll see you later, okay?"

"Can't wait. I'll call you about dinner tonight." I wink, which earns me a subtle you-will-die-in-your-sleep glower.

She grins so hard that it causes her to squint, and she appears to be in pain.

Just like I will be by the time she's done with me.

As I leave the trailer, I just know Madison's going to get me back for this like she did the worm incident. But worse. I mean, she's had over ten years to plot my demise, and now I've given her more than enough bait to carry out each excruciating revenge act.

In all fairness, I did just fucking ask her to pretend to date me so that my delusional co-star would get off my back. I didn't plan on this, but it could work.

It seemed like Annalisa bought it and will finally end the insanity of constantly texting me.

We'll be able to film in peace and avoid compromising our careers in the process.

But there's one major problem with all this—Madison Taylor.

I don't know the when, what, or how, but she is definitely going to make me pay for this.

FOUR

Madison

Ian Brock is going to pay for what he did.

A fake relationship and a kiss on the cheek? Seriously?

It's been almost a week since his little announcement, and I already miss having anyone in my chair other than Ian. Our busy schedule has done nothing to distract me or curb the fury inside me, especially since I've had to be nice to him to keep up appearances.

Once he explained how badly he needs this movie to go well, I felt bad enough for him to play along, but I don't like it one bit.

I'm contemplating which is worse: pretending to like my asshole ex, that he put his stupid soft lips on me, or that he told *Annalisa freaking Hughes*—mega-talented Hollywood star with gorgeous silky hair and naturally bronzed skin—that I'm his girlfriend.

Annalisa is a lot cattier than I imagined her, and it was surprisingly satisfying to make her jealous. But it wasn't enough to keep bile from rising in my throat, especially since Ian kissed my cheek again this morning—that takes the cake for the day.

The only reason I didn't knee him in the balls right then and there was because he swiftly produced a fresh cup of coffee from behind his back with my name on it.

How dare he. How *fucking* dare he!

Seething, I clean my brushes without the gentle care I would normally use. My skin is prickling with heated rage, and all the hairs on my arms stand at attention just like my nerves, ready to fire the minute my brain gives them the go-ahead.

All it would take is one more dumbass comment or lie from Ian.

I toss the brushes onto the counter and rub my hands down my legs, my fingers tingling as I remember touching his face.

The cheek he's now kissed twice suddenly burns.

I've been flustered, trying to learn the dos and don'ts of a movie set. Yesterday, I even knocked over a table of donuts in an embarrassing attempt to jump out of the crew's way while they moved props.

On top of all the chaos, I've resented the fact that Ian's only gotten hotter since we were teenagers. Watching him on a screen did not do him justice in the slightest. His jaw is so much sharper. His voice is deeper and sexier too.

His cologne—God, his cologne—is more intoxicating than ten bottles of champagne.

Here I actually believed that the universe would go easy

on me. Instead, it's sitting in the front row, eating popcorn, and laughing hysterically.

Because instead of having a magical first week on a movie set, I've spent it shocked and angry because of the guy who broke my heart as a teen.

Given the events of this week and the lies he's told, Ian is still the asshole I remember.

Standing alone in the middle of my salon, the sun long set by now, I stretch my neck from side to side, then raise my hands over my head, feeling the pull in my abs. Bending down to my toes, I stretch my back the way Erin's taught me from all her years of doing yoga. Because of my crazy schedule, I don't usually go to classes with her, but she's done so many that she's practically an instructor herself.

Which is why she's my health and wellness accountability partner.

"Ow," I mutter to myself when something in my lower back pops.

This has been a long, tense week, and it's evident in every muscle.

More importantly, I still feel Ian's dumb lips on my cheek like he branded me.

I stare at my flushed complexion in the mirror and frown just as my phone rings. Sighing with relief for a distraction, I swipe to answer and greet my friend.

"Are you coming? We're on our second pitcher of margaritas." Tessa's voice comes through my speaker.

I spin on my heel for one last check to make sure everything is in its place for tomorrow. After each day of filming, I've rushed over here to relieve Sofia from cleanup duty since she's covered—aka *saved*—my ass this week and every day before this. She's been my number two for the last few years, and she's a big reason the salon runs so smoothly.

Sofia is also insanely supportive and agreed to cover for me without hesitation, so the least I can do is finish cleaning and locking up each night.

"I'm on my way," I say to Tessa.

Keys and purse in hand, I leave through the front and lock the door behind me.

"Hey, Madison. Working late tonight?" a woman asks from behind me.

I turn to find Missy, a regular at the salon, walking backward to cross the street. "How else am I going to earn my spot in *Forbes*?" I wave to her as she giggles and disappears around the corner.

The community the salon has cultivated is one of the things I'm most proud of. Although we have our fair share of complainers—or joy stealers, as Sofia calls them—most of our clients are fun and amazing to work with. It's what makes the job enjoyable, and even though I've been absent for only a few days, I miss them.

I just couldn't pass up this opportunity, especially when Sarah offered to pay me an obscene amount of cash.

Once I hail a cab and settle in, I rest my head against the back. I contemplated missing girls' night out, but I'm too wired to sleep, anyway.

Besides, I need to vent before I explode, and they're the best listeners.

We come to a stop in front of the corner restaurant and bar that's become like a second home for us. After I'm finished paying, I step out and into the busy establishment, where I quickly spot my group of friends.

I make it just in time to overhear Bree's conversation with Harvey.

"When are *you* going to be on the menu?" she teases, her smile suggestive but completely harmless. It's nothing she doesn't say on any other Thursday night—to him or to any other hot dude in New York, for that matter.

I swear, the woman is on the prowl twenty-four seven.

Harvey leans down and says, "You can always consider me on the menu." He gives her a wink, which earns howls from Tessa and Erin.

I take my jacket off and join them, tugging up the sleeves of my sweater. "I'd ask what I missed, but it doesn't seem like anything's different since the last time Harvey was here."

Bree shrugs as he backs away to tend to other customers. "You should ask him to participate in the bachelor auction," she tells Tessa.

"What?" I ask, searching each of the girls for any indication of what they're talking about but come up empty.

"The Everyday Bachelors Auction we're hosting this May to raise money for charity." Tessa snags a chip from the basket. "I would've asked Harvey had we not filled up faster than I could blink. Ava had to start a waitlist."

I point to the empty pitcher in the center of the table. "Looks like I've missed out on more than just margaritas tonight."

Erin twists her lips, glancing suspiciously at me. "Where have *you* been? Are you already too famous and superior for your friends?"

Bree slaps the table, and I practically jump out of my skin. "What the hell, Mads? You have some serious explaining to do." She holds her finger up, stands from her seat, and leans over the table toward me. "I might be drunk, but I'm thinking clearly enough to be miffed by your deceit."

"I couldn't tell by the hundred texts and voice mails I've gotten from you," I deadpan. "You didn't even text me that much when I had the flu last winter."

Lifting her shoulder, she laughs along with me as she lowers herself onto the seat again.

"You've been here for five whole minutes, and you haven't told us all about the movie set you're now working on," Erin whispers, her words almost as slurred as Bree's. "Congratulations, by the way. We're super proud of you. Like, *super*."

Oh, hell. Erin's using her high-pitched sorority girl voice, which means she's toasted.

I'm a lot later than I planned.

The second Harvey sets a fresh pitcher in front of us, I ask for two tequila shots and pour myself a glass. "I need to catch up." I grin at him and turn back to my girls, who all stare at me. At least, they try to. Tessa seems to be the only one who's remotely sober. The other two watch me through lazy gazes like their eyelids weigh too much.

I take a gulp, then lick my lips for every last drop. "So, thanks to Tessa, you already know about Carter's little stunt to get me on the team for the movie before I could announce it, but there's more."

"Yeah!" Bree scoffs. "You're working with Ian fucking Brock, bitch."

Time to rip off the Band-Aid.

"Y'all are going to lose your shit." I gulp down more of my drink.

Once I finish swallowing and take a deep breath, Bree slaps the table again. "You're killing us!"

I clear my throat, then blurt, "Ian Brock and I used to date."

In unison, they repeat, "Oh my God" three times.

And this moment definitely calls for the Holy Trinity of gossip.

I thank the server, who sets down two shots of clear liquid with limes on the rims. I bring them both to my lips, toss them back, then suck on the lime for dear life. This was exactly what I needed in order to get through the excruciating details of my week.

Even if I didn't need to get all this out for my own health, they're my best friends. I can't not tell them, especially since I'll be working with the spawn of Satan for the next few weeks until they go back to LA to finish filming in a studio.

"Wait. Wait. *Wait.*" Bree is the first to speak—unsurprisingly. "Start from the beginning. What the hell are you talking about?"

All heads turn toward me at once.

I let out a long exhale as I pour myself another margarita. "I went to high school with Ian, and I knew him when his name was Ian Bowman."

Bree's jaw drops so low I'm afraid it'll hit the table, and Tessa and Erin have their own versions of that reaction—they're all too shocked for words.

I wave my hands. "It's not a big deal, and I never mentioned it because he wasn't a fucking movie star before. He was just Ian, the guy who took my virginity. I mean, I happily gave it to him, of course, but—"

"Oh my *God*," Bree exclaims again. "You mean to tell me that Ian Brock was your first, and I'm just now finding out about it?"

I shrug and purposely leave out the part where the pig told Annalisa Hughes that I'm his girlfriend. Not only do I need them sober for that part, but also, the fewer people who know about the charade, the better.

Besides, only a handful of people know, and I'm positive that the whole thing will blow over faster than a snowstorm in Texas.

"Holy shit," Bree says, rubbing her lips as she stares at her phone. "Ian fucking Brock is sexy as all hell, and I've never been so jealous of anyone in my entire life." She jerks her head up and looks at Tessa. "I mean, this might be bigger news than Tessa getting engaged to a billionaire, especially one as hot as Carter."

Tessa clutches her chest. "You bitch."

Bree holds her hands out. "I call them like I see them, and Ian is a chiseled masterpiece. I knew Texas cowboys were hot, but they bred something extra special on those farms when they made him." She purses her lips and pins her icy stare on me. "And I can't believe I've known you for almost two years and am just now finding out this secret of yours!"

"I have *so* many questions," Erin adds.

Bree leans back against her chair, her eyes twitching like she's working a math problem in her head. Then, she holds her finger up. "Before we get to yours, I have one important question I need answered. How do I have two best friends who know famous people? Erin, do you have a famous brother or cousin I should know about?"

"My dad used to live next to a porn director before he married my stepmother."

My head swivels toward Erin. "What?"

"Your stepmom was married to a porn director?" Bree blinks at our friend.

Tessa's laughter bursts out of her. "She meant her dad lived next door to one."

Erin shrugs. "I didn't know it at the time, but it's why my mother wouldn't let me visit him much as a kid."

"Okay, how did we not know about *that*?" Bree asks.

"It's never come up," Erin says indifferently. "I didn't go to my dad's often, so it's not like I saw anything good from his neighbor."

Tessa and I snort as Bree mutters, "Shame."

"I was nine when he moved out of that place. I'm actually glad I didn't see anything, and therefore, wasn't scarred." Erin stares pointedly as she picks up her drink.

Tessa points her finger at Bree. "Don't play all innocent, ma'am. I only found out last week that you have a sister!"

"Fuck," Bree mumbles, sinking lower into her chair. "And don't call me *ma'am*. That was just cruel."

"A sister? What the hell?" I throw my hands up. "Are we even friends at all?"

"I haven't mentioned her because she doesn't live around here, and it's been ages since I last saw her." Her lips form a line so tight they disappear altogether.

"What's the story there?" I prop my elbow on the table.

"Don't change the subject." Bree rubs her temples like she's trying to wrap her head around rocket science. "Your first was Ian freaking Brock?"

I nod and am about to share the ending to that tale when Tessa turns her concerned gaze to me. "Wait…" She searches my face, and I grimace.

I see the exact moment understanding dawns.

We were roommates in college, and as my oldest friend, she knows me better than anyone, so I'm not surprised when she asks, "He's the one who disappeared on you after graduation, isn't he?"

"One and the same," I confirm.

Erin reaches over to rub my hand in comfort.

Bree drops the shocked and entertained gleam in her expression and furrows her brows. "Start from the beginning, and please let me know if I should start a nasty rumor about him for the gossip mill. I'll make a hashtag so fierce that it'll go viral, for sure."

"It's not necessary." I wave her off, giggling. "But thank you."

"We're here for you." Tessa gives me a sympathetic smile.

"There's not much to tell." I exhale. "Ian was the class clown and our star football linebacker before he made his way onto the screen. I didn't know he was acting until a few years ago, and then there was that Netflix movie."

"I forgot about that!" Bree snaps her fingers—she tries to, at least. She doesn't make much of a sound since her fingers barely even touch each other. "And you didn't feel the need to tell us about him back then?"

"I'm glad she didn't since I wasn't there and would've missed all this." Erin sips from her straw, attention glued on me like I'm a big veggie burger, which is her new favorite thing lately.

"Are you sure you're even going to remember any of this tomorrow?" I ask Bree, who's now leaning so far forward over the table that I'm surprised she isn't out of her seat.

She nods so fast it makes me dizzy. "Spill."

"Okay," I draw out, squirming in my seat and psyching myself up for this. "He was the butt of a few jokes, but it was all in good fun. Everyone loved him. He was always pulling crazy stunts on people, even our teachers." I clap my hands as I lose myself in the fonder memories of my teen years. "His pranks started small when he worked at a video store one year. He was always hiding in the booth outside where people dropped off their rentals." I shake my head, smiling wistfully. "Ian got into trouble every other week, but he just found other ways to mess with people. By the time graduation rolled around, he'd scaled up for his final hoorah."

"What did he do?" Bree freezes with her drink halfway to her lips.

"The night of graduation, he'd rigged the podium to release confetti and balloons the second our principal walked up to it. He'd also paid off the AV club with GameStop gift cards and seized control of the final slideshow. His version had not been pre-approved by the principal, and although it wasn't family-friendly, it did paint a more accurate picture of our high school experience. Jocks in the locker room giving each other wedgies, cheerleaders smoking, and what not."

"Wow." I'm not sure who this comes from. I'm taken back to that night on our football field, where rows of chairs faced the stage that we walked across to receive our diplomas and become adults.

I swallow to try and wet my dry throat. "Ian Bowman became a legend, and those memories are the last ones I have since I never heard from him again. We'd promised to stay in touch and try the long-distance thing, but he'd moved out west without a word or explanation."

"That sucks, Mads." Tessa leans her head on my shoulder.

"You know what you should do?" Bree rubs her hands together, mischief written all over her face. "You should make him look like a vampire for this movie. Put white makeup on him, draw thick black eyebrows, and have red streaks running down his mouth. That'll show him."

"And I'd also lose my job," I point out, suppressing a smile. "I might've just started, but I'd like to see it through for at least another week."

"I guess," she says sarcastically.

"Besides, it was over ten years ago." I shrug, downplaying it.

Ian is in the past, after all, and we're not even friends, let alone dating—not for real, anyway.

"I'm coming with you to the set, by the way," Bree announces. "For backup."

I clink my full glass to hers, and we continue talking about our week, what's new on Netflix, and our current argument against whatever healthy food Erin recommends.

By the time I get home, I've made up my mind to keep things with Ian professional, no matter what stupid lies he tells his co-workers.

We've made it almost a week without our lives being upended, right? A few more will be no problem.

He can fend off his ex for whatever reason he thinks is valid, and I can work an exciting job.

We'll each get through this in one piece, I'm sure of it.

FIVE

Ian

I won't make it out of this alive, I'm sure of it.

Annalisa stares at me, her gaze unwavering and terrifying. When did she stop blinking?

Things were going so well too.

The first week of filming has been incredible. I've been on point with my acting, chemistry with Annalisa on the screen has been exactly what the director wants, and my co-star hasn't made a move on me since finding out about my relationship with Madison.

However fake the latter might be.

The only thing that's been off is Madi's uncharacteristic silence. When I knew her, she never stopped talking for longer than it took to take a sip of her Coke, which she constantly drank back then. It was all part of her charm. I could've listened to her talk about her hair, poetry, flies—anything, as long as it was coming from her sweet lips.

But she hasn't said more than two words to me since that first day, and although it stings, maybe it has nothing to do with me at all. Maybe this is the new Madison Taylor—quiet, contemplative, and mysterious.

It makes her all the more intriguing.

In any case, she's professional. And aside from a tiny mishap where she left a small line of foundation unchecked and unblended on my jawline, she's been doing a great job. Sarah told me so too.

When I relayed the compliment to Madi, she blushed, and it made me stand a little taller. Ever since, I've been trying to get another blush out of her to no avail.

"Well?" Annalisa taps a slender finger against the side of my head like she's knocking to see if anyone's home. "Do you have anything to say for yourself? I swear to God, if you've been lying this whole time, I'm going to lose it."

"As opposed to—" I tighten my lips and cut myself off. What I really want to say will only make things worse, so I fold both arms over my chest and steel myself.

It's my fault, anyway. I should've known better than to let my guard down. Then again, I underestimated Annalisa's level of… passion.

Is that the right word?

She scoffs, her cheeks puffing out like she's holding her breath. "Ian Brock, the more you divert, the more I'm going to think I'm right." She tosses her hands up. "I mean, I *know* I'm right, but I have to hear it from you. You're lying about the makeup artist. You're not together. You rarely talk to her, let alone flirt or anything else. Just tell me so I can forgive you, and we"—she points between us—"can get back together. The fans will absolutely lose their shit if we're a couple on and off the screen. Can you imagine?"

I cringe as her tone lightens by the end, and she audibly sighs like this is a fairy tale.

I reach out and rub her shoulders, trying my best to let her down softly, even though I've done it countless times over the last week with zero success. What will it take to convince her?

I thought Madison was my out, but our cover isn't looking too solid.

"Annalisa, you're very wrong," I say, my voice as gentle as I can manage.

I'm an actor, after all, so it's not too difficult to pretend I'm calm.

"You and I will not be getting back together," I insist.

She pushes my hands off her, huffing.

As I'm about to say something more, Madison appears over Annalisa's head, bag slung over her shoulder and hair untamed. She jumps out of the way as two crew members wheel props toward the filming area, then tousles her hair to the side as she continues walking up to us. She exudes confidence with each sway of her hips as she places one boot in front of the other.

Madi belongs on a damn runway.

She licks her lips.

Her green eyes are ablaze like she's on a mission.

The whole thing happens in slow motion, and I practically have to pick my jaw up off the ground.

"Yes?" Madi asks, stopping right in front of Annalisa and me.

I blink, gathering my wits.

Annalisa snickers and wraps her arm around me. "We were just talking about getting back together. He and I are too solid to pass up. We fit," she says in a singsong voice that grates on my fucking nerves.

She says she and I fit like we're one in the same.

Like Madi would never have a chance, and that's the worst part of it.

My eyes bug out of my head as I dip out of her clutches. "That's not what I said at all. Why is it so hard for you to believe that I've moved on?"

"We haven't been broken up that long, and you already have a new girlfriend—that's why," Annalisa fires back and tosses her hair out of her face. "But fine. If this thing between you two is real, then prove it. What's her favorite food? Or her last name? Or how did you two even meet?"

Madi straightens her posture and stands to her full height, which I'm happy to say is the same thing she used to do when she stuck up for herself or whoever else needed it back in high school.

It wasn't easy for her to fit in, being the new girl and all. I knew the feeling myself. How hard it was to make friends when cliques had already formed years before. Opinions and conclusions were made based on little information. The usual asshole teenage things.

But Madi never backed down, and it's one of the reasons I was so drawn to her right away. Our pranks got us off on the wrong foot, but it didn't stay that way for long.

"Ian and I have known each other since high school," Madi explains. "He walked right up to me at lunch in the cafeteria one day and asked—"

"Why is New York called the Big Apple? The state looks more like a plane from the side," I finish for her, grinning so wide my cheeks hurt.

Her gaze locks on mine, and the tension between her brows softens.

The hairs on my arms rise, and heat pricks my skin.

Madi sashays to my side, and I instinctively inhale a sharp breath as she throws her arm over my shoulder. "We picked up right where we left off," she says absentmindedly, still staring at me like we're the only ones involved in this conversation.

"Right." I gulp as her perfume invades my senses, consuming me like the hot blood in my veins.

The best part? Madi and I only lied about our current situation. The rest is true, which bodes well for my rising level of guilt. I hate misleading Annalisa, but she hasn't left me many options.

"As for her favorite food, it's any kind of pasta, and her last name is Taylor," I say evenly.

My attention is still glued to Madison as Annalisa says, "Okay, but Ian and I only broke up, like, three days ago." Her voice is full of skepticism, but I sense a hint of defeat.

"It's been over a week," I correct her, but she doesn't budge.

I need to seal the deal.

Something Annalisa can't dispute.

A touchdown.

Madi's breast is pushed into my side, driving me wild, and when she flicks her gaze to my lips, I float outside my body. Before I can think better of it, I plant my mouth on hers like I imagined doing countless times since she came back into my life.

Her lips are soft and warm and sweet.

I deepen the kiss like a thirsty man in a desert, and I drown in her taste as if it's my only chance of survival.

In a way, my life does depend on it because if I don't convince Annalisa to back off, I fear our performances on camera will suffer.

I can't let that happen.

But more than that, something else happens…

Madi kisses me back.

Once the obvious shock wears off, she leans into me, letting a moan escape as I part her lips with my tongue and reacquaint myself with Madison Taylor.

She tastes of mint and a trace of flavored coffee—is that vanilla? Caramel? Mocha? I delve my tongue deeper in hopes of finding out, bringing my palm up to cup her cheek and losing myself in her.

Goddamn, this kiss is…

A throat clears next to us, and I spot movement in my periphery. Madi tries to jump back, but one of my arms is still wrapped around her waist, holding her close. Tearing myself away from her, I blink out of my stupor and study Annalisa. Her arms hang lifelessly by her sides, and her mouth is open as if she's trying to eat a double decker sandwich.

Bingo.

Annalisa swallows, raises her eyebrows, and shakes her head like she's getting into character. When she speaks again, her voice is unusually squeaky and chipper. "I'm sorry for the trouble I've caused, and I am *so* happy for you two."

A commotion sounds to our right, drawing our attention. A woman holds an iPad to her chest as if it's a lifeline and rushes to keep up with the others. A tall man holds a camera on his shoulder, pointing it at another woman, who wears a tight knee-length skirt and AirPods as an accessory. Her head held high, she struts across the street toward us, her heels clicking with confidence and finesse. Once they reach us, the woman taps at one of her earbuds and smiles.

"Annalisa, darling, how are you? Ready for our interview?"

She kisses both of Annalisa's cheeks in grand European fashion. Before she can answer, the woman turns to me, then does a double take. "Ian Brock." Her smile widens as she offers me her hand. "I'm Rayanna Mills."

Madi's eyes widen. "As in the host of *Morning Coffee with Rayanna*?" she asks.

"That's right." Rayanna turns to her. "And who might you be?" Beside us, the woman with the iPad frantically taps at her screen, swiping left and right like she'll find the answer on it.

Madi steps forward. "No, no. I'm not in the movie or anything. I'm a makeup artist, and I'm a huge fan of your podcast."

"She's also Ian's girlfriend," Annalisa chirps, using her squeaky voice again. I'm surprised she doesn't choke on the words.

Rayanna's eyes dart between us as her pleased expression deepens. She's obviously just cooked up an idea, and I'm not sure it's going to bode well for me. "Your girlfriend, you say?" Rayanna places her hands on her hips. "Care to comment, Annalisa? You were just dating Ian, right?"

Her lips tighten as she peers from me to Madi to Rayanna, and then something dangerous happens.

She smiles.

And it's not an evil queen, I-want-to-ruin-Ian's-life smile. It appears genuine.

Damn, she's good.

"I'm just happy for my co-star." She lets out a content sigh. "Did you know they're high school sweethearts?"

"Oh?" Rayanna lifts her eyebrows, obviously intrigued. Shouldn't journalists be more interested in world hunger or climate change than my dating life?

Jesus.

"I only know what that's like from playing a high school girlfriend for the teen drama *Only Young Once*, but if I learned anything from my character, it's that no one should stand in the way of true love. I'm such a romantic." Annalisa nods.

A guy pulls out a camera and snaps a picture of Madi and me. "Hey." I hold a hand up to shield Madi like she's physically in harm's way, even though I'm more worried about the emotional toll a picture in the hands of the media might do to her.

Already, this has been one crazy-ass morning, and we haven't even started filming yet.

One of our production assistants scurries our way with coffees and gives Annalisa and me one from the tray. As I thank her, Annalisa nudges Rayanna toward her trailer, rambling about being a celebrity on the next season of *Dancing with the Stars*.

Beside me, Madi lets out an exhale like she's been waiting to breathe this entire time. Flushed, she brushes past me and into the makeup trailer. I follow, jumping up the steps behind her, but she slams the door in my face, making me sway backward.

"Fuck," I mutter, rubbing my nose. It's not a real and heavy door, but still. I didn't expect to be ambushed this morning, nor did I want my ass kicked.

I deserve it, though.

I kissed Madison like she's actually mine.

I didn't ask if she has a boyfriend or anyone in her life who might be upset about a picture of us coupled with an article of our new "relationship" landing online. Because there's no doubt it will end up on the internet for everyone to see.

I swing the door open and rush inside, where I find Madi swiveling the chair to face the mirror. Next to her, Searcy laughs at something Patrick says, and at the end of the line of stations, two more actors are getting their hair done.

It's crowded. Loud. Chaotic.

This isn't the place to address things with Madi, although I want to sooner rather than later.

"Sit." She grinds out the short word like it's difficult.

Sighing, I hold my hands out and plead, "Madi, I'm so sorry about all that. Can I please take you to dinner and make it up to you?"

"Already have plans tonight."

My jaw tics. *With who?* "Coffee?"

"Already had some."

"Gum, maybe?"

"Why?" She glares at me. "Did my breath smell bad when you stuck your tongue down my throat?"

"God, no!" I blurt, drawing attention from Patrick.

"Hey, I-guy." Patrick glances over his shoulder as Searcy works on one of his eyebrows.

I suppress a groan at Patrick's nickname for me. Is my entire name of two syllables that hard? "Hey, Patty Cakes," I offer.

"Good one." Patrick wags a finger at me. "I love it."

"That's not at all what I meant," I tell Madi, staring at her in the mirror since she's turned her back to me. "I meant it as a joke. As in, can I get you anything at all to help you forgive me?"

Her steely gaze is unwavering as she says, "No."

I hang my head and take a seat. She jumps right into work, roughly dabbing at my cheeks with tan goop that clears my blemishes, and I grimace when she plucks a couple stray hairs from my eyebrows like they offend her.

The only time her face lights up is when the trailer door opens, revealing a shorter woman with large sunglasses on top of her head, holding back her black hair.

When her eyes land on Madi, both women squeal and hug like long-lost friends. Then her attention falls on me, and her jaw drops. "Hi," the mystery woman breathes, clutching her purse to her side like it's helping her balance.

"Ian, this is my friend Bree. Bree, as you know, this is Ian Brock." Madi and the woman move toward me as a couple actors leave the trailer, opening more space, although privacy is still non-existent. "My new *boyfriend*," she says sarcastically.

"What?" Bree screeches, grabbing Madi's arm.

"I can explain," I start, feeling Patrick's curious eyes on me, along with Searcy's.

Fuck. I've dug myself into quite a hole, haven't I?

"So, I guess you're well over Chaz, huh?" her friend mumbles, but I'm standing only a few inches away and hear everything.

"Who's Chaz?" I cross my arms over my chest.

"Don't do that. You have no right." Madi shakes her head. As she edges toward the makeup by the mirror, she shoos me on my way like I'm a horsefly.

I don't push her any more.

I'll give her space, but no matter how many steps I take away from her, I can't help the taste that lingers on my lips.

Her taste.

I touch my mouth, and my grin spreads before I can stop it.

But it quickly falls. I need to find out who this dick Chaz

is. What kind of name is that, anyway? It sounds like a name for a twelve-year-old.

I plan to find out exactly who he is and what he is to Madi, because after that kiss, I refuse to give up so easily.

SIX

Madison

*H*e kissed me, and it knocked the damn breath out of me.

That motherfucker.

We often used to kiss—and more—when we were together. We were in love back then. Inseparable and happy. If I was studying, he'd study with me. If I went running, he was right alongside me, even if he'd just finished two-a-days with the football team.

He always lacked personal space and liked taking up most of my time. I nicknamed him my space-time continuum.

But that's all in the past.

It was supposed to be, anyway.

The last few days have been a dream—literally.

I'd never thought about it before, but while I talked to Carter and Sarah about this job, I had a feeling in my gut that this was the kind of side gig I was craving. Something to call my own beyond the walls of my salon. I'm proud of my business, but being a boss, no matter how small the staff, can be challenging and disheartening. No matter how well we get along, I'm still in charge of their livelihoods, and it's a lot of pressure.

It's rewarding too, but I still want something fun. Something temporary to get me out of the everyday routine. Working on this movie set has already been the zap I needed to boost my creative system.

But working with Ian has been a fucking nightmare.

I'm out of my element around here as it is, but he's just made things ten times more difficult for me.

Not only did Annalisa tell Rayanna Mills that Ian and I are in love, but that guy took a damn picture of us. There's no telling when that will surface, and there's nothing I can do about it.

I don't know much about the world of Hollywood, but I've watched enough of the Britney Spears documentary to know anything's fair game for the public.

Even if it's a lie—a little white lie that was meant for one person but is now going to be broadcast from the rooftops.

What the hell am I supposed to do? Am I going to get fired when Sarah sees this? What will she think—that I just jump into bed with all my clients?

Shit.

I need to talk to her directly.

My phone vibrates in front of the mirror with a new text.

Bree: How are you doing?

Sighing, I lean my hip against the counter, clutching my phone. I told her about Ian's ambush and the picture earlier. I told her about Chaz's silence. It's been over a week, and I haven't heard from him.

But, as I told my friend, I'm not hurt that Chaz hasn't called or texted since our date. With each day that's passed, I've realized exactly how lame and naïve I was to think it was something special.

That's how badly I want something real, but all I've ended up with is a fake relationship with a movie star.

> **Me:** I'm okay. Thanks for bringing breakfast earlier.
>
> **Bree:** Of course. It's the next best thing since I couldn't get off work to be an extra. ;)

I roll my eyes as another text comes in.

> **Bree:** Call me later.

I pack up my brushes, palettes, and other products and rush toward my post on the set to be ready for touch-ups, while also keeping an eye out for Sarah. She needs to hear about this rumor from me instead of Rayanna.

I set my bag down by Ian's chair, which has his name scrolled in bold letters across the back.

A man lunges in front of the camera to snap a clapperboard, or a *slate* as I've learned they say, and steps away as the director calls, "Action."

In character, Ian and Annalisa argue over the attack on their lives, sparring for who's right. Out of sequence, the scene doesn't make sense to me, but I'm mesmerized, nonetheless.

The movie is a sci-fi one, which isn't usually my thing, but Ian is really... good. He sells his character's panic. Owns the setting. And his voice commands his lines.

I inch toward a camera next to the director and peek at the screen far enough behind from the cameraman.

And my lips part as I realize how well Ian works the camera. I've seen him on TV before, but the live show is something else.

Especially now that I'm catching it after he and I made out.

I made out with the lead in a freaking movie.

"Cut!" the director yells, jolting me out of my trance.

I clear my throat and search around me, not recalling how I got so close to the action. Seemingly unnoticed, I slip back to my spot by Ian's chair and crouch down to retrieve a blending sponge and a couple napkins. When I stand back up, Ian's so close, I jump. "Shit," I blurt.

Smirking, he takes a seat and waits for me.

Tightening my lips, I get to work, placing the napkins inside the collar of his shirt to keep from getting makeup on his clothes. I've done this before several times now, but this feels different.

More intimate now that we've sucked each other's faces again after ten years.

His kiss was… hot.

I remember kissing Ian as a teen, but this was hot in a different way today. We're not just a pair of clumsy kids anymore, and it shows.

He kissed me with precision. Passion. Expertise.

My mouth dries just thinking about it, especially as my fingertips brush against his warm, smooth skin.

"I saw you watching me during the scene," he says, pulling me from my thoughts. "Did you see anything you liked?"

I flash my gaze to his as I dab at his forehead. "The person in the green suit was cool."

The smug twinkle in his expression dulls just a bit. "The one they'll edit to be a spirit?"

"That's the one." I gloat in an attempt to disguise the fact that I was actually captivated by Ian alone. I finish smoothing the subtle creases from his forehead and pull the napkins from his collar. "Also, you raise your eyebrows too much, and you're making my job difficult."

He squints, his jaw ticking. "You're just trying to get inside my head so I don't think about our kiss."

I narrow my eyes. "You *shouldn't* be thinking about it."

"Hard not to."

My cheeks are on fire. Is it hot out here or what? Never mind the fifty-degree weather and slight chill in the air. My blood is boiling.

"Ian, you're on," someone from behind me calls.

"Let's put a pin in it." He winks and saunters off.

I cross my arms over my chest and get sucked back into the scene like I'm watching a different person.

And not the Ian Brock I want to smack for confusing the hell out of me.

My nose twitches as I stand on my tiptoes to watch more of his scene over crew members' heads.

Annalisa's perfect too. She's confident in her role. Her character is poised and motivating. She and Ian have chemistry, which, from what I can tell by the murmurs around me, is making filming that much easier.

I might squeeze my sponge in frustration like a stressor ball when Annalisa grabs his hand to save him, but that's only for me to know.

An hour later, Ian rushes back toward me and plops into his chair.

"I'm telling Sarah about what Annalisa told Rayanna," I tell him firmly as I touch up his makeup once again. He's sweating quite a bit now that the sun's come out and wrapped us in its warm rays like a hug. He's also been running down the street in a frenzy while the guy in the green suit chases after him.

Quietly, he studies me, and I start perspiring myself.

"I'm still mad at you for doing this to me," I clip.

He holds his hands up in surrender and drops any humor from his voice when he says, "Look, I'm sorry. I didn't mean for it to get out of control like that, but it's not necessary to tell Sarah."

"Why? Are you in a fake relationship with her too, or is it real?"

He tilts his head, and I squirm under his scrutiny. "Are you jealous, Madi?"

"Yeah, right." I scoff. "And stop calling me Madi. It's Madison. If my friends call me anything else, it's Mads."

"Mads," he repeats like he's tasting a new food for the first time, and I instinctively lean in as if I care what he thinks of it. "I like it."

I blink and stand back. "I'm telling Sarah."

"She's not going to care."

"That's for her to decide, but I can't have her opinion of me tainted. I refuse to be the last-minute floozy she brought on to the scene just to sleep with the lead actor."

His irises flash a bolder brown than usual, the color a mix of whiskey and coffee. "Now there's an idea," he says slyly.

Ignoring my fluttering stomach, I say, "Don't even go there."

He stands from his chair, rising to his full height, only a couple inches taller than me. Peering down, he deeply inhales and hums like he enjoys the smell of my hair and whispers, "It would be fun to go there, though. Wouldn't it, *Mads*?"

My knees weaken, but I don't give in.

I refuse.

"It would be just like old times but…" He leans farther down to talk in my ear, his breath on my skin sending shivers down my spine as he finishes his sentence. "*Better*."

He's called over again, and he backs away without taking his eyes off me.

They hold desire.

And promise.

Like he's going to try and make his suggestion come true.

But I'm not falling for it. The ache in my core will just have to get the hell over it because turning this fake relationship with Ian Brock into anything real would be a mistake.

One I'm not too keen on repeating.

I reach for my coffee that a PA handed me earlier and take a few drinks to wet my dry throat as the director calls, "Cut," two seconds after they start. While he instructs the actors to make eye contact during their exchange, Sarah sidles up next to me, an iPad in hand.

"Sarah, hi." I tap her arm gently, pulling her attention away from the screen.

"Yes, Miss Taylor?"

"First of all, thank you again for this opportunity. This has been amazing."

"No thanks needed. After all, you prevented me from having a stroke."

My laugh gets caught in my throat when I realize she's serious. *Damn, movie people are dramatic.*

"Is there a second of all?" Sarah studies me.

"Yes. I want to make you aware of a little misunderstanding. It's going to pop up on the internet any minute, and I'd like to tell you the real story before the rumors run rampant."

"What're you talking about?" She drops the iPad to her side.

"Well, there was a journalist here earlier who snapped a shot of Ian and me, and they were asking all kinds of questions," I ramble. "But there's nothing going on. I'm a professional, and I don't want you to think that I don't appreciate this job or that I want to cause any trouble. I've enjoyed this so much, and—"

Sarah holds her hand up, cutting me off. "Honey, I don't care."

I flinch.

She smiles, but it's not the kind one Searcy gives me. This one is more of a how-adorably-pitiful-am-I kind of smile, which makes me uneasy. "Everyone's sleeping with one another around here. The media and tabloids run all kinds of stories, real and fake and ridiculous. If you're going to stay in this industry—which I think you should because you have a knack for this—you're going to have to learn not to care as well." She places her hand on my shoulder and dips her head to meet my gaze, softening her expression. "Do the job, and that's all we care about. That, and any relevant press is advantageous as far as I'm concerned, so… thank you."

"You're welcome?" I say, but it's more of a question as she disappears into the sea of crew members and film equipment.

I rub my temple, feeling like she just gave me whiplash.

When I glance back up, Ian's staring at me as the director talks with the guy in green.

The thorn in my side nods, and he doesn't have to utter the words "I told you so" for me to know he witnessed my exchange with Sarah and is thinking exactly that.

He winks, then turns back into his character, transforming his expression to one of wide-eyed innocence.

By this point, I've put together the gist of the story. Justin discovers a spirit realm and refuses to accept his role in the fight to save humanity from the ghosts of that realm, who want to use Earth as their new home.

I clutch a compact mirror to my chest as I watch Ian run down the sidewalk, away from the cameras.

His jeans cling to his curved ass and lean hamstrings, reminding me of all the times I'd stare at him from behind when he was in tight spandex football pants back in high school.

When he turns back around to face us, he licks his lips, and his neck glistens with small beads of sweat, reminiscent of summer days spent by the lake.

My hand itches to fan myself, and my throat screams for a drink.

What fresh hell is this?

Suddenly, I wish the ghosts could take me to their realm and far away from here.

"**M**adison Everly Taylor!" Bree screeches into the phone.

Good thing I have it on speaker on my bed, or that would've taken my eardrum out.

"It says right here—and I quote—'Brock's new fling is a bigger surprise than results of this keto diet. You're probably thinking, who is this fiery redhead who's stolen the heart of the Hollywood star? She's none other than his new makeup artist. Our sources say the pair have known each other since high school. Isn't it amazing when stars fall for average people?'"

"That's enough," I say.

It didn't take long for the pictures to circulate—it was mere hours, in fact. A few articles have popped up alongside them too. They quote Annalisa and air out my history with Ian as if it's anyone's business.

Movie stars and the rest of Hollywood might get this sort of thing a lot, but to me, it feels… icky. Even if the kiss was real and I was actually dating Ian again, I'd feel just as violated. How do people get used to this?

Bree's giddy voice fills my quiet apartment, and every excited word she utters makes my stomach flip more and more. I have yet to decide if it's because I'm angry with Ian or because the world thinks we're sleeping together.

And I'm fighting against wanting the latter to be true.

"I mean, you're fucking famous, Mads!" Bree squeals.

I shake my head. "I'm not. They don't even mention my name in the article, and they definitely don't flatter me. Instead, they basically congratulate Ian on slumming it with a nobody."

Bree hums, but it's not the excited tone she's nearly deafened me with since I answered her call. "They do compare you to Annalisa quite a bit," she says distantly, and I can only assume she's skimming the rest of the article for the millionth time.

I also suspect she wants to spare my feelings, but unfortunately for me, I've already read the damn thing.

"And I'm not winning that comparison, either." I throw my head back onto my pillow with an audible *oomph*.

I had plans to do the laundry that litters my apartment, but I've put it off for two weeks. What's another day?

Staring at the ceiling, I let out a frustrated sigh. "Like I told you, the whole thing is a lie, Bree. Not the part about

Annalisa being hotter than me, but the rest." I laugh, but it lacks any humor.

"Hold on. Is this Madison I'm speaking with?" Bree uses the professional voice I always imagine she uses at the career counseling center, where she works alongside Tessa. "Because that's who I called, but you don't sound like her. My friend would not sell herself short like this. My friend is one of the three sexiest ladies I know, and she better not forget it, no matter what LA goddess is involved."

I giggle. "Thank you for the reminder, babe."

"That's more like it." She settles back into her normal voice. "Now, what about the kiss?"

My smile slides off my face faster than my new high-end curling iron gets hot.

She whistles. "That is one hot kiss, but I need more details. Is he the same kisser as he was in high school, or has he gotten better? Are his lips soft? And does he wear boxers or briefs?"

I pull myself to sit upright with the first ab crunch I've done in weeks. "He's much better, they're very soft, and I have no fucking clue," I humor her. "The last time I saw him naked was when we were making the switch from VHS to DVD."

"But you can remedy that *so* easily," she says. "I mean, the way he's cupping the back of your head while you kiss is the stuff of, well, movies." She snorts at her own pun.

"Are you still staring at the picture of us?" I ask, referring to the image of Ian and me kissing that's circulating the internet.

I don't know who took the shot or when, but I shouldn't be surprised someone was in the right place at the right time to capture the moment Ian's lips touched mine in a scorching kiss that's plagued my thoughts all day.

I do curse the individual, though.

"Of course. I can't analyze evidence without the evidence," she throws back.

"You're not a detective."

"Never said I was. I'm just a concerned citizen—I mean, *friend*." In the background, a door opens and closes. "Hey," she says to someone, and it's followed by murmuring.

"Bree?" I ask.

"I need to go, Mads," she whispers.

After we promise to talk tomorrow, we hang up, but not before I hear the other voice more clearly. It's low and gruff, which means it's Bree's male company for the evening.

She's got a bigger appetite for men than a professional pie eater does for dessert, and it's refreshing and healthy. Much better than some of the girls I knew in high school, who trash-talked me behind my back because they heard Ian and I had fooled around in the commentary box in the football stadium.

I check the time on my phone and lie back against my pillow again, squirming until I fall into a comfortable nook underneath the covers.

Since they changed the schedule, I have to be up in three hours to make it to the set on time. If I fall asleep now, I'll get enough of a power nap to survive tomorrow.

I won't be as refreshed and glowing like Annalisa, but according to the magazine, there's no comparison, anyway.

With a huff, I turn onto my side and repeat Bree's praise.

Besides, why the hell am I comparing myself to her in the first place? The magazine did, but that's their job.

Mine is just to do her makeup and make her look more gorgeous than she already is.

Creamy freaking skin.

Lashes for days—she doesn't even need fakes!

I can see why Ian was into her.

Ian.

If only I could stop thinking about him.

I'll see him again in a couple of hours, and I'm sure his eyes will be sleepy, falling lazily in the corners. Not even one of his famous smiles can crinkle them up into place until he's had plenty of black coffee to wake himself up. He drank it straight and plain even at eighteen, probably because that's how his older brother took it.

Ian idolized him.

It was cute how his face would light up any time Cash would want to toss the football around in the yard while I played with their black lab, Shadow.

The memories flood, slamming into me so hard I get dizzy. If I wasn't exhausted before, I'm absolutely drained by the time I finally doze off, still in my clothes from the day and the phantom feel of Ian's lips on mine.

SEVEN

Ian

She's had a dazed look about her all morning.

Maybe it was the early—or late?—hour, but Madison showed up to the set at three a.m. in black leather leggings, worn combat boots that tied up just above her ankle, and a forest green jacket that matched her eyes, which shined with little help from any mascara or other product.

She's glowing.

Her wavy red hair hung low down her back, and my mouth hung open as she tossed it into a ponytail on top of her head before she started on my face. I wasn't even embarrassed that she had to pay extra attention to the creases on one cheek from where I slept harder than I have in months.

These last couple of weeks have been brutal with filming at all times of the day and night. In between, I've been memorizing and running lines with Annalisa, who up until yesterday spent most of our time together trying to feel me up.

After my little stunt of kissing Madison, though, things are shifting—in more ways than one.

"What're you smiling about?" Madi's breath is minty and cool against my cheek, sending blood down south. It's too early to be this close to her, especially after thoughts of our kiss replay in my brain like my dad's record Cash and I broke as kids.

"You," I whisper honestly. I've never been able to lie to her face, so why start now? "I'm smiling because of you, Madi."

Tensing, she stands upright and watches me in the mirror as Searcy scurries between the others in the trailer.

"I mean, *Mads*," I correct myself with a smirk.

Her eyes flash with something I can't decipher, but she's not cussing me out or throwing me from this chair, so I think it's a good sign.

Her throat bobs as she swallows slowly, and she jumps when Searcy appears next to us, adding a third presence in the mirror like we're posing for a portrait. "Need me to finish up here?" she offers.

"Sure." Madi glances down at me one more time before turning to do the rest of the cast's makeup.

She stops at Patrick's chair and leans down close to him, rubbing makeup under his eyes to cover dark circles. "I didn't get any sleep last night. I was hooked on a show about a deadly surgeon who botches operations and paralyzes his patients. Can you imagine?" Patrick asks her. I've seen that glint of appreciation in his gaze before—when he was appraising the Empire State Building.

I met him for a beer a couple days ago, thinking it was a good chance for us to get to know each other. I really wanted to figure the guy out. He surprises me at every damn turn.

I was also starting to go stir crazy with the schedule of shooting, running lines, and pacing my hotel room until I pass out. Since the only person I know in the city is my fake girlfriend, I thought I'd branch out and make a real friend.

After beers, Patrick and I stood under the epic Empire State Building in awe. But when I suggested we go to the top, he shook his head vehemently—he's petrified of heights.

I felt sorry for him but respected his honesty. Right now, though, as he follows Madi's every movement and talks her ear off, I clench my jaw and feel nothing but rage.

Is talking about deadly surgeons his way of flirting? Like I said, I can't read the guy.

"Relax. You're all done, Mr. Impatient," Searcy teases. "Movie stars and their moods."

"Oh, I wasn't…" I turn toward her.

"You were making sure other actors aren't closing in on what's yours." She nods knowingly, an amused air about her. "I think it's cute. I mean, what an epic love story—a real second chance romance in the making between you two."

"I'm sorry?" I search her expression, utterly confused.

"High school sweethearts reunited over ten years later by pure fate?" She sighs, and a dopey smile graces her lips.

"Right," I draw out. "It's a real fairy tale."

I thank Searcy for her help and head out of the trailer for some fucking air. On my way, I steal one last glance at Madi, who's working on someone else, leaving Patrick to follow me out.

"Good news about you and Madison." He claps my back.

"Oh, you heard too?" I lift a brow, peering over my shoulder as I take the last step and land on solid ground.

"Of course. It's everywhere." Patrick shrugs. "Plus, Annalisa's telling everyone she runs into."

"Why am I not surprised?" I ask sarcastically, teetering on my heels.

All I can think about is how pissed Madison probably is—that, and how relieved I am that Patrick wasn't actually trying to flirt with her.

"Let's get another beer sometime," Patrick suggests. "It'll be a nice break from shooting and watching rappers play video games."

"Huh?"

He gives me a sly grin like we're planning to take over the world and not just talking about beer. "We still have a lot to learn about each other."

I nod, my head a giant mess. "We do," I agree, and I mean it. Everything out of his mouth is a mystery as if he's giving me pieces to three different puzzles.

"Break a leg today," Patrick chirps as he does every time he sees me before we film a scene. Hands in his pockets, he flips around and maneuvers through crew members, leaving me alone with my turmoil.

I squint into bright lights past a couple trucks and trailers where people are taming wild cords and rogue parts of the set. Instead of following him, I whirl around and hop back into the makeup trailer. "Madi, what's your phone number?" I blurt.

Searcy clutches her chest. "You don't have your own girlfriend's phone number?"

"I... well, what happened was..." I gulp, sliding my sweaty palms down my pants as Annalisa's curious eyes rake over me.

Madi cuts through my sad attempt with a laugh. "You didn't drop your phone in the toilet again, did you, baby?"

A slow smile spreads as I fixate on how she called me *baby*. It was so natural and fucking hot, leaving her lips like it did once upon a time. "I did, actually. Lost all my contacts." I lean forward and into my character of the clumsy boyfriend as I try my best to hide the very real stiffy crowding my jeans.

Once she's finished running a miniature comb over Annalisa's brows, Madi stands upright, bravado intact, then brushes past me, red hair flying backward like Katniss's flames in *The Hunger Games*.

Outside, she paces by the steps of the trailer. As I descend to meet her on the pavement, I do a slow clap. "Nicely done. Are you sure you don't moonlight as an actress? You could act circles around—"

"What was that?" She scowls. "You asked for my phone number, Ian. Why the hell would you want that?"

"So I can text you sometime," I say, shrugging coolly.

But the laugh she lets out holds zero humor, and she shakes her head more adamantly than if I would've asked for a sample of her blood. "In case you've forgotten, we're not actually together. You shouldn't need to text me."

I catch her arm as she brushes past me. Her eyes immediately fall to my lips, and I inhale a sharp breath, tensing all over again from being close to her. "I couldn't find you on social media, so I thought I'd ask for your number, instead."

"Did you not hear me?" she asks, but her voice is less stern than before. "We don't need to talk outside this base."

"Did you block me?" I press, ignoring the sting in my gut from her resistance.

But I know better.

This is her front. Her way of putting a wall between us.

But the truth is that she saved my ass in there when she didn't have to. In fact, she could've used it as an opportunity to drop the whole charade, but instead, she kept pretending we're together.

What wasn't a pretense was how she felt against me yesterday when we kissed. She kissed me back, and it's all I can think about.

There's something here, and I'm determined to explore it.

I just have to figure out a way to convince her to let her guard down.

Madison turns her eyes up to meet mine, fire burning in them. "I blocked you seven years ago. You're telling me you just now realized it? You never tried to look me up after you vanished?"

I soften my grip on her, but I don't stand back or let go completely.

"Wow. How special am I?" She purses her lips, and my chest tightens. I've hurt her feelings again—*shit*. Why do I keep getting this all wrong? "Let me get this straight. You randomly come back into my life, tell the world we're together, kiss me in front of said world, and now, you're admitting you've never even thought about me since you left?"

"That's not what I said," I whisper. "I've thought about you a lot over the years."

"Not good enough."

"Is this about Chaz?" I ask, and she jerks her arm from my grasp, then spins on her heel to surely storm back into the trailer.

But before she reaches the door, I call out, "You shouldn't have helped me in there."

That gets her attention.

She freezes halfway, and I take measured steps to where she stands, one hand on the side of the trailer. When I reach her, I tuck a mess of curls over her shoulder and behind her ear. "Because one might think you don't actually want this to be fake. One might think you care about me."

All I get in return is a quiet murmur, but it's enough.

I'm under her skin, which works out very well since she's under mine too.

I'm still watching after Madi as she disappears, and Annalisa emerges, makeup natural for the scenes we're shooting today.

"Do you need my number?" she asks, stopping in front of me.

"What?" I tilt my head, the hairs on the back of my neck sticking up.

Annalisa points behind her. "Inside, you said you dropped your phone in the toilet and lost your contacts."

"Right." I rock back on my heels and force a smile. "I definitely need your number for movie stuff." I make sure to emphasize the last part to ensure there's no confusion.

She holds her hand out. "Phone me."

I freeze with my hand on my pocket, under which my phone is nestled safely out of her reach. "I'll just do it. What is it?"

I steel myself and hold my ground as she studies me, her gaze inquisitive. Even the crew members a few yards away seem to halt. Finally, she relents, and I pretend to input her number, carefully tilting my phone to the side so she doesn't notice that I already have it.

"See you out there." She brushes past me wearing a smile that is oddly nice, and my phone vibrates with a new message.

Keith: I thought I told you not to get too attached out there!

It's followed by a screenshot of Madi and me—a picture of us kissing.

Me: It's not what you think.

Keith: Call me later. Gotta go explain the concept of puberty to Rhett Stevens and why he's being fired from a children's show.

I slide my phone back into my pocket, rubbing my chin. What will I even say to Keith about Madi when I call him later?

"There you are." Sarah appears next to me, throwing her hands up. "We're waiting for you, or did you forget you're the star of a movie?" she asks sarcastically, challenging me with an exasperated tap of her foot and shoving the watch on her wrist in my face.

She doesn't wait for my response and turns on her heel back toward the set.

I follow her, and the closer I get to my spot, it takes more and more energy to focus. To switch off my real thoughts and get inside the mind of Justin, the naïve guy who has so much to learn.

Which is ironic for my reality.

Madison thinks I haven't thought about her at all since I left. That leaving her didn't gut me. When in fact, I was a fucking wreck for months after graduation. It took every ounce of willpower not to answer her calls or texts, even though I was hurt, and I really wanted to talk to her.

She was my best friend, after all.

But I couldn't face her. Not after I learned the truth.

She might be mad at me for ignoring her all these years,

but she's obviously forgotten the truth about what happened back then.

EIGHT

Madison

"Well, well, well." Sofia clicks her tongue, her lips twitching as I enter the salon. "It's about time you showed up here. I was starting to forget what you looked like," she teases, leaning into her thick New York accent as she ribs me. Not only does she draw out her vowels, but she infuses her own charm and attitude into each word too.

"It's only been a couple weeks." I roll my eyes and greet a few of our regulars sitting in swiveling chairs. Some sit under dryers with foil in their hair, and I nod to them too as I shuffle toward my office in the back.

I don't get very far when there's a shriek from behind me, and I jump around, searching for the source. Missy jolts from the dryer chair as the circular hood clamors to the floor, along with a single bolt rolling in circles.

I rush to Missy's side and grasp her shoulders, checking her over while she cups the back of her head. "Are you okay?"

"I'm fine." Her throat bobs as she swallows. "It just scared me, is all."

"Are you sure?" I search her expression one more time, noting the shock there as color fills her cheeks again.

"I'm sure. I really am fine." She nods. "It barely touched me, honestly."

I exhale, clutching my chest with one hand as I guide her toward another chair. "Hang on." I hold my arm out to stop her and check the hood for any issues. "Okay. You're safe."

She giggles and swats me away.

"I'm really sorry about that. I will comp your appointment and finish you up myself," I offer.

She's normally my client, anyway, and I know how attached people get to their hair stylists once they find someone they like. It's been difficult enough for me to give up control while I've been gone, and the second I'm back for a brief check-in, a loyal customer is attacked by a treacherous chair.

Welcome back, Mads.

"Oh, honey, that's not necessary." She pats my hand. "It was an accident. You know I won't make any trouble for you. Like I said, it was nothing. My job working for a bail bondsman is much worse."

"I'm not sure that's comforting, Missy."

"I can hold my own." She shrugs like it's no big deal and settles into her chair. "Go on now. You're busy. We'll catch up later."

Sighing, I relent and pick up the scattered pieces of the chair, putting them back in their places for now until I can properly fix it or order a new one. Then I make my way to the back for a sign to put up to warn others not to sit.

In my office, I hang my jacket on a hook on the wall, and the moment my ass hits the chair, there's a knock on the door.

Suppressing a groan, I force pep into my voice instead and call out, "Come in."

Thankfully, it's Sofia.

I sink into my chair, relaxing. I've been up and working all night after another filming schedule change. I had time to run home for a power nap and shower before I got here to catch up. "I'm making a sign for the chair."

"Oh, that's not what I wanted to tell you."

I power up my laptop and fold my hands on the desk in front of me, giving her my full attention. "What's up? Has everything been okay while I've been gone?"

"While you've been smooching on sexy as *hell* actors, you mean?" Sofia taunts me with her devious grin. "Damn, chica, you've got game to land someone like Ian Brock."

I glare.

"Not the time. I got it." She holds her hands up and nods, her tight curls bouncing above her shoulders. "Everything's been fine. I've been earning that bonus you're giving me, and I haven't smashed Cheryl's windshield with my tire iron yet, so we're perfect." She shrugs innocently.

"What did she do this time?" I ask, my voice professional. I make sure my staff know they can confide in me, but I avoid engaging in gossip like it's a bad perm—nothing ever good comes from it, and it's hard to fix after the damage is done.

"She botched a coloring job and ran off before the client saw it just so she wouldn't get yelled at. When I called her to come back, she claimed she threw up and had to go home. Like I was born yesterday." She tilts her head in doubt.

"Noted." I give her a tight smile, tamping down the string of curse words I want to unleash. "And I appreciate you picking up the slack around here."

"You got it, boss lady." She halfway turns before snapping her fingers and facing me again. "Oh, and you're here to do Mrs. Frita later, right?"

I hum as I find the schedule of appointments on my laptop and filter it to mine. "Looks like it."

"*Phew.*" She clasps her fingers together in front of her, more relieved and excited than she is when her Amazon orders arrive early.

And I totally get it. Mrs. Frita is one of our most difficult clients, nitpicking everything, including her hair color.

Which we never even change.

We always offer to touch it up, but she insists she likes her natural color.

Until she comes back for another appointment, only to repeat her previous complaints about the color.

Sofia turns to leave again, but the second I retrieve red duct tape from my drawer, she bounces back in. "Last thing—I swear—but Ian's here for you."

I blink. "What?"

She sways from side to side, a mischievous grin spreading across her face like she's an evil queen. "Ian Brock is waiting for you out there."

Instinctively, I smooth a hand over my untamed hair.

With a wink, Sofia slips out the door, leaving me alone while I ask myself, "What the hell is he doing here?"

Taking a deep breath, I snatch a sheet of paper from the printer for an "Out of Order" sign and grab the red duct tape. Then I give the long legs God gave me a purpose and take large strides back toward the lobby.

I hear a loud "Ow!" and know before I see it that Ian has sat in the broken chair. Again, I inhale deeply and enter the separate space where the dryers are lined against the wall. Sure enough, Ian's leaning forward in the chair, with the lonely hood skidding across the floor for a second time. Wincing, he cradles the back of his head like Missy had moments ago while Sofia gets him a bag of ice.

It might help his head, but it won't take care of the embarrassment evident in his flushed cheeks. Only a time machine would work better for his ego, but I keep that to myself.

Quietly, I sink down in front of Ian, set my materials down, and hold up my hand. "How many fingers am I holding up?"

He jerks his head up, peeking out of one eye. It reminds me of the times he'd wake up next to me in the middle of the night before he'd sneak out the same way he'd tiptoed inside so that my parents wouldn't catch him.

His dark hair is messy and longer than it was a couple of weeks ago when we first started filming.

His coffee-brown eyes are bold, and a flash of amusement crosses them like a shooting star as he gives me a once-over, then runs his gaze over my fingers. He reaches out to touch each of them, sending heat through my veins faster than an electric current. "Three," he answers, paying extra attention to the final digit—my ring finger. He sucks in a sharp breath, drawing my eyes to his bottom lip.

Immediately, I'm overcome with the urge to kiss him like I did a few days ago.

"Here you go." Sofia's voice trails off as her eyes dart between us, and we both jump upright, brushing against each other on the way.

"Thank you." I take the bag of ice from her and hand it to

Ian, then step around him to tape the sign to the chair. "I was putting up a warning, but you sat in it a moment too soon." I wave toward the piece of paper.

"Ah. And here I thought it was a prank gone wrong. Or very right." He studies me. "I'm still not sure which."

I quirk an eyebrow. "If I wanted to hurt you, you'd have a black eye right now and not a sore head."

"Ouch." He clutches his chest.

"You'd deserve it."

"I agree."

"You two are so cute. You make me want to throw up." I turn to find Sofia still standing beside us. "It's my goal in life to find a partner to wish harm on."

Clearing my throat, I fight a blush, knowing good and well that I can't hide it once it's unleashed. "What're you doing here, Ian?"

"We finished up early today, so I wanted to come see you and ask if you're free for coffee."

"I'm busy." I wave around the buzzing salon.

Several women's asses are halfway out of their chairs as they try to catch a glimpse of Ian. I'm not even sure they all know who he is, but they know he's a hot guy. That draws enough attention around here as it is—not that I've brought many around myself in the past.

This is my place of work, and aside from visits from my friends, I try to keep my personal life separate.

"Of course." Ian's shoulders slump a fraction, ruining his perfect posture. "It was a long shot, but I thought I'd try."

He slinks backward, and something about the defeat in his eyes before he turns around has me grabbing his arm and blurting, "We can do dinner. Come back later?"

His lip twitches. "It's a date."

"Just dinner." I narrow my gaze.

"We'll see." He winks, and I purse my lips, trying to get the butterflies in my stomach under control.

NINE

Ian

When I return like Madi suggested, the salon is locked, and the lights are out.

I knock on the door and pace by the windows, careful to spot any movement inside as my heart races. I've wanted to take her out since the first day I saw her again, and now that it's happening, it feels like I've waited for years.

Reuniting with Madi has been a breath of fresh air. A taste of fine wine. A welcomed plot twist to my life.

I didn't realize how focused I was on my evolving career—how many nights I spent alone or running lines with my reflection in the mirror—until I ran into Madi again.

Dating Annalisa was a high, but it was different. It felt more like work than a good time, given how often I had to go shopping with her or wait behind the scenes with sparkling water while she did an interview.

It might've stung to know Madi blocked me on all her

91

social media, but she's made me feel like myself again.

Like Ian Bowman instead of Ian Brock.

After a few minutes of pacing, a raindrop falls on my cheek, and I stop in my tracks to look up. "Shit," I mutter.

So much for wanting to walk to the restaurant.

Two giggling boys and their guardian pop out of the bodega on the corner. When they pass me, I notice the kids chewing on a piece of candy, and the scene takes me back to when Mom would take Cash and me to the grocery store. She'd buy each of us candy at the register to eat on the way home, although we hadn't had dinner yet. I dip my head, smiling at the few good memories I have of us boys together when the door swings open.

Madi pops out, swinging her ponytail over her shoulder.

Damn, she put it up.

It looks good any way she does it, but when it was down earlier, it was wild and sexy and free.

"I just need a minute." She tilts her head and bites the inside of her cheek. "Can you come in?"

"Of course." I inch toward her, and she moves aside to make room, assessing me from head to toe as I pass.

"I just need to close out the register, and we can go to dinner."

I rub my hands together. "So, I get a front row seat to watch Madison Taylor at work."

She laughs as she turns a lamp on at the front counter. "Such exciting foreplay, right?" She straightens. "I mean…"

"I know what you meant." I hum, pacing by the door.

"Besides, you've watched me work every day for weeks," she says, keeping her head down—is it to hide her blush?

I rest both elbows on the counter and lean forward. "This is different."

She pauses with her finger an inch from the iPad, and my gaze travels up her forearm, where I notice small goose bumps scattered there.

I can't wait to have her all to myself tonight.

I'm the luckiest bastard in New York, aren't I?

The screen of her iPad casts a soft blue glow across her face as she tucks a strand of loose hair behind her ear. As she works, the concentration lines in Madi's forehead deepen. They're the same ones she had when she'd show me how to do a complicated math problem for our algebra class. I used to rub that line smooth with my thumb, which would make her sigh, partly in exasperation but also in contentment. She'd say I wasn't paying attention, but the truth was, I *was* paying attention... to her, anyway.

She was far more intriguing than a few numbers.

"Being the boss looks good on you," I say, breaking the silence. "Much better than being an English expert. Not that you weren't good at that too, but this is better."

"I think so too. Which is why my English major didn't work out for me."

"How did you end up here?" I wave around.

"I went to college for a year, but it wasn't for me. I enjoyed doing hair and makeup. I was known as the beauty bitch on our floor in the dorm." She smiles and turns back to the screen as she continues. "Everyone came to me before a sorority event or a night out. So, cosmetology school seemed like a good fit, and it was the first time I was excited for the rest of my life."

After another brief pause, I break the silence again. "And the salon?"

She doesn't answer me immediately, twisting her lips,

instead. "My parents loaned me the money to get started. I did refuse at first because I didn't want to complicate things between us—"

"And because you can be a bit stubborn," I add with a wink.

She rolls her eyes. "Being independent and determined does not make me stubborn."

"That's one way to spin it." I chuckle as she turns off the iPad and grabs a few pieces of receipt paper from the printer below her.

"I'll put this up in the back, and we can go."

"I'll join you."

She raises a brow as I fall into step with her toward the back. On the way, we pass swiveling chairs in the main room, stations with all kinds of products I've never seen or heard of, and black and white paintings decorating the walls.

I imagine her life here. Working with fun and interesting people every day. Doing what she loves. Making the world a prettier and more confident place.

I work on piecing her life together with what little she's told me, along with what I've witnessed, and I hope to learn even more tonight.

I want to know all of her.

Stopping to lean in the doorway of her office, I wait for Madi to unlock a desk drawer and shove the pieces of paper inside. When she stands up, she smooths her top down and grabs her green jacket.

"New York looks good on you too," I say. "Almost like you never were a Texas girl."

"Tell that to my accent when I talk to my parents or when I'm angry."

I laugh. "You say *yee-haw* when you're drunk too, don't you?"

She shakes her head, and her ponytail dances behind her. "I've never been *that* drunk."

I enter the room, and it feels smaller with both of us inside, especially with the tension swirling around us in thick waves.

Just being near her sends my nerves into overdrive.

"I can tell why it was so hard for you when your family moved from here to Texas. And why you moved back here after high school."

We lock eyes, freezing in place, and something settles in my chest, warming me from the inside out. As I stare at Madi, I wonder how I ever could've let her go.

"LA seems to be good for you," she says, reaching up to let her hair down. Running her long fingers through it, she untangles the thick strands and pulls it over one shoulder. "Although I miss the farmer's tan on your arms from when you worked on your uncle's ranch."

I narrow my gaze. "How do you know I don't still have those lines?"

She stiffens. "I don't. How would I? You've been wearing all your clothes the entire time we've worked together. I was just… assuming."

"Good assumption." I step farther inside her small office, invading her space as I inch closer to her, enjoying how she squirms. "But this guess wouldn't have anything to do with my shirtless scene in a rom-com I did or pictures found online, right? You wouldn't have googled me, would you have?"

Her nostrils flare. "I may have run across one or two online." Her voice trails off, but she quickly juts her chin up at me and jabs her finger into my chest. "You should really learn to keep your shirt on more often. I mean, your mother sees those pictures too, you know."

I throw my head back and laugh. "I'm sure she doesn't," I say, my voice shaking. "She's busy with Cash and his new job and family to worry about anything I'm doing." I instantly curse myself for letting that slip.

It sounds like I'm jealous. Like I'm yearning for my parents' attention and affection as if I'm five. And it pisses me off.

Because that's not what this is about—it's about Cash.

Madi doesn't seem to notice, though, and innocently asks, "How is Cash? I saw he got married a few years back and has an adorable son."

I stand back, my ego taking a hit as hard as those sacks I took in football. "You saw? As in, you didn't block him on Facebook like you did me?"

Her lips part.

My blood boils.

And the fun and easy dance we were just doing turns into a tug-of-war of emotions.

I take more steps back as she stiffens, and her guilty expression speaks volumes.

I don't wait for a verbal answer. Instead, I rush out of there like I'm on fire and head straight for the front door, grumbling over my shoulder, "This was a mistake."

When I came in here tonight, I thought there was something between us worth rekindling. That I could earn her forgiveness for the shit I've dragged her into.

But knowing that she still has my brother in her life in any capacity is too much to wrap my head around. It brings up old wounds with a fierce vengeance.

"Are you fucking kidding me right now?" Madi calls out, and her stomps quicken behind me, growing into a threat.

Sweat runs down my back. When did I start sweating? *Shit.*

She catches up to me and yanks on my arm, chest heaving. "What is your problem?"

"You still wanting Cash in your life but not me. *That's* my problem," I grind out.

"I have him on my social media, and we've never talked. All we do is like each other's pictures once a year, at most." She crosses her arms. "But even if we did talk, Cash and I were friends, Ian. We were friends because I was your girlfriend, and I made an effort to get to know your family. And not just that. I *loved* your family because they made you, *you*, and I loved you. But none of that mattered, obviously."

I fully turn to face her, placing both hands on my hips and squeezing my eyes closed. I feel every bit the teenager I was when she knew me. When she loved me.

I've never been jealous like this.

I've changed, and it's partly because I left my issues with Cash in Texas.

They have no place here, although the fact remains that Madi hated me enough to completely delete me from her life, but Cash—he made the fucking cut to stay.

Sirens sound from outside and grow louder the closer they get. Blue and red lights flash across the sky, lighting it up like the Fourth of July as police cars zip down the road. Rain taps against the windows in rapid succession, and my chest constricts as I war with myself.

"I'm sorry." I lift my gaze to meet hers. "I am sorry for what happened back then. I ran away, and I'm storming off right now. But you—*fuck*." I pinch the bridge of my nose.

What can I say? Where would I begin to air out how devastated I was with happened all those years ago? And besides, would it make a difference?

"You still can't be honest with me." She frowns, searching my face, which has morphed into a conflicted expression. "Save your apologies. They're as fake as our *relationship*."

I clench my jaw, and my hands itch to run through her hair and comfort her.

"I'm not even sure what I expected. You always chose *dare* when we'd play truth or dare way back when, like telling the truth was worse than licking a frog." She scrunches her nose, and I'm reminded of the time I did just that.

And it was, in fact, better than telling the group what size boxers my brother wore because the girl asking the questions was obsessed with him. Yet another person hypnotized by my brother's charms like he could do no wrong.

A fire truck shines its bright red lights and honks its horn outside, jostling me from the memories.

But Madi doesn't flinch. "You're right. This was a mistake." She brushes past me, her strides long and angry as she moves toward the door and yanks it open. "Go," she says at the same time lightning strikes, illuminating the night sky.

The screeching sounds of the obvious crisis outside blares into the salon, and the chaos is perfect for what I'm feeling right now.

I sigh, glancing around the dark salon. "I'm not leaving you alone here."

"Fine. I'll lock up, and we can go our separate ways." She lets the door shut and rushes toward her tote next to the register, grumbling about keeping our relationship professional. "We'll pretend we don't even know each other from here on out. Good luck with Annalisa."

"You're just proving my earlier point about being stubborn, so thank you," I say sarcastically.

Without another word, she rummages through her bag more frantically than before, and guilt eats at me.

"Madi…" I start, moving toward her.

"Don't." She sighs and lets her head fall back, her eyes shut. "Shit," she murmurs.

"I don't want to leave."

"Well, I don't want you to stay, and I most certainly don't want to go to dinner with you." She pins her glare on me. "But right now, I need to figure out where I left my damn keys because they're not here."

"What do you mean?"

"What do you think I mean?" she throws back. "My keys are not in my tote where I usually keep them, so I can't lock the fucking door."

"Okay, okay." I hold my hands up. "Why are you taking it out on me? I didn't take them."

"But you're flustering me, and I can't think straight."

An ambulance races back in the opposite direction the caravan was headed in earlier, and its siren echoes inside my head—it's definitely not helping to ease the tension in here.

Opening and closing my fists, I turn on my heel and power walk to the office, my heart thundering. If I stay here any longer, I'll burst and tell her exactly why her being in contact with Cash, even as online acquaintances, pisses me off.

Or I might kiss her again.

My head is a fucking mess.

"Where are you going?"

"To search for your keys," I call over my shoulder louder than is necessary, but my nerves get the best of me.

None of this is what I had in mind when I came here tonight. I expected to laugh over old times while we shared a bottle of wine, not fight over my asshole brother and yell at each other over lost keys.

Exhaling, I check the hook on the wall inside her office, then search her drawers, but I come up empty.

As I close the last drawer, Madi rushes inside. "Anything?"

I shake my head and stuff my hands into the pockets of my jeans.

She mutters a curse and scratches her forehead. "I know I had them on set this morning. I must've left them in the trailer."

"Let me guess—that's my fault too," I deadpan.

"You're not helping." She scoffs and flees the office faster than if it was infested by bees.

I take a few deep breaths—the woman is infuriating—then follow after her. She stands at the counter, the phone to her ear, but her frown tells me all I need to know.

We're going to be stuck in here for a while.

TEN

Madison

"I left my keys on the set and can't leave here without locking up," I explain to Sofia, clutching the phone in my white-knuckled grip.

"Shit. Okay, no problem, chica. I'll be there as fast as the subway will bring me," Sofia reassures me. "I don't want to keep you waiting too long. I hate being in there alone at night. So creepy. It feels like everyone's watching me."

"I'm not alone, actually. Ian's waiting here with me." I exhale, but it does nothing to relieve the weight on my chest.

"Oh," she draws out, and her voice takes on a much different—and suggestive—tone. "How nice of him to wait with you."

"Yes, but if you could still hurry, that would be great. I'd really appreciate it," I emphasize.

I can't stay in here all night with Ian fucking Bowman. That's right—I'm referring to him by his real name because even though we're both adults now, he's the same *boy* I used to know.

A scared and immature one at that.

Which is what I told Sofia this afternoon before Ian got here. She was making far too many jabs at my love life, so I explained to her the reality of our situation. Having worked with her for years now, she's a good friend, and I trust her to keep our secret.

But I don't like where this conversation is headed.

"Sure. I'll definitely hurry." From the sound of how slowly she pronounces those words, I wouldn't bet on her being fast. "Just so you know—I'm not dressed yet, and of course, the subway is always delayed. But at least you have snacks and champagne while you wait for me, right? Isn't this why you keep the salon stocked better than your own refrigerator at home—for emergencies?"

"No," I hiss.

"So, this is not an emergency?"

"It is," I quickly grind out.

"I see. I'll be *right* there, boss lady," she practically sings, then clicks off.

"What's going on?" Ian asks, the firm pinch in his brows deep.

"Sofia is on her way, but she wants us to party while we wait," I say sarcastically and cross my arms over my chest. "You don't have to stay."

"And miss the party?" His mouth lifts on one side, flirting with a smile.

"This isn't funny. None of this night is funny."

His face falls. "This isn't what I had planned for tonight, either, okay? But I'm trying to make the best of it."

I scoff. "That's what you're good at. Laughing off every shitty thing you do."

"And we're back to blaming me. Wow."

"Who else should I blame?"

"I don't even know what the hell we're fighting about anymore." He buries his face in his hands.

Just when I think I've won, his shoulders tremble, and he lets out a howling laugh.

"Are you serious right now?" My eye twitches as I stare at him. He has a death wish, doesn't he?

"Your accent does get stronger the more riled up you get." He uncovers his face, and his megawatt grin freaking blinds me, rendering me speechless. There's no doubt that smile is part of the reason he landed this big movie role.

It softens his edge.

It's as playful as he is.

And it's infectious.

My shoulders slump forward as I give in and smile. The way he's looking at me with appreciation makes it hard not to.

After all, my accent is comforting and reminds me of my parents. It's also a connection to the time I spent down south, and the way Ian appraises me is unique and special.

He can relate to it all, and that does something funny to my heart.

"Do you miss it?" he asks after a while. "Do you miss living in Texas?"

I shrug, glancing around the space that I've made my own. The original wallpaper was really just a bunch of torn scraps hanging on the walls like mold on stale bread, and we had mold too. The floor was naked cement, and the pipes were rusted, adding an odor that still sometimes haunts me.

But with patience, a hard-working team of professionals, and more patience, the place came together to turn out better than my vision.

"I often miss my parents, but I've created a life here. I have my friends and my business, and I'm happy," I say. "My parents fly out often too."

Ian nods and spins in place, seemingly taking it all in. Then his focus lands on the broken chair in the other room. "I love it, except for that evil contraption."

"You didn't have to sit there, you know." I hook my thumb over my shoulder and point to the perfectly structured chairs behind me. "There were plenty of other options."

"They were occupied." He stares at me pointedly. "You seem to be very popular around here."

"And that's a bad thing?"

"It is when I'm physically harmed because of it," he teases.

"I wouldn't say physically, not since it's obviously your ego that took a hit," I toss back.

He thrusts his tongue in his cheek like he's chewing on it, then relents. "To my defense, there were a lot of women staring."

Just like that, we've settled into easy conversation again.

It's how it always was with Ian. One minute I wanted to ring his neck, and the other, I wanted to pull him on top of me.

Not that I want the latter right now, but I like the change in subject at least.

I definitely, definitely, *definitely* do not want him on top of me.

I head toward the mini fridge, and over my shoulder, I say, "Sometimes I forget I ever lived in Texas. Like that period in my life happened to someone else. It was so long ago." I pull out an open bottle of champagne, retrieve two plastic cups from the cabinet along the wall, then pop the cork out of the bottle. As I pour us each a drink, the subtle bubbles and fizz fill my senses and the brief silence. I turn to face him, leaning my hip against the counter as I continue. "Other times, it feels like it was just yesterday. Either way, I made a home there for a few years, and it'll always be part of me."

His gaze bores into mine, so many emotions flashing across the depths of his eyes, and I know he catches the double meaning there.

That *he'll* always be part of me.

"I know what you mean," he whispers.

I push off the counter and hand him a cup, which he holds out for me to clink.

"What're we toasting to exactly? Fighting like we never stopped, your new movie, or being stuck in this salon for God knows how long?" I eye him over our raised cups.

"Definitely the first one."

His answer catches me by surprise. Did he not hear the part about being trapped in here? I don't know about him, but I have other things to do than hang around at my place of work after hours.

But as he sips his drink, a slight tic in his cheek winks at me, and I start to think maybe it's not such a bad thing.

With one last gulp, I finish the wimpy cup and set it aside on the mirror.

Ian and I each settled into a chair and have been

spinning around like we're back at the Texas State Fair and riding questionable rides as the fearless teens we were.

"Can I get a haircut?" he asks, interrupting my very *fascinating* internal game of counting the dots on the ceiling tile.

I whirl my chair around and stop once I'm facing him. "Are you allowed?"

He tilts his head. "You're right. I should get my parents' permission. Hold on." He holds a finger up and pulls his phone up to his ear, pretending to talk to someone on the other end. "Hey, Mommy. Is it okay if the nice lady cuts my hair?" he asks in a high-pitched voice.

"You're the biggest smartass I know, and that's saying something, considering I know quite a few of them from living in the city."

"You did start it."

"I was only asking because you're an actor in a movie. I'm new to your world, but aren't you supposed to maintain a certain appearance throughout filming for consistency purposes?"

When his amused expression falters, I can tell victory is mine, but he shakes his head, quickly catching himself. "My hair grows fast, and it's been three weeks since I last cut it. If you did the honors, you'd actually be helping me maintain consistency."

I tap my chin, pretending to mull it over. "You're on. But you should know it'll be two hundred dollars."

"I want a haircut—not a tattoo."

"Let's just say I added a very generous tip for all my trouble of being your fake girlfriend," I quip.

The grin that spreads across his incredibly handsome face

reaches his eyes, smoothing the thick brows arched above, and my breath hitches. Suddenly, I'm squirming under his appraisal like we're discussing something out of a dirty fantasy instead of a haircut.

He's a freaking wizard. That's the only explanation for how he can infuriate me so much one second and then turn that rage into fuzzy warmth the next.

"Let's do it." He hops out of his seat.

"You'll need to sit, actually."

"I knew that." He sits back down, clasping his large, strong hands in his lap, and I fan out a cape, lay it over him, and clasp the button at the back of his neck.

His sharp intake of breath draws my attention to him in the mirror, and I tilt my head to the side. "Do I make you nervous?"

"No, ma'am," he asserts, obviously trying too hard to appear firm as he shifts in his seat. I grab a pair of scissors, and his tone is infused with sarcasm when he deadpans, "I love when feisty redheads come at me with scissors after they've had a drink, even if it was champagne. Which might as well be Kool-Aid."

"If that's your roundabout way of asking if I'm too drunk to operate on your hair, then rest assured because I'm fine." I snap the scissors open and closed, making his eyes widen.

"I forget—were you a *Sweeney Todd* fan?" He follows my every movement as I begin trimming the ends of his wavy hair. Even though his question, cologne, and presence could be a major distraction, the truth is, I'm at my most Zen— as Erin would say—when I'm cutting hair. No small cup of champagne is going to change that.

"I haven't seen it. Actually, I wasn't too big a fan of

musicals, in general, until I saw *Wicked* on Broadway a few years ago. I've been to some others since then and really loved them too." I grab a few strands of thick hair between my fingers, smooth it up to the edge, and gulp as I cut the end pieces.

His hair always had volume and body, and I spent many nights running my fingers through it like we were in a shampoo commercial.

I've always lost myself in him and got excited for the next adventure. I never thought about what would happen if we broke up. It was never an option, and when it did happen, I was devastated.

Since then, I thought I'd hate him forever. Never did I imagine being here with him now, laughing and joking after all this time.

I tousle his hair and study my work in the mirror, feeling his heated gaze on me. My heart flutters as I slide around him for a pair of clippers, then resume my position behind him. The gentle buzzing fills the space as I continue working in silence and trying to ignore the way he watches me.

It's comforting and familiar, yet he makes me feel exposed.

When I moved back to New York for college, I started fresh. I didn't know anyone anymore, and no one knew me. Tessa was my freshman roommate, and we immediately hit it off. She was the one who encouraged me to pursue a career in cosmetology—which is why I always say that I was her first client since she's now a career counselor.

But before my friends in college, no one knew I wanted to do hair and makeup. That I enjoyed it more than making it a hobby. I soon became a different version of the person I was in Texas, and having Ian here, crashing into my life and seeing me now, is doing strange things to my stomach.

It's confusing.

Overwhelming.

Exciting.

I suddenly want to impress him and show off the life I've made here.

Licking my lips, I round the chair to face him, then lean down to study his sideburns as his eyes dart between mine. "What're you doing?" he asks.

"Trimming your sideburns, Elvis," I tease. "Relax. I do know what I'm doing."

"Oh, I know. And watching you work is a damn turn-on." He smiles, and my lips part as I suck in a sharp breath.

Ian's aftershave is faint, but from this close, I smell all man and feel his heat against my cheek like I would the sun on a hot day.

I'm too aware of his intense focus on me.

In order to calm the sudden jolt of adrenaline coursing through me, I hold my breath and graze the end of the clippers against the side of his head, first one, then the other, talking myself through each second of it like I'm a newbie at the salon.

I'm never deterred while I work, but being alone with Ian from this close has my brain and heart in chaos.

Once I'm finished, I assess my work, and when I'm happy with it, I say, "You're all set."

"Ask me," he rasps, snaking his hand out from under the cape to grasp my free hand. "Ask me to pick truth or dare."

I glance down to where our skin touches, and instinctively, my fingers curl around his. Being with him is as natural as laughing and breathing and swallowing.

Although it's hard to do the latter right now.

When did we stop joking around? And when the hell did it get so hot in here?

Tingles skip down my spine as I lock eyes with his in the mirror and whisper, "Truth or dare, Ian?"

ELEVEN

Ian

The words leave her mouth like a gavel sealing my fate.

I slide my damp palm down my jeans, then slowly pull off the black cape sprinkled with my hair. "Truth," I answer as the cape falls to the floor, removing the barrier between Madi and me.

She stands upright, and I drop my hand from her wrist.

Heart thundering, I unleash my admission in what feels like a single breath. "I didn't want to break up with you after graduation. I wanted to keep in touch and do the long-distance thing. I was prepared and ready and had our lives planned out, but..." I search her surprised expression. Did she really not know how crazy I was about her? "I thought you wanted to date my brother," I blurt.

Her jaw drops, and then she laughs.

It's one of those belly-aching, side-splitting laughs that echoes across the ceiling. Like dating Cash is the most ridiculous thing she's ever heard.

She wipes at the corners of her eyes, catching the runaway mascara in time before black lines run down her cheeks. When she finally somewhat composes herself, she checks me over, hiccuping between each word. "Oh. Wait. Are you serious?"

I nod, pissed that I'm not clued into this little joke she obviously thinks I'm playing. Although, confessing out loud that my high school girlfriend wanted to break up with me and date my older brother does sound… asinine, for lack of a better term.

But at the time, I thought it was very real, and a good reason to stop dating. After all, we weren't going to the same college or even staying close to each other. The distance was a lot, but adding my brother to the mix made my head spin.

And I admitted long ago that I was a teenager who made poor and impulsive decisions, so there's that.

"Why the hell would you think that?" Her smile fades. "Cash was like a brother to me. I never saw him as anything else, and I definitely did not want to date him."

I pinch my brows together. "The weekend before graduation, he made a comment about wishing he would've met you first. That you and I wouldn't make it past the summer and that he would be *there* for you afterward." I make my fingers into quotations, fighting the bile rising in my throat. The words taste bitter as I say them out loud for the first time since Cash spoke them to me.

What a giant asshole he was.

But no one saw him as anything other than the golden boy— honor student, star football quarterback, ladies' man. I knew differently, though. I saw the conniving side of him when no one was looking, and I experienced the brunt of it a few times.

Case in point—Madison Taylor.

"He told me he was going to talk to you."

She throws her head back to stare at the ceiling as if it's a time portal, sifting through all her past memories. "I don't remember... oh my God."

And there it is.

She laughs again, but it's more nervous and less hearty than the sound she made before. "He was joking."

"That's what I thought too."

"He said something about hanging out when I'm in town for a visit, and he joked about it being a date. I laughed, and he admitted he was kidding."

"Then why didn't you tell me? I asked you about him, and you denied ever talking to him."

"Because he wasn't serious." She pins me with her gaze. It's intense and vulnerable. Regretful and pained too. "I didn't think there was anything to tell. Besides, even if he was serious, you idolized your brother, and I refused to be the one who tainted his image."

"That's exactly it. I admired everything about him. I played football because I wanted to be like him and convinced myself that all those sacks, two-a-day practices, and grass burns on my shins were all worth it so I could be even half the man Cash was." I scoff, despising how pathetic I sound to have respected him so much, only for my brother to act like a jackass and kill my fucking spirit. Sighing, I run my fingers through my freshly cut hair. "Every girl wanted Cash, and they all thought being close to me would get them there. I didn't think you'd be any different." I bite out a curse. "I mean... *Shit*, I didn't mean it like that."

She crosses her arms over her chest. "You should've given me more credit."

"I didn't mean it like that," I repeat, and when she takes off toward the back, I lunge after her.

"How did you mean it, then?" she calls over her shoulder as she reaches a white porcelain sink along the wall. With choppy and frustrated movements, she washes her hands like she has slime on them.

I wait until she cuts off the loud stream of water to answer. "I was a stupid kid back then, who was insanely jealous of his big brother, okay?"

She tenses, her back still turned to me.

"I was an idiot to think that about you, and I'm sorry." I spin in place, laughing humorlessly. "Saying this out loud to you now makes me feel like an even bigger dumbass. It's all so juvenile and ridiculous."

"Yes, you are." She faces me.

"I'm what?"

"A dumbass."

"Agreed. Can that be on the official record, please? Ian Kurt Bowman is a dumbass."

That earns me a small smile from her, which is more than just a relief.

I drop both arms to my sides. "I should've been honest with you back then, but you should have too."

She sighs. "You're right. I should've told you the truth about him."

"We can add that to the official record as well." I grin as she places her newly dried hands on her hips.

After a beat, she holds her shoulders high, and if I were sitting down, I'd be on the edge of my seat as I wait for her to say something.

"You know what?" She assesses me with curiosity etched

in every sparkle of her green eyes. "It's in the past. Truthfully, if you and I would've stayed together, I probably wouldn't have stayed here and started a business. You probably wouldn't have started on the path to being a huge movie star. And we probably wouldn't be stuck in here tonight, though I could deal without the last one."

"I don't know." I shrug, lightening my tone. "If we weren't stuck in here, we wouldn't be having this conversation, and we wouldn't be feeling this heat between us."

"Ian Brock is just as charming and smooth as Ian Bowman, isn't he?" She hums and chews on the inside of her cheek as she sashays toward the bottle of champagne for another pour. "Why did you change your name, anyway?"

I follow her for a new cup of my own. After I take a sip, I ask, "Do you remember Decker? Wiley kid with crazy hair and an unyielding appetite for Skittles and the school librarian?"

She almost chokes on her drink, using the back of her hand to swipe at the drops on her chin. "I remember him," she sputters. "He had large hands too. Did he ever grow into them?"

"He did, and he also cut his hair, became a lawyer, and is the creator of Ian Brock."

"Oh?" She toys with her cup, running the tip of her finger along the rim as she waits expectantly for the rest of the story.

"Brock was the name of his goldfish, and being so sentimental, he named my online character after him," I say sarcastically as she giggles.

Thank fuck.

I couldn't take the disappointment in her voice anymore. But now that the past has been aired out, this conversation doesn't feel forced. I never realized that something was always holding us back before until we were finally honest with each other.

We can talk freely, and it makes me… fuck, it makes me want her even more.

I dip my head—*stay focused, Bowman.* "We were just being dumb kids, playing pranks on everyone we met while we hung out. I didn't know he was posting videos of it all on an Instagram account he'd created for me, but he was. For whatever reason, people enjoyed it, and my agent and I agreed to keep the name since that's how the world knew me." I scratch the back of my head, thinking back to all the times Decker and I made bets with bystanders that I could make the target spit their drink out, buy me a new shirt, or talk to my mother on the phone.

It was a special brand of nonsense, but it was fun. It made people laugh, and it helped me realize I wanted to do more of it on a bigger scale.

"I'm sure it also makes it harder for Principal Stratton to find you and give you detention for ruining his graduation speech. You know how much he loved to hear his own voice echo from a microphone in the middle of his old football field."

I nod, my lips curling upward. "God, I don't know if he was more pissed that he couldn't finish his speech during the commotion or that he got glitter in his hair from the confetti explosion. I bet it took him a month to wash it out."

"Probably longer than that." Madi shakes her head and takes another sip of her drink. "Now I want Skittles. Is that weird?"

"I was thinking the same." I chuckle, pacing in front of her.

"Too bad I only have crackers." She makes a face, then claps and waves for me to follow her. "Come on. Let me shampoo you and get rid of the prickly hairs on your neck—on the house."

"Finally. I was told celebrities get free shit, but this is the first I'm experiencing it." I take a seat and wink up at her. "This must mean I made it, huh?"

As she laughs, a new sense of peace settles in my chest.

It's like we're back to normal—back to the Ian and Madi we used to be. The fun and easy pair. But it's different too. Better and more comfortable without this wall of secrets between us.

And we're only just beginning to reacquaint ourselves, so there's a lot more to look forward to.

No matter what we've said about our situation, being stuck in here with her has made me feel more at home than my own house in LA does.

I suddenly hope Sofia never comes to let us leave.

TWELVE

Madison

"Your dad seriously isn't still mad at me about his garage door?" Ian arches his brows as he spins his chair to face me, a dazed tilt to his eyes, probably due to the bottle of champagne we just finished.

We're now on our second, and the only food of substance we've had to curb the drunkenness include crackers and chocolate raisins. Why do I even stock the fridge with that random combination?

"He's more pissed about you scuffing up his beloved car than the garage." I step down from my chair to retrieve the bottle from him.

Sofia texted a couple of minutes ago to share that she's just now switching lines and will be at least another half hour, so we gave up on cups. Drinking straight from the bottle is much easier.

"I think it's the only time I've ever seen my father cry, and he shut his hand in a car door before," I continue.

"My uncle used to say that there's no bond as strong as the one between a man and his truck." Ian holds his hand out like he's giving a speech as he mimics his uncle. "Of course, he'd interchange truck with tractor, cars, or just toys in general."

"Cheers to your uncle. He's got it all figured out." I raise the bottle and drink, trying not to stare at him.

Ian's hair is still damp and sexy, and I've imagined him stepping out of the shower more times than I can count over the last two hours.

In that time, the world outside has quieted, and every time a person walks by the window, I think it's Sofia, even though she told me she's on the subway.

No matter what hell I was planning to rain down on her, though, I'm relieved she's taking her sweet time.

I like being with Ian, especially after what he revealed about his brother.

It's hard to believe that's what happened between us all those years ago. That we broke up because of a miscommunication and stupid assumptions.

But the truth is, his brother was just the catalyst to the inevitable demise of our relationship.

We were young and lost. Ian and I were in love, but life and growing up would've pulled us apart eventually. Teens are tugged in every direction like branches of a tree in the winter, and we weren't any different.

Besides, I meant what I said before. I was in love with him all those years ago, and it broke my heart to let him go, but it's all worked out the way it was supposed to.

Shit, I've really grown up.

Ian crinkles a bag of crackers as he pulls one out and pops

it into his mouth. As he demolishes the snack, his tongue grazes his bottom lip for any rogue crumbs sprinkled there.

Idly running my hand through my hair, I follow the movement of his lips and jaw as he finishes chewing like he's performing a mating ritual.

Even when he eats, he's sexy.

"Want me?"

"Yes," I breathe, then sit upright.

He hands me the sleeve of crackers, and I stare at it. When I don't immediately accept, he studies me. "I asked if you wanted any. Don't you?"

"Right." I laugh, but it's high-pitched and nervous. When have I ever giggled like that?

I snatch a cracker from him and use my other hand to fan myself like I'm a ridiculous meme. "I'm going to grab us a couple bottles of water." I make a beeline for salvation, my mouth a dry desert after a few crackers—and Ian.

Even though we've settled our past differences, I'm not in a position to date him or do anything with him that resembles dating, outside of the headlines, anyway.

We're attracted to each other—that much is obvious. I've seen the way he checks me out, and they're not friendly once-overs, that's for sure.

On the contrary, he rakes his gaze ever so slowly from my feet to the top of my head like he's studying the lines on a sculpture. And he has stars in his eyes by the time he's done.

But the fact remains, he and I are from different worlds, and taking the relationship from fake to real is not an option.

Right?

Ian stands from his chair and stretches his legs from

side to side, straightening his crinkled jeans back into place. "You're hot."

"Excuse me?" I squeak with another sound I've never made before.

It's the booze. It has to be. I mean, he's just a freaking guy.

Ian Bowman.

My high school boyfriend.

That's it.

I'm drunk, and being alone with him is too tempting—that's all. I just need to sober up. Keeping my back to him, I untwist the cap to the water bottle and chug.

After I swallow, I already feel much better.

That's what I tell myself, anyway.

"Do you need me to turn the AC on?" He now stands in front of me, pointing a strong thumb over his shoulder.

I lick my lips and touch the back of my hand to my forehead to find I am, in fact, very warm. I wish I could say it's because I'm getting sick and have a fever. Anything to make Ian stop walking toward me with such purpose, his piercing gaze boring into mine.

What is he doing?

I gulp, but it's hard to swallow.

He reaches me in three steps and dips down to meet me at eye level. "Are you feeling okay?" he rasps, pulling my hand from my face and replacing it with his own.

My eyelids flutter closed as his knuckles skate and pause over my forehead. "I'm... fine," I manage.

"You're very warm."

"It's hot."

He chuckles, and he's so close to me that the sound feels like my own, rumbling deep inside my chest. "I'm actually pretty comfortable, but I'll turn the AC up."

I hum as he disappears down the makeshift aisle between stations, giving me the perfect opportunity to check out his backside—again.

I should stop doing that, shouldn't I? I don't know anymore. Ian's caused all kinds of turmoil in my head and heart since he returned, and after his confession, I'm only growing crazier, it seems.

When he reaches the thermostat, he presses a few buttons, and I imagine those fingers digging into my skin. I bet he's learned how to really use those fingers since they were last on me. Judging by his kiss the other day and the expert way he massaged my tongue, I'd bet his touch has evolved too.

God, I need to find out where Sofia is before I let this get out of hand.

Phone to my ear, I take a seat at one of the stations and wait for her to answer, but she doesn't. I do get a new text from her, though.

> **Sofia:** Sorry, boss lady. Hung up at the store—my niece is sleeping over. NEEDS cereal.

I much preferred it when she was lying to me about hurrying.

"That should help." Ian returns and places his hands on either armrest of my chair, caging me in, and my breath catches.

"I told you I'm fine," I say weakly, lowering my phone into my pocket.

He searches my face, and I stiffen under his scrutiny, feeling his gaze over my eyes, cheeks, and lips like he's touching me. He studies me in that way he does that leaves butterflies in my stomach. "You know what you need?"

You.

"To dance," he says simply.

This tickles a giggle out of me. "What're you talking about?"

"You have champagne and snacks. Don't tell me you don't have a Bluetooth speaker or some kind of sound system for music in this place."

"I do, but that doesn't answer my question."

He leans back, putting much-needed distance between us. "I promised you dinner and a fun time tonight. I know crackers are not the gourmet meal I had planned, but we can still make good on that later." He wiggles his eyebrows and grabs his phone from the other chair. "Now, what station do you want to listen to?"

"Country. Definitely country."

"I was hoping you'd say that." He winks and taps on his phone, connecting the music to the sound system.

As he walks into the space between the short rows of chairs toward me, a soft guitar melody floats above us. I smile as Kelsea Ballerini's voice sings the first verse. Naturally, I sway my hips to the slow tune.

"We should've started music the second we got here instead of sitting in silence like we're in detention," I say with a laugh. "Not that you would know anything about detention. You always knew how to prank, but you were even better at not getting caught."

"That's why they called me MC Prankster." He spreads his arms, then arches his brow. "Besides, you wouldn't know anything about it, either, darlin'."

I shrug coyly.

He uses one arm to scoop me up into his embrace, and a

laugh rips from my throat as I cling to his shoulders, kicking my feet back. Once I'm safely on the ground again, instead of steadying myself, I use Ian as an anchor.

I'm weak in the knees.

My stomach flutters with excitement and joy.

My thundering heart joins the song as it grows louder during the chorus, the notes heartbreaking, then hopeful.

I gaze into Ian's eyes as we fall into the rhythm of the song, his hand splayed across my lower back. He then brings our joined hands between us, holding them to his chest, and for a few long moments, we simply sway to the music.

When the song eventually ends, Ian doesn't let go as the next one begins. It's another slow melody, so we continue stepping from side to side, spinning in place between the rows of chairs. "Remember that Mexican restaurant we'd eat at every weekend?" he asks, breaking the silence.

I sag against him, lowering the side of my cheek to rest on his shoulder. "More like, every other night." I giggle, recalling countless evenings at our favorite spot. We'd complain about homework or a bad call at one of his games, and we'd laugh about who fell asleep in boring Mrs. Lance's history class too, all over bowls of chips and queso. "It was our place. Somewhere to unwind and have fun. I loved it."

"Have you found a place like that here?"

Immediately, margarita nights with my girls come to mind. Smiling, I grip his shoulder tighter and peek up at him. "My friends and I have a restaurant we frequent every week. It's more for the amazing margaritas, but the queso reminds me of that place in Texas. The tables have similar colorful squares around the edges, and it's always packed like the one I remember." I lick my lips and furrow my brows. "Actually, that's why I kept dragging Tessa and the other girls there, and then it became a tradition."

"Does it also look disappointing from the outside?" he asks as he dips me until the ends of my hair brush along the floor.

This makes me laugh, and when he rights me again to continue swaying, blood rushes to my face. "No. The outside is not misleading like the old place."

"It was so dingy on the outside, like an abandoned shack—"

"Until you went inside and out to their covered patio, which looked more like a rainforest without all the creatures," I finish, reminiscing about the restaurant that boasted not only the best tacos in town, but also its beautiful setting. It was filled with greenery, stone pathways between tables, and large columns separating sections.

"You had to give it a chance before you could get to the good stuff," he says, but it sounds distant.

And not just because we're nostalgic.

There's something else going on here, something deeper than digging up memories of a time long past.

"What made you think of that?" I ask.

His hold on me tightens as he answers, his smile a strange mix of sad and wistful. "I haven't found a place like that in LA, and I didn't realize how badly I missed it until I saw you again."

I raise an eyebrow, equally surprised and intrigued. "Have you tried googling it?" I whisper, my body buzzing with energy I haven't felt in a while. "It's LA. They must have a ton of restaurants."

One corner of his lip rises. "I'm not talking about the restaurant, Madi."

That's what I was afraid of.

"I was drawn to you the moment I saw you in the cafeteria that day our freshmen year. You were hot."

I try and fail to control my blush.

"But it was more than that. You were scribbling in a notebook while you ate like you didn't even see anyone else." He drops his voice as he slows his swaying, and the music becomes muffled like I'm hearing it through a wall. "I wanted you to see me."

I gulp.

"You didn't like me very much at first." Amusement dances across his features. "It took a bad pickup line and a worm in your hair to make you fall for me."

"I don't know which was more romantic," I muse.

He quickly grows serious again, working his jaw back and forth as his focus settles on my lips. "You were one of the very few people in my life who saw I was more than jokes and pranks. Our connection went beyond just bonding over the fact that we were both transplants, me from California and you from New York. We were real."

My lips quiver under his scrutiny, and my breathing quickens until I'm panting faster than if this were the beginning of a jog. Each of his words is like one fast stride after another, building up to the peak.

Just a couple more strides…

"I miss you," he confesses.

And I leap into his arms, closing the final few inches between us to crash my lips against his, assaulting his mouth as he hoists me up to wrap my legs around his waist.

This kiss is unlike the one we shared at the base. While that one re-ignited our chemistry, it was also hesitant and wrong, since it was just for show—a pretense.

This kiss, though…

This one is desperate.

Pleading.

Intimate and hot.

My fingers weave in his hair, and then I work them down to interlock at the nape of his neck, pulling his face closer, needing him.

Badly.

It's like I'm trying to crawl inside him, and I can't get enough, especially since he kisses me back as if he wants to devour me whole.

His hands squeeze my ass, and he plunges his tongue between my lips to explore and tease as we reacquaint ourselves.

He steals my breath with every sweep of his tongue.

"I guess you missed me too, huh, sweetheart?" he murmurs against my lips, and I smile back, enjoying the raw intensity of how our teeth clash together like we're two glasses raised in a toast.

A toast for this reunion—one of many celebrations.

Because I need more of this man.

His passion. His touch. His everything.

As his chest presses against mine, I'm thankful yet again that I forgot my keys and was able to feel him again.

THIRTEEN

Ian

Madi is ravenous, tugging on my bottom lip with her teeth as she feasts on my taste, and it drives me insane.

The moment I put my hands on her to dance, I was a goner.

She felt too good and right in my arms not to pour my truth out to her.

And I meant what I said.

Madi is the kind of woman I've always dreamed of ending up with, and it's hard to believe that our paths crossing again is a coincidence and not something more like fate.

Her heavy pants drive me forward, and when she starts squirming in my hold and rubbing against the most painful hard-on I've ever experienced, I'm fucking crazed.

I bury my nose in her thick red waves and nip, lick, and suck on the soft skin of her neck, peppering kisses down the column. Then I pull her sweater to the side to expose her collarbone and kiss at the hint of her shoulder.

I fucking worship her.

Her moans mix with my pounding heart in my ears, and I can barely hear the country song overhead.

Our emotions run free.

This is real and earth-shattering.

Crazy and inspiring.

I continue raining kisses everywhere I can like I'm on a timer as I walk us toward one of the stations. My dick stirs and strains against my jeans like it's trying to undo the zipper for me, but I refrain.

I want to taste more of Madison first.

Once I set her on both feet, I whirl her around and pull her back flush against my front. I groan as I rub myself along the curve of her ass. It's perky and especially sexy in her leather leggings.

"Ian," she breathes, resting the back of her head on my shoulder.

I gather her wild hair and move it to the side so I can whisper in her ear. "What will I find if I reach inside your pants, Madi?" I ask, flattening my palm over her chest and dragging it down to her stomach. I growl when I palm between her breasts, and it takes more energy than usually necessary to bring our reflection in the mirror into focus.

Madi writhes under my touch, and a sliver of her stomach teases me as she responds to my movements and words.

She's driving me to the brink, and we still have our clothes on.

My hand reaches the hem of her thick sweater, and when my fingers glide over bare, soft skin, my mouth waters.

"Are you wet for me, baby?" I run the tip of my nose along the outside of her ear as I dip my hand into the elastic waistband of her leggings.

Whimpering, she rubs against me harder, rising onto the balls of her feet in an attempt to get my fingers where she needs them.

But I'm a greedy son of a bitch.

I tsk. "You should know what I want."

Her eyes fly open and meet mine over her shoulder in the mirror, telling me she remembers my favorite type of foreplay.

A sense of pride swells in my chest as I use my foot to spread her legs apart and take a deep breath, inhaling her sweet smell.

"Wait." She shakes her head and takes off toward the front door.

What the hell?

I blink, trying to gather my thoughts of where we went wrong. Wasn't this what she wanted too? I search after her, my mind and body still reeling.

Until I notice Madi's frantically closing the blinds on the large windows in the lobby.

I sigh and tilt my head back as I whisper, "Thank you."

"What are you thanking my white ceiling tile for exactly?" She walks toward me with her hands on her hips, her smile knowing and seductive.

"Well, it's not every day that a very sexy woman such as yourself—"

"Wants a goofball like you?" she teases.

"—turns down a handsome gentleman like myself," I finish, grabbing her hand and twirling her around into the position we were just in before she thought to be the responsible one of us two.

"Is that right?" Her eyes narrow, and a devious gleam shines brighter in them than the lights on set.

"No." I shake my head as I run my hands back to the waistband of her pants and yank them down, kneeling behind her. "I'm actually no gentleman."

I spread her quivering thighs and inhale her sex. From my spot between her long legs, I notice she grips the counter—*good girl.*

Panting, I slide between her opened legs, palm her ass with both hands, and finally get that taste I've been craving for what feels like years, licking and sucking and fucking her with my mouth as she moans my name in a mixture of reverence and pleas.

One of lust and satisfaction.

It sounds good coming from her perfect mouth.

Almost as magnificent as her sweet taste soaking my tongue. She was, in fact, wet and ready for me, and I want to prolong this as much as possible.

But I didn't factor in how much I would enjoy this. How quickly my cock would threaten to combust.

I slide my tongue over her clit as my nose presses on the tight bundle of nerves at her center. I watch as she squeezes her eyes closed and hisses her approval. "Keep… going," she sputters as the tremble in her legs travels up to her stomach and arms.

She grips the counter harder.

My assault becomes frantic.

The song breaks through the blood rushing to my ears as it transitions into the chorus, growing louder and louder as if in tune with Madi and her screams.

"Yes," she says as she hangs her head and locks eyes with me. "God, Ian."

She's close.

The muscles of her thighs tighten.

This is it.

She removes one hand from the counter to grip a tuft of my hair, holding me in place as I fist handfuls of her ass. "Right there," she pants. "That's it."

I keep sucking on her clit, relentlessly working her until she clenches and explodes in a bright blend of satisfied moans and appreciation.

Humming, I swallow the last of her climax and use my thumb to wipe each corner of my mouth, my tongue tingling with the taste of her. It's buzzing like I just took a few shots of vodka or tequila, and it burns down my throat with the sweetest bliss.

I want more.

I need it—I need *her*.

Madi falls slack against the counter, and I help her onto the seat, after which I yank her leggings the rest of the way off.

Her head lulls to the side as she points to my pants. "Off."

"Yes, ma'am."

She bites her bottom lip, raking her hungry gaze over me as I expose myself, my hard length standing at attention.

"I have an idea." She snaps her fingers and pulls my arm toward the other room. As I follow, her bare ass peeks out from underneath her sweater that sashays as she walks.

I lick my lips.

I won't last long.

"Sit," she demands, nodding behind her.

The firm tone she uses makes my knees buckle—good thing she needs me to sit.

I peer over her shoulder and let out a strangled laugh. It's the broken chair. She's removed the hazardous bowl from the top, along with the pieces of paper.

The second the cool leather hits my bare skin, I bite out a curse, but I'm immediately speechless when she removes her pants the rest of the way.

With a deep breath, she hovers over me, places a hand on either armrest, and kisses me as she slides onto the chair to straddle my lap. "I figured we could properly send this demon chair on its way."

"I like the way you think."

The chair squeaks, and the leather makes a grating sound as Madi adjusts herself. We laugh into each other's mouth, swallowing up the sounds without breaking our heated kiss.

My tip grazes her wetness.

Her fingernails dig into my shoulders.

My nerves are shot.

Fuck…

"Wait." I lean my forehead to hers, gathering my wits. "Condom," I rasp. "I have a condom in my wallet in my jacket pocket."

She wiggles off me, and I shift in the leather, painfully hard, not to mention my blurred vision.

When she returns, Madi sheaths me herself and practically hops back into place on my lap.

I fist her hair as I kiss her neck, and her breath is hot and heavy in my ear. I palm her breast over her sweater on my way down to grip both her hips, and once there, I position her center at my tip.

I'm dying to feel her.

With my hold on her, I drop her onto me, no longer patient or in a teasing mood.

I just fucking need her.

She throws her head back, and the ends of her hair tickle my bare legs, fueling my thrusts to go faster and fit myself even deeper inside her.

She's so damn wet.

And hot.

And wild.

My Madi.

I bury my face in her sweater between her breasts as she slides her hips back and forth, creating friction and driving me to a place beyond insanity. "Yes, yes," she repeats as she cradles my head.

"Fuck, Madi," I growl as I take over again and rattle what's left of the metal pieces of the chair. If it wasn't broken before, it definitely is now.

"Call me… Madi… again," she stammers, and her request temporarily throws me off.

I knew she liked it when I called her that.

Smirking, I find our rhythm again and tug on a handful of her hair, urging her to open her eyes. "Madi, you're so damn sexy and perfect. Madi…"

Her hands roam through my hair and down my shoulders, until she leans them on my knees behind her and arches her back, freeing her hair from my grasp, but this view of her works too.

Especially since I can do more from this position.

Grunting, I yank her sweater up and over her chest to bite down over her bra on a nipple, earning me a sexy scream from deep in her throat.

Our rhythm becomes urgent and manic.

Our hips rock into each other at a furious pace, and her

core clenches a little more each time she drops onto me, squeezing and sucking me into oblivion.

She keeps her hands on my knees, giving herself to me and this moment, and right when I think I'll burst, Madi's cry rips from her pretty lips as a second climax slams into her.

I clench my jaw when my own release hits me hard and fast, and she sucks me dry.

We're dripping in a mix of lust and contentment, and I'm spent.

Captivated.

Completely enraptured by Madison Taylor.

FOURTEEN

Madison

We both get cleaned up, and when I emerge from the bathroom, Ian is standing in front of the broken chair and staring at it.

He's fully dressed, but his hair is unruly as if a gust of wind messed it up. His cheeks also have extra color in them, and I ache to touch him again.

"I was going to fix this chair, but we have to burn it now," I joke as I rejoin him.

"I did clean it, if that counts for anything." He gestures toward the new shiny leather and stuffs his hands into his pockets. "Although you're probably right. No amount of cleaning products can erase the traces of what we just did."

I smile and close the gap between us. Intertwining my fingers through his, I kiss his lips, and we linger, melting into each other like we're preparing for round two.

Sighing into him, I place my hand over his chest. "More

champagne?" I whisper, raking my teeth over my bottom lip as he watches my every movement.

His eyes are dazed and cloudy as he idly nods like he doesn't care what I ask for—he'd say yes to anything.

I tap my chin. "Or you could clean the bathrooms? Maybe fold the clean towels that I forgot about? The floor could use an extra sweep too."

He still nods as he stares at my lips, but after a brief pause, he snaps his attention up to my eyes, his jaw dropping. "Wait. What?"

"Just testing a theory." I burst into laughter and pat him on the back, then brush past him toward the mini fridge for a new bottle of champagne. "Come on, MC Prankster," I call over my shoulder.

Spotting my phone by the fridge, I turn it over and see I have a few messages from clients, as well as a few texts from the girls, checking in to see if I've strangled Ian yet.

I had texted them earlier to let them know that we weren't getting out of here anytime soon just so people on the outside other than Sofia knew two people were stuck in here.

Quickly, I tap out a message in our group chat to tell them we're fine—more than fine, actually.

My God, I'm *great*. Fantastic. Blissfully sore in all the right places from riding Ian Brock all the way to Jupiter.

He remembered my body like it was yesterday when we were stealing kisses and sneaking around for a quick rendezvous.

His fingers and mouth and *everything* were skilled.

But this time, Ian also paid attention to who I am now. He was in tune with my body and listened to it like his life depended on it.

I was the center of his universe, and I've missed that feeling. Even though it's complicated between us, he's made me realize that the guys I've gone out with haven't made me feel even half as important or worshipped, but Ian blasted through my lull with as much force as a tornado.

"Cheers." I tap my cup to his, and we settle back into our chairs.

Once he swallows, he eyes me curiously. "So, there never really was a Chaz, huh?"

I snort, and my drink of bubbly makes it halfway up my nose before I choke it down.

"I knew it." He wags a finger at me as I catch my breath between the fit of laughter and a drink gone wrong. "It was all a ploy to make me jealous."

"No," I draw out and clear my throat for good measure. "He's a very real guy I went out with once, but that won't be working out."

"Have your eye on your fake boyfriend, do you?" He winks, holding his chin and moving it from side to side like he's at a modeling shoot.

"As a matter of fact…" I lean forward, smiling over my cup. "I do."

I crawl into the chair with him and rest my head on his shoulder as we continue talking in hushed tones.

It's darker in here now that I've closed the blinds, which is keeping the moonlight out. In the confines of the salon, Ian and I steal champagne-soaked kisses and coy glances while we wait for Sofia to rescue us, although we're perfectly content to be here too.

It's almost eleven when we hear the door opening. "Hello?" Sofia calls out.

I jump, spilling my drink over the sides of my cup.

"Scared the shit out of me," I whisper to Ian, who laughs.

While he rushes to grab a towel for the mess, I hurry toward the front to meet Sofia.

"I didn't interrupt anything, did I?" Her question is laced with innuendo as she searches behind me.

A gust of wind bursts through the door before it shuts again, but when Ian comes up beside me, his warmth courses through me like all the champagne I've had tonight. It's been a whirlwind, and I'm still tingling from the two orgasms he gave me too.

Suddenly, I'm upset that we have to leave.

"Sofia, right?" He flashes her a smile. "Nice to see you again."

"You too." She dips her chin onto her shoulder, eyeing him like a piece of candy. I swear, if she starts twirling her hair, I'm going to ask her to get out because, clearly, she isn't Sofia.

The Sofia I know wouldn't be tongue-tied and blushing over a celebrity like this.

I clear my throat, drawing her attention, and she stands upright.

"Thank you for taking care of my sweet boss lady," she says.

"Pleasure was all mine." He winks down at me.

I groan. "Can we please get out of here now?"

"I'll grab our things while you close up." He kisses my cheek and leaves me alone with this sudden stranger.

Averting my gaze, I move behind the counter to gather the items I dumped out of my bag when I was looking for my keys earlier. "Did you forget how to talk?" I whisper, suppressing my laugh. "You seem to lose your accent around him."

"And you seem to gain one," she shoots back. "You're a regular cowgirl with him next to you."

I scoff, scooping up my lip glosses, along with stray change.

She nudges me upright. "All jokes aside—I'm happy for you."

"It's not like that," I say, but it's weak.

Before we can say anything else, Ian appears beside us, and my sharp intake of breath echoes between us.

"Right," Sofia draws out. "I'm just sorry it took me so long to get here."

I roll my eyes at her not-so-subtle sarcasm. "Come on."

Giggling, she practically skips to the door.

"Did I miss something?" Ian asks as we bundle up and follow her out.

"Just years of Madi's loneliness," Sofia chirps over her shoulder.

"Sofia!" I glare, and Ian chuckles behind me, wrapping his arm around my waist.

"If only I filmed this movie sooner," he says into my hair, and I instinctively lean in, giddy and totally lost in his embrace instead of planning Sofia's demise for her embarrassing candidness.

She hums as she finishes locking up, then nods toward the road, where a few cars pass in a blur. "Want me to hail you a cab?" she offers, one eyebrow quirked.

Ian shakes his head, and if I'd had even one more cup of champagne, I'm sure that would've made me dizzy. As it stands, I'm pleasantly buzzed on alcohol—and him.

"I'll make sure she gets home safe." Ian squeezes my hip, and I lean farther into him, sniffing his neck with what I believe is subtlety.

But when Sofia snorts and mumbles something akin to, "I bet you will," I don't think it was that inconspicuous, after all.

It does make me giggle, though.

"I'll see you tomorrow, boss lady." She walks backward, smirking. "And Ian, I better see you soon too."

He lifts his hand in a wave, and once she's gone, I bury my face in Ian's checkered flannel shirt under his leather jacket.

His chest rumbles too, shaking underneath me, and as our laughter subsides, I rest my chin on his shoulder. "She was so jealous," I say, followed by a snicker that tickles my nose.

"And what exactly did she have to be jealous about, darlin'?"

"Because she knew we had *sex* in here." I whisper the word like it's against the law and cover my mouth.

He smooths my hair back. "How drunk are you?"

I lick my lips and toss my hair over my shoulder as I try to stand upright. *I am standing up, aren't I?* "I'm not at all. I'm just having trouble—what's the word?"

"Standing still? Opening your eyes completely? Enunciating?" Ian reaches out to steady me.

"Enunciating!" I clap. "God, you are so smart. When did you get so good at English? It was your worst subject." I fall into him and plant what might be considered a sloppy kiss against his half-open mouth. I think I interrupt him, but it's too hard to care when it feels this good kissing him.

"And even after this long, you won't let me forget it," he says lightheartedly as I pull back and lick my lips to savor the taste of him that still lingers there. "Let's get you some food."

"Oh, I'm starving!"

"I figured."

"And you did promise me dinner tonight, mister." I jab my finger against his hard chest.

"I believe I promised you a date, not just dinner." He slings his arm around my shoulders and leads us toward the crosswalk.

"You were always so sure of yourself. Like a cat."

"Cats are sure of themselves?"

"Yes. Everyone knows that."

"Of course." Ian glances around. "Is there anything in particular you're in the mood for?"

I purse my lips as I search our surroundings like I'm wading through thick mush. "Not really…"

"How about pizza?" he suggests. "We should be able to get pizza somewhere at this hour, right?"

"Duh." I spread my arms wide, reveling in the freedom. The signal changes for us to cross, headlights blinding us as we make our way to the other side. "This is New York, after all. The city is basically a giant pizza." I point to the buildings around us. "That's a mushroom. There's a pepperoni. Oh, and that's the cheese." I point across the street to a fenced-in basketball court, which is visible only by a flickering streetlight.

Ian's laugh is soft and comforting as he places his hand on my lower back, and we continue down the sidewalk.

"I really need to eat." I sigh, the pounding in my head growing more intense than before.

As we walk, I lean into his side to help shield me from the cold wind. It stings, but it's helping sober me up, that's for sure.

"Shit, does the cold ever let up around here? It's spring and freezing."

I smile. "You should be here in the summer. It's sweltering. Reminds me of Texas."

"I'd have to experience that for myself to believe it." He rubs comforting circles on my lower back as cars drive behind us.

Out into the city, we walk huddled together like we're riding into the sunset at the end of a movie, but once we find the first pizza joint with an "Open" sign turned on, I know I want more of Ian.

As we smile over our enormous slices with gooey cheese hanging off the sides, I know this is no ending.

Rather, it's just the beginning for us.

FIFTEEN

Ian

"I have to admit, you look great together," I hear Annalisa say from behind me.

I drop the sandwich onto the table topped with a variety of foods for meat eaters like myself and vegans like Annalisa too. "I'm sorry?" I ask, spinning on my heel to face her in a move only professional dancers have perfected, but I'm nervous.

Annalisa's voice is unlike her normal one. It's too calm, even, and genuine.

It doesn't help that she's in full special effects makeup, which consists of dark eye shadow and pale skin complexion. She's supposed to be possessed by the Second Worlders in today's scenes, and the artist certainly nailed it.

She turns her phone screen toward me and attempts a smile, but it comes out as more of a grimace. I'm not convinced the latter wasn't the goal. "You and Madison."

I don't need to be up close to recognize the long red hair in the picture. It's undeniably Madi, and instantly, the tension in every part of my body relaxes.

The image is of us through a window at the pizza place the night we were stuck in her salon last week. We're holding hands across the table like we're in a scene of *Serendipity*.

If it were a movie, we'd only need the one take to nail the romance.

A night to remember.

"Madison's very lucky," Annalisa says.

"Thank you for saying that," I offer, still cautious.

"I'm sorry about acting so crazy before." She laughs, but it's shaky. "That was bizarre, right?"

I shrug, not sure if this is a trap or trick of some sort.

"Relax." She rolls her eyes. "This is a real apology."

"Of course." I chuckle, running my fingers through my hair.

"I just... I want us to start over." She places a gentle hand on my forearm. "We'll shoot for a few more weeks once we're back in LA, and I don't want there to be any weirdness between us for the remainder of filming. I want us to be friends. As you might've noticed, Hollywood can be pretty lonely, so it's nice to have someone you can trust."

My stomach churns, knowing the feeling she's describing well.

I'm also suddenly nauseous at the mention of leaving New York next month—of leaving Madi when I only just got her back.

Brushing it off, I smile at Annalisa and mean it when I say, "I'd like that."

Her shoulders sag with relief, surprising me that this

means so much to her. "I think that's why I do this sort of thing. Why I get attached to guys and act like a spirit out of *The Conjuring*, or well, *Ghost Predators*." She dips her head, and when she glances back up at me, her eyes reflect the sadness I was starting to know well before I left LA. "It's unbelievable to have so many fans around the world, yet I couldn't be lonelier. And that would make anyone act crazy as fuck, right?"

I grip her shoulder in comfort, my earlier caution taking a backseat. "Don't be so hard on yourself. It's not easy doing what we do. I'm still fairly new, but already, I can tell it's a good idea to surround myself with people I care about if I have any hopes of staying sane. I'd really like to be friends, Annalisa."

"Thank you." She throws herself at me, and I catch her in a friendly embrace, my heart softening for her as I start to understand how much more there is to this starlet beneath the dolled-up surface and face of magazines, billboards, and beauty commercials.

"You two are on," Sarah interrupts, pointing toward the set.

We pull apart and get into character as we step in front of the camera, replacing the other actors whose scenes are finished for the day.

I flick my gaze toward the crowd behind Richard where Madi usually stands, but she's already gone. As with the last few days, we've mainly seen each other in passing, long enough to sneak a kiss here and there. She hasn't been on the base as much since we've needed special effects makeup instead, which has been done by Rocco. He's fun and talented, but it's nothing like starting my days off with Madi.

He doesn't smell as good, either.

Nonetheless, he knows what he's doing. When I looked at myself in the mirror earlier, I was thrown off by the dark black circles painted under my eyes, thick lines expertly drawn on either side of my face like my cheeks are sunken in, and the dark red smudges around my mouth. I shrieked like I did when my character sees a ghost for the first time.

Since my character is becoming more and more zombie-like, today's makeup is heavier than it has been. It's a new level of acting for me as I lean into the frenzy that once-plain Justin is feeling now that he's possessed.

Annalisa and I need only a couple of takes for each scene, and I thank our newfound agreement for that. We've found a balance in our personal relationship that has definitely helped. Richard praises us as if he's a proud father, and I thank him.

I'm also silently grateful and relieved I haven't gotten any more warnings from him.

Safe to say—life is good.

But by the end of the day, my chest is heavy.

It's one more day crossed off on our schedules, bringing us closer to the end, and I'm not ready for the credits to roll just yet.

After the sun has long set, I enter my trailer and proceed to wash the day's makeup off, painting the white sink with lines and splashes of reds and blacks and dark blues. Once I'm finished and burying my face in a towel to blot it dry, my phone rings.

"Hello, Ian? Is that you?" Keith's voice sounds through my speaker as I finish drying my face.

"Yeah, man, what's up?" I call out into the phone sitting on my sink.

"Just wanted to make sure since I haven't heard your fucking voice in forever." He laughs.

Smiling, I pick up the phone and sit on my couch to put my shoes on. "I've been a little busy filming a movie and all."

"And this has nothing to do with a certain makeup artist, right?" he asks in an all-knowing tone. "Here I thought it wasn't what it looked like since that's what you told me, but you never did explain."

"It wasn't…" I rub the pad of my thumb over my curling bottom lip. "Until it was."

"Care to elaborate, or do I have to pull it out of you? Get on with it, asshole." Keith's extra cursing makes it obvious he's at the office and not at home with toddler ears listening in. It's confirmed when I hear the thud of him throwing his feet onto the desk.

I check the time on my phone and give him the quick version of how our fake relationship to get me out of Annalisa's clutches ended up with Madi and me hooking up in her salon where we quickly turned very real.

"Nice," Keith approves.

"I'm actually about to go meet her here in a second." I stand, shaking out my denim pant legs that had ridden up while I sat.

I hear muffled groans from Keith's end before he says, "I have to go too. Rhett, the son of a bitch, has called me five times in the last ten fucking minutes, probably to *boohoo* over losing his spot on that children's show. How many ways can I explain that he can't play a thirteen-year-old when he sounds like he's forty? The kid's voice is deeper than my old man's, fucking Christ. I told him I'd get him a new role, and I already have something lined up for him."

I cringe.

After a pause filled with the sound of a clicking keyboard, he sighs.

"Was that Hollywood talking, or were you up all night again?" I ask, treading lightly.

Like me, my agent didn't grow up in LA. He moved out there from Oklahoma and sometimes gets caught up in the pressures of Hollywood. He often confides in me that he's pulled in so many different directions between work, clients, and his family that he sometimes feels like he's going insane.

Every now and then, he has to unload—he's only human, after all.

"A little of both," he confesses.

"Everything okay with the twins?"

"They're great." He sighs again. "My wife and I finally got some grown-up time last night, but we stopped because she thought she heard one of the twins moving around, only to find they were fast asleep. When we finally went back to bed, she passed out, and my damn balls are bluer than that girl in the Willy Wonka movie."

"Shit."

"Fuck, I have to go. It's Rhett again. Wish me luck."

He clicks off before I can offer any help, not that I'd know how to respond. I've never been in his professional or personal positions. I've never been married or even had a relationship last longer than three months, other than Madi. That was in high school, though.

My phone buzzes in my hand, and I find a message from Madi about our late dinner plans in half an hour.

> **Madi:** Can't wait to see you soon. It's been too long since I last got a squeeze.

This makes me laugh. My girl loves my ass more than any other part of me, including my mouth, which is surprising considering how much she loves when I bury my face between her thighs.

And I've done it often over the last week.

We've spent a lot of time in her bed together, absolving me of lonely nights in my hotel room.

She's given my life the fire I needed.

Waking up with her next to me, her eyes lazy with sleep and hair mussed from a long night of sex, is my new favorite kind of high.

Not to mention, cooking with her. It's usually done wearing only aprons and nothing underneath, which makes it easier to fill the time while chicken bakes.

We even got a recipe from her friend Tessa for brownies. She and Madi insisted they're the best around, and although I was skeptical at first, I turned into a believer after a single bite.

It didn't hurt that Madi fed it to me while straddling my legs, my hard cock pressed against the curve of her ass.

Going out to dinner tonight with Tessa and her fiancé, Carter, will be the first time we've left Madi's apartment together other than to come to the set, and I'm excited to be a real couple in the world beyond ghosts and zombies.

Changed and looking more human, I let the door shut behind me and take the steps down until my feet hit the concrete. As I round the corner toward the next block, I type out a reply to Madi.

> **Me:** I'm happy to report my ass is extra squeezable tonight, so be ready.
>
> **Madi:** Tease.

Madi: Hurry up. I'm waiting.

Me: On my way, one step at a time. You people walk too much around here.

Madi: You haven't seen anything yet. A 10,000 step day is child's play around here.

Me: How barbaric.

I smile at my phone as I exit the base and cross the street, on the other side of which I duck under a scaffold, skirting around a guy doing pull-ups. Huh. Who needs a gym when the city is its own obstacle course?

Right on.

I silently applaud the man's dedication and continue down the sidewalk, strolling shoulder-to-shoulder with other pedestrians and bumping into the occasional speed walker, until I finally reach the small Italian restaurant we agreed to meet at.

I stop in front of the faded brick building next to the stairs that lead to the entrance below, and I'm nearly drooling over the rich aromas of basil, garlic, and other herbs drifting from the restaurant like salt from the ocean back home.

I lick my lips like I can already taste the Italian dishes, which I bet are as authentic as it gets around here, given this isn't a chain. It doesn't seem to be much of a tourist spot, either, since there aren't any museums or attractions nearby.

My phone vibrates with another new text.

Madi: Who are you waiting on out there? We're inside.

I peek over the wrought-iron railing and into the window downstairs to find her and a blonde woman waving at me. Grinning, I bounce down the steps and cross the threshold into a space that's not much bigger than my hotel suite. I pass the only other occupied table—a young couple who seem to be out on a romantic date—and reach my group in a couple of strides.

Before I sit, I plant a kiss on Madison's mouth like we're entirely alone, but when plates clink in the kitchen, we both jump. "I've spent my day with ghosts. You'd think a few plates wouldn't make me blink twice." I chuckle, shrugging my jacket off.

Madison dips her head, but I can still make out the subtle twitch of her nose as she runs a finger along her bottom lip, drawing my gaze there and following its soft back-and-forth motion like a boat swaying at sea.

A throat clears from the other side of the table, breaking my spell. "We're here too, by the way," the man, whom I assume is Carter, teases, his grin all-knowing and amused.

"Howdy." I rise from my seat to shake his hand for a proper introduction, and I nod to Tessa too, then point to Madi. "This one wasn't on set much today, so I had to make up for the time lost."

"Do you get much time on set for... extra activities?" Tessa narrows her eyes.

"No. We are professional," Madi insists.

Carter attempts to hide his laughter behind the menu, his shoulders shaking, and Tessa tsks. It's obvious that neither of them is buying our denials.

"Professional with the occasional ass squeeze on my way out of the trailer," I say, giving in. From what Madi's told me and the comfortable vibe I'm already getting, I sense I'm in good company.

Madi smacks my arm, but when I glance over, she's smiling. "I can't resist," she relents.

Carter drops the menu onto the table. "You're welcome for that, by the way."

"Oh, God." Tessa folds her arms across the table in front of her as Madi passes me a bottle of red wine with a name I've never heard of scrolled across a white square sticker.

As I pour myself a glass to catch up with them, Carter's eyes widen toward Tessa. "What? It's thanks to me that he and Madi reunited since I'm the one who got her the job."

"Your assistant did," Tessa corrects him, her voice light and teasing.

"Technicalities." Carter shrugs and raises his half-filled glass of wine up for a toast. "To love in unlikely places."

Sighing, Tessa relaxes into his side as she clinks her glass with his. "Can't he be so romantic sometimes?"

"So dreamy," Madi draws out, following it up with a laugh, and I know we're going to do a lot of that tonight.

The server comes by to take our order, her thick Italian accent confirming my earlier theory that I'm about to get authentic cuisine, and once Carter orders another bottle of red for us all, I add, "Can we also get the bruschetta for an appetizer, please?"

She smiles politely and holds her hand out, touching her thumb to two fingers. "It's pronounced *bruh-sketta*."

We fall into a round of *ahs* and repeat after her until she nods with approval, her brown eyes full of wisdom and longing, which I assume is because she misses Italy.

I know a fraction of what she's feeling since I, too, miss my home in LA, and I've only been gone for almost a month. New York is far too cold, and I don't own anything heavier than a leather jacket. Even that wasn't broken in before I stepped foot off the plane at JFK.

As someone who lived in southern California, then in Texas, and back in LA, my blood isn't accustomed to this kind of cold.

The server finishes writing down our orders and waltzes through the curtain back to the kitchen as a pair of women enter, gushing about the glass and ceramic trinkets along the shelves behind a clunky square register.

This is the kind of traditional and quiet place that won't accept Apple Pay, and I already like it before I've even tasted the food.

"I knew the right way to pronounce it. I just didn't want to come across as a know-it-all." Carter sips his wine and almost spits it back out when Tessa calls him out.

"You did learn a lot about Italy during all your trips over there, including women, their naturally curvy hips, and that they parade around topless at the beach."

"I'll take you to one of those beaches in Greece for our honeymoon." He wiggles his eyebrows.

"You're right, Tess. He *is* romantic." Madi squints sarcastically at him.

Carter kisses Tessa's cheek as our appetizer comes out, and for the rest of dinner, we swap stories about how we all met, although my and Madi's story isn't as eventful as Tessa calling the sheriff on Carter because she thought he was a stalker.

Turns out, he was just her brother's best friend.

By the end of it, I almost choke on my bite of *bruh-sketta*, which is tasty perfection. The bread is thin and crispy, yet fluffy at the same time. The tomatoes are cooked just the right amount to be blackened on the top. The basil tastes fresh too, like they just picked it off a real plant.

But better than that or any of the rest of our food is the company.

Throughout the evening, Madi squeezes her slender fingers around my quad, and I wrap my arm around the back of her chair, comfortable and content to be here.

"Oh, I have a story." Madi holds a finger up, her eyes animated as she describes a time from when she and Tessa were roommates in their college dorm. "We were celebrating my very last teen birthday, and I wanted to do something wild, like get a tattoo."

"You don't have any tattoos," I interject, recalling every inch of her skin.

"That's part of the story!" She grips my shoulder and gives it a shake. "So, I couldn't wait until my birthday, and the night before, Tessa googled a tattoo parlor. We picked the one with the highest ratings, but our taxi dropped us off at an Irish pub that was hosting a St. Patrick's Day party."

"We'd given the driver the wrong address," Tessa explains.

"But we agreed to put our new fake IDs to good use for a drink, then find another place. I was determined to get a tattoo, damn it." Madi brings her fist down onto the table next to her half-empty plate. "But Tessa and I got carried away with the drinks—they had a ton of specials—and we joined a bachelorette party, who thought we were their sorority sisters."

Tessa snorts as she picks up her wine glass. "Didn't we also pretend to be French?"

"Yes!" Madi claps. "I think I made up words and convinced them it was French."

"Fun times." Tessa clinks her glass to Madi's. "Oh, and speaking of your birthday, what St. Patrick's Day party are we attending this year?"

"One of my clients told me about karaoke night at Bar Underground." She turns to me, her smile effortless and glowing. "I celebrate my birthday on March seventeenth every year because of the tattoo-pub-bachelorette party fun."

I quirk a brow, and as I twirl her hair around my finger, I say, "Then karaoke it is. For you, anyway."

"You have to sing too." She pulls on my arm. "Free shots go to the ones who sing and wear green."

"Before we get into all that, I think it's in Ian's best interest to know about Bree." Carter turns to me and smirks. "You only have a few days, so I hope you're a fast learner."

"Actually, that's not a bad idea." Tessa nods, her cheeks flushed.

As we finish our entrees, I learn all about Bree—more than our brief introduction on set had offered me.

"I can't decide if I'm scared or not," I joke.

Madi laughs. "You should be scared."

Empty plates aside, Carter tops off Tessa's and Madi's glasses with the rest of our second bottle of wine. "Should I order another?" he asks.

"I think that's enough for tonight. We still have to get home, you know." Tessa leans into him.

He sets the bottle down and shrugs. "I'll call us a car when we're ready to leave."

"I didn't think you had any money," I tease, adding to the number of times his famous billionaire status has been brought up over the evening.

Carter narrows his eyes as Tessa laughs.

I wag my finger at Carter. "If I would've known I'd have competition for fame tonight, I would've brought my special chair to sit in. The one with my name and everything. Someday I'll have my name on a star on Hollywood Boulevard, and I'll really show you."

The table erupts, and Madi leans over, her nostrils flaring. "That's hot." She sharply inhales like she's taking all of my cologne and keeping it for herself.

I capture her lips in what I thought would be a chaste kiss, but Madi cups my cheek and slips her wine-soaked tongue between my lips to deepen it.

Pulling back, I blink and squirm in my seat.

My damn blood is on fire.

Humming, I drag my foggy gaze toward the other side of the table and announce, "We have to go."

"Nature calls." Tessa giggles, giving Madi a once-over.

"Bye, babe." Madi hurries around the table to give her friend a quick hug and wraps one arm around Carter as well. "Feel free to finish my wine. And as always, be good to my girl," she says to him, the underlying tone dripping with innuendo.

I rub a palm down my face, unable to contain my grin as my chest stirs. She only had a couple glasses of wine and isn't at all drunk—Madi's just happy.

The brightest light shines from her soul.

And I want to bask in the warmth of it for as long as I can.

SIXTEEN

Madison

I bring the hot cup of coffee to my lips, and the steam warms my nose as I take a sip. My apartment is quiet and peaceful, and the early morning sun shines through the blinds, illuminating my gray couch and black accent pillows.

I run my gaze over the corner of the wall that looks like my own murder board out of a cop show. Since I've been dividing my time between the movie set, Ian, and my salon over the last few weeks, I haven't been able to sit at my desk and practice or catch up on *YouTube* vlogs.

But working on the set has allowed me a different kind of outlet, and I've enjoyed the challenge.

On top of it all, I've been especially busy at the salon since the media caught wind of Ian hanging out there, and they've plastered it all over the internet. It's brought an ungodly amount of new business that I never dreamed of. Even if we worked twenty-four seven, we wouldn't be able to take every appointment.

It's been hectic, and sometimes, it feels like I can't come up for air.

Then Ian shows up in person or sends me a text to let me know he's thinking of me, and he manages to calm any overwhelming stress and pressure I'm feeling. And he celebrates with me too.

I miss my old routine, but at the same time, I've appreciated the disruption.

Even if I'm exhausted.

And sore in all the right places.

Actually, I welcome the latter any time of day or night.

I smile as I take another sip of my coffee and step over the trail of shoes, pants, and bra littering the floor until I reach my bed. Ian is gloriously naked and spread across the middle of it.

After we were done with filming yesterday, we went to karaoke with the girls and Carter. Sofia joined us too, along with a couple of friends I know from the salon. We sang, drank, and yelled so loudly over squeaky karaoke singers that my throat is dry and scratchy this morning.

Ian and I slipped out earlier than the others—I pulled my birthday card to avoid Bree's pout and slurred comments about abandoning them. But I had big plans to spend some of the first few hours of being thirty with Ian.

We stumbled through the door to my apartment and ripped each other's clothes off in record time.

It's how it is with us—passionate and intense, yet tender.

"It's like you're starting halfway through a relationship," Tessa said to me last week at dinner before Ian had arrived and while Carter had been in the bathroom. "You and Ian have a history and already know each other so well, but it's also exciting, right? Because there's a lot to catch up on too."

I gulp, but it's not because I think she's wrong. While it's true that someone else would see it as a bad thing that he and I know each other so well, I don't. I like that we're more than just two weeks into a relationship, given our past.

With the string of terrible and boring first dates I've had in the last few years, I'm more than relieved and happy that Ian and I got together, even if I wasn't thrilled to see him in the beginning.

I run the tip of my forefinger along my bottom lip, still tasting Ian there after we tangled ourselves in my sheets last night.

"What are you smiling about over there?" Ian's groggy voice cuts through my thoughts.

"Coffee and pastries from the bakery three blocks from here. Interested?" I ask, my head still pounding from the free shots we had at karaoke.

"Very." His husky voice is seductive, like he's referring to eating something other than breakfast, and just as I start to crawl up to him from the edge of the bed, both of our phones go off with a new text. And another. And another.

"Shit. What's going on?" I grab my phone from my nightstand.

Ian sits up, running both palms down his face, mumbling into them, "Did the set burn down or something?"

"No," I say as I scan the influx of new messages. "There was some mix-up with the security company they hired. No one showed up to keep people out of the location for filming today, and squatters took over the building."

"Seriously?" Ian scrambles for his phone just as he gets a call. "It's Annalisa." He puts it on speaker and answers while I look over my shoulder at him.

"Oh my *God*," she screeches. "Did you see what happened to our set?"

"Yeah. What—"

"Sarah said they trashed the place, and she almost stepped in a puddle of piss. Can you imagine?" She exaggerates every word, her outrage obvious and very valid.

Puddles of piss? *Gross.*

Ian looks at me and grimaces.

"I'm just glad I didn't show up early or something because if I would've gotten even a whiff of urine—you know how sensitive I am to smells—I would be on the phone with my lawyers right now to sue those squatters. All of them."

I suppress a grin as Ian paces by the bed, his dark hair mussed and wild, his boxer briefs clinging to every lean muscle. Automatically, I lick my lips, and my nose twitches.

"How are you going to spend this impromptu day off? We can gather the others and go for a beer. You like beer, if I remember correctly." She giggles.

And suddenly, I remember why Ian and I started the lie about being together to begin with. It was because of the woman on the phone.

How could I have so easily forgotten?

As she names off a few bars around the hotel, not giving Ian a chance to talk, I sink farther into the bed, and an odd feeling settles in my chest. It's one of jealousy. Not because he dated this woman—we all have past loves and lusts.

It's because she's in his world.

She'll go back to LA with Ian, and I won't.

161

My home is here. On the other side of the country from him.

And even though what I said to Tessa last week about loving how far into this relationship I am with Ian, the reality is that he and I have only really been dating for a couple of weeks.

An amazing two weeks, but still—fourteen days isn't that long to have the conversation about our future.

My studio apartment is tiny as it is, but the walls feel like they're closing in on me as my head spins.

"Jesus." Ian tosses his phone on the bed and plops next to me.

I wave away my nagging thoughts… for now.

They have no place for this moment. Not when Ian is here with me.

I prop my elbow up and lean my head on it, facing him. "What did you tell her about drinks?" I ask, realizing I missed the end of his conversation.

He turns toward me. "I said probably not, because it's your birthday, and besides, this is the first morning I've had off since we started filming. I want to spend it with you."

"You're very sweet." I smile and lean over to kiss him, then roll off the side and onto my feet. "But first, I'm going to call Sarah and make sure I'm not needed. Then I'll call Sofia about the salon. She may need my help. Thanks to you, we're backed up like crazy, but at least I'll be able to buy a replacement chair and other supplies a lot sooner than I'd planned. Maybe even new and better snacks too," I say coyly.

"So businesslike." He waggles his eyebrows. "I like when you're the boss. Can you spank me around later for being such a bad boy?"

"Leave the toilet seat up again, and I'll do more than spank you," I tease with a layer of very real warning underneath my sweet-as-honey tone. "But wait. It's my birthday today. Aren't I the one who gets to be spanked?"

He narrows his gaze. "Now there's an idea."

I playfully swat at him as he tries to reach for me. "I need to call Sarah first."

I check in with her, and she confirms that I, too, have the morning off because of the dirty assholes that ruined their set, so they need to get it cleaned or secure a new location. Either way, they should be able to pick up filming tonight to avoid wasting a whole day in their schedule.

I'm inwardly relieved when I click off the phone with her. It's been fun doing the cast's makeup, but I'm ready for a break, no matter how brief. I don't celebrate just yet, though, since I still need to make sure I'm not needed at the salon.

I hear Ian turn the shower on, and it's not long before steam drifts through the cracks in the door. He left it slightly ajar too, as if inviting me in, and fuck, do I want to join him.

"Hello?" Sofia's voice sounds. "Madison, are you there?"

I blink and pull back my phone to see Sofia's on the other line. When did I call her?

Ian is too distracting.

Soap sliding down between his pecs and over his abs.

Water droplets coating his lips.

Wet hair curling over his forehead.

"Hello?" she repeats.

"Yes. Sofia. Hi," I sputter.

"Have you been running, or did you just have sex? Because you're out of breath, and with Ian around, it could just as well be the latter. If I were you, I'd never stop doing it with that fine piece of—"

"Although I'd love to hear the end of your wishful, but definitely crass, comment, I'm calling to check in. Are you at the salon?"

"Of course. I'm not late like Cheryl," she quips, and I imagine she's rolling her eyes.

"Here's the thing: we're not shooting this morning, so I can come in and help. Maybe take over for—"

"Wait. You have a few hours off?"

"Yes, until tonight." I toy with my bottom lip as the shower squeaks off.

"You are not coming in," Sofia states firmly, leaving no room for debate. "You haven't had a day off in ages, and you need it. I started noticing some circles under your eyes the last time you were here, and I'm afraid to tell you that they might become permanent, chica."

Instinctively, my fingers fly to my eyes.

"Oh, and as soon as you can, I need to color your hair."

"It's that bad?" I gasp.

"It needs a refresh," she says bluntly, and I hear the ding above the door in the background, signaling someone just entered. "Listen, Mads, go have fun with Mr. Movie Star, and I'll take care of things around here. You were going to be gone today, anyway, so I have it under control. Besides, it's your freaking birthday! Enjoy it."

"If you think so…" I run my teeth over my bottom lip like I'm tasting something sweet—and I am. I'm two seconds away from a blissful morning off with Ian.

"I do. Consider this my gift to you, because I haven't had time to get you anything yet."

"You've done way too much for me already, Sofia."

"And I'm doing one more. Now, get off the phone, and let

your man get *you* off."

I hear a woman's muffled voice, and the call cuts off right as Ian emerges from the bathroom, a towel hung scantily across his hips.

He holds the soft fabric together in his fist just under the lean curve of his obliques.

And I salivate.

Drool is dangerously close to falling out both sides of my mouth like the water droplets running down the valley between his round pecs.

"If you keep looking at me like that, we'll be late for pastries," he says while reaching for his shirt from the edge of the bed.

I reach out and grab his arm to stop him from getting dressed. "So? We have plenty of time."

"We do? I thought you might have to go to the salon…" He leaves the question hanging in the air.

I shake my head from side to side in slow motion as I close the distance between us.

His innocent eyes turn a shade darker as lust consumes them, and I yank the towel out of his hold—not that his grip was reluctant to let go.

His gaze falls to my mouth, and I blink once before his lips are on mine, sweeping across them similar to the way we make love—tender but hungry.

Effortless and feverish.

His damp chest soaks through my shirt, and my fingers slide through his wet hair, slinging more water onto our shoulders.

He deepens the kiss, thrusting his tongue between my greedy lips. Kissing Ian Brock is like riding a roller coaster.

My stomach flips, and my heart races as each swipe of his tongue causes a thrill through my body.

It's electric.

I moan as Ian strips my panties down my legs, then jerks my shirt over my head. My hair falls back over my bare breasts, the strands tickling my nipples.

They're hard and sensitive.

Desperate for his touch and attention.

As if reading my mind, he drags my hair over my shoulders, his knuckles softly brushing against my skin and lighting me on fire.

All my senses are heightened.

Once my strands are out of the way, he takes one bud between his teeth, nibbling just the way I like it.

I throw my head back and moan, feeling the pleasure of his tongue deep in my core.

"Hang on, baby," he murmurs as he pulls away. The sun's rays beam down, highlighting every groove and ripple of Ian's back muscles as he bends to the floor to retrieve a condom from his pants pocket.

As he sheaths himself, the head of his thick cock points straight at me, so hard and ready. I squeeze my thighs together as need pools in my center.

He tsks under his breath, smirking. "Don't you dare," he warns, drinking in every exposed inch of me. "Open for me," he says in a tone that's a request wrapped in a plea.

I swallow, anticipation coursing through me like a drug as he stalks toward me, backs me up against the wall, and hoists me up to wrap my legs around his narrow waist.

I dip my head to kiss him, and he parts my lips right as he plunges inside me, the initial sting transforming into a delicious friction the more he rocks his hips into me.

Ian rattles me, my back hitting the wall to the rhythm of his movements, and I welcome each thud.

"Oh, God," I pant in his ear as I lose myself in him.

Ian takes me higher with each thrust, nip on my shoulder, and squeeze of my ass in his hands.

I'm completely at his mercy, and it's my favorite place to be.

"Yes, yes," I chant as my toes curl and tingle, my heels digging into the top of his firm ass.

"You're so fucking sexy, Madi," he whispers in my hair as he wraps a hand in it, fisting it like he's hanging on to the edge of a cliff.

I love when he calls me Madi. He's the only one I've ever allowed to call me by that nickname, and it's become our own little private thing.

He shifts me from the wall and onto the bed behind him, grunting like an animal.

It's wild and hot, and an ecstatic shiver vibrates up my spine.

Ian pushes back into place and rolls his hips into me at a different angle, making me claw at him for release.

When he runs his tongue from the base of one breast up to wrap it around one nipple, I gasp.

Everything in my body tightens.

"I'm… going… to come," I sputter, heat dancing along my skin.

He pulls away from my nipple with a pop and buries his face in the crook of my neck, his pace now quicker.

More relentless.

Cool air hits the sheen where Ian sucked on my nipple,

and I arch my back, loving the sensation that washes over me.

"Me too." The tip of his tongue skates against my shoulder as he licks his lips. "Me too."

His name rips from my throat in a satisfied cry as a euphoric climax pulses through my core, and his own release soon follows. He drops his forehead to my shoulder, his breaths labored and hot on my slick skin, and I grip his head, humming my pleasure.

My chest heaves against his.

Words fail me.

Ian has an effect on me I've never experienced, and each time with him only makes my feelings for him stronger.

It's a high I never want to climb down from.

"Shit," he mutters as he smooths my hair back. "I can't keep my fucking hands off you."

"Is that a problem?" I ask, gripping his waist between my legs more tightly.

"Not for me."

"I don't remember complaining, either," I say, happily sandwiched between his hard body and the soft sheets. "But we have work to do today."

"Work?" He cringes like the word tastes of olives—his most hated food.

"We have to figure out what adventure we're going on since we have some time off," I say, my voice hoarse.

I'm spent.

Sated.

Warm inside.

As much as I'd like to stay wrapped around him all day, he hasn't had much time to see the city since he got here, so I'd like to take advantage.

Heart still racing, I fuse my mouth to his, tasting the salt of sweat on his upper lip.

"Think of some ideas," I manage.

After one more kiss, I disappear into the bathroom for a quick shower, running my hand over every spot Ian just worshipped, my breasts still tingling. At one point, I think I hear the door open, followed by shuffling, but it's too hard to tell with the water running and shampoo dripping past my ears as I rinse off.

Once I'm finished and step out of the shower, steam rising to the ceiling and fogging up my mirror, I notice a heavenly smell mixed with my lavender soap.

Which is when I see one of my clay mugs full of fresh coffee sitting next to my sink.

I smile as I take it between my hands and bring it up to my lips.

He's so thoughtful.

After I take a sip, I set the cup down, wrap a towel around myself, then pick it back up. "Ian?" I call out as I tiptoe out of the bathroom like it's a secret I'm here.

"At your service, gorgeous." He pops around the corner, his own mug of coffee in hand. His hair is mostly dry now, except for a few damp strands here and there.

And when he leans on the wall next to us, he seems comfortable being in my apartment. Like he belongs here, and my heart soars.

"Thank you," I manage over the overwhelming knot in my throat and hold up my cup.

Except I forget how full it is, and the hot liquid spills over the top and onto my hand.

"Shit!" I rip the towel from around my chest and dab at the coffee running down my wrist.

"I'll take that," Ian says, grabbing the mug from my hold. "I was trying to be nice. Didn't mean to harm you."

I giggle, shaking my head. "I'm the clumsy one."

Once I finish cleaning up, Ian steps close to me. "Let me see," he whispers, bringing my wrist to his lips and kissing the reddening spot. "Are you okay?" He kisses up to my open palm.

My lips part, and I think I nod.

"Need some ice?" he offers.

"No." I swallow. "Just keep doing that."

My eyelids flutter closed, and I feel his smile against my palm, spreading wide and happily and making its way into more of my heart.

SEVENTEEN

Ian

"I can't pick what to do on your birthday. That's blasphemous," I insist. "You have to pick."

"You haven't explored much since you got here, so you have to call the shots. I'm just your lowly tour guide," Madi teases, sauntering into the living room as she pulls a black shirt over her head.

"We can do *anything*?" I raise my voice an octave.

She narrows her eyes and smooths the wrinkles of her shirt down over her lean waist. "Do you really want to stay in bed during your one morning off?"

"If you're in the bed, yes. It would be better than any view, museum, or crowd in Times Square." I shrug, meaning every word.

"Well, there will be plenty more time for us later." She tilts her head. "What's the one thing you've been wanting to do since you got here?"

Her lavender scent washes over me, and I lick my lips as I try to focus on the question. I'm not one for sightseeing when I go to new places. I prefer to simply see how the locals live. To shop like they do and try unique restaurants or food trucks.

It's another reason I liked the Italian place so much—it wasn't exactly a hot spot for tourists, but the food was incredible.

On top of that, I also went jogging with Madi once through swarms of people as we raced toward the nearest park from her apartment. That was a near-death experience I never thought I'd have. One woman tried to claw at me because I accidentally bumped into her purse. I never even touched her.

But it felt like a true New York experience.

I sift through ideas of what I'd like to do since it'll make her happy, and when I finally have a lightbulb moment, I hold my finger up. "Actually, there is one thing…"

"Let's hear it." She stalks toward the door and grabs her sinful combat boots.

"I want a Nathan's hot dog."

She drops a booted foot to the floor with a thud and raises up. "That's it? A hot dog?"

I nod. "One from those carts outside."

She shakes her head as a slow smile spreads. "Put your shoes on, Ian. We're going to Coney Island."

A train screeches to a halt farther into the underground subway as Madi and I stop by a map.

"I need to check which train will take us all the

way out there." Madi holds her coffee to her chest with one hand and traces a free finger along the multi-colored lines running over a map of the city until she comes to a stop at the end of one. "Got it."

"Have you ever been to Coney Island?" I ask, raising my voice to be heard over the people on the platforms and the rush of air as a train takes off, zipping down its track.

I hold my own paper cup close to my body as we squeeze through huddles of people and keep walking down the platform between the two tracks. We pass a bearded man singing into a microphone and several other people, ranging from businessmen with briefcases clutched to their sides to teenagers wearing headphones twice the size of their heads.

It's like a secret city down here.

Once we're settled into our seats at the back of a subway car, leaving the loud chaos outside, Madi finally answers. "I've never been to Coney Island."

I lick the stray black drops from the lid of my cup and nudge her with my shoulder, urging her to go on.

She sighs, peering down at her hand, which was red a moment ago from the chill in the spring air, but it's slowly getting back to its original color now. "I never went as a kid, but I wanted to go when I first moved back up here as an adult. I was so busy with college and waiting tables part time, though. Then I quit college for cosmetology school and opened the salon, which took up even more of my time. I always said I'd go someday, and I am." She turns to me with a grin and taps her cup to mine. "Only, my *someday* came ten years later."

I interlock our fingers and pull both our free hands into my lap as we get comfortable for this hour-long ride. After the first stop, Madi retrieves a wrinkled brown paper bag from her leather tote. "Snack?" she asks, unrolling the top of the bag with a crinkle barely heard above the whipping of the subway through the tunnel and low chatter of the rest of the car.

"Sure." I pull my arm from around her shoulders to accept the blueberry muffin she gives me. "Let's see how the best bakery on the planet tastes."

She grips my forearm and keeps me from taking a bite. "I didn't say it was the best, but it is damn good."

I drop my hand with the muffin into my lap, arching my brows. "Okay, then what is the best bakery? Clearly, you have one in mind."

Her green eyes lighten as she answers. "It's this little place in California called Olive Branch Bakery. They make the most delectable lemon poppyseed muffins." She wipes at her mouth. "I'm practically drooling."

"Me too." I rake my gaze over her, loving her playful side. I've seen a lot of it since we were stuck in her salon, and I much prefer it to her scowls and glares from when she thought I was the epitome of evil.

The train makes another stop, letting handfuls of people on and off each car. When it takes off again, Madi sways into me, her mouth hanging onto one side of her muffin and refusing to let go. It makes me chuckle, and warmth spreads through my chest.

"When were you in California?" I ask, curious about her life in the years we spent apart, especially since we were in the same state at one point and didn't know it.

She finishes chewing her mouthful and licks the crumbs from her bottom lip. "A friend from cosmetology school lives in Sonoma, this cute little town in wine country, and she invited me to come out for a beauty expo nearby. While we were there, we visited the bakery."

"And this friend of yours—do you still stay in touch?"

When she smiles, it's wistful, but there's something else too—something between sadness and guilt that tugs at my chest. "Other than the occasional check in, we lost touch a while back. We're both busy with our salons, and she got married and has a kid now too. It's hard to stay close when you're so far away." Madi's lips form a tight line before she turns away.

And we fall silent as her words swirl around in the pit of my stomach, making me nauseous.

But it's a conversation for another time.

Today is about having fun together and celebrating her birthday. Enjoying the sunshine. Being spontaneous in a new place.

So, I do what I'm good at and push the hard feelings deep down inside, where they sink like the rocks we used to throw across the lake, ignoring the ripples they caused while skidding across the water.

The train emerges above ground like a submarine, and I have to shield my eyes with my hand. The sun is abrupt and blinding as we roll to a stop along the platform.

"We're here." Madi flashes me her light green eyes, her smile glowing and radiant in the sunshine, and she grabs my hand to lead me out.

I follow with excited steps, tossing our empty cups into the trash can once we're off the train. "It's a lot emptier than I would've thought." I push my sunglasses into place and study our surroundings. A handful of other people litter the area, strolling along the boardwalk while others walk their dogs on the beach.

"It's fifty degrees and early spring. Not exactly bikini and board shorts weather, which is the main reason people come here." Madi laughs.

"Fair enough." I join her, taking in the famous Coney Island.

The wind blows a lot stronger without skyscrapers to tame it, although a few tall hotels and other buildings do stand in the distance. The sun beats down without much to provide shade, and many of the shops and restaurants around us are colorful and fun, adding to the exciting energy of this slice of the world.

In a way, it reminds me of Venice Beach, and I'm hit with a sting of homesickness again, although this is stronger than the other times I've felt it.

I grip Madi's hand more tightly as we walk toward a wide yellow building with a white sign hung at the top that reads "Nathan's" in green letters.

Grinning, I pick up my pace as Madi stumbles to keep up. "Slow down!" she calls from behind me. "They're not going to run out of hot dogs, I promise."

I slow down for her sake, throwing back, "Okay, but if they run out of condiments, I'm blaming you."

"Plain hot dogs are the way to go, though."

I stop completely now and face her. "*Plain*? What kind of monster are you?"

She shrugs. "I rarely eat them, but if I do, I'm not going to dress them up." Leaning in close, she whispers, "I just want the wiener."

I rub my palm down my face. "How old are you?" I tease as we resume walking.

She throws her head back, her thick hair falling in waves

like the ones washing to shore beyond the boardwalk—unrestrained and restless. "Like you're *so* mature," she says between giggles as she tries to catch her breath.

I angle my body to face her, walking sideways, and spread my arms. "I am. I'm the new and improved Ian Bowman—Ian Brock."

"You might go by a different name now, but you still compared your cannoli to a penis the other day and wanted more whipped cream to make the *balls* bigger."

"I'm only human." I wag my finger at her. "And don't tell me you've completely changed, either. I saw the bag of peach rings in your pantry."

She covers her face, and her shoulders tremble as the wind whips her hair over her cheek. "You are so nosy!"

"Irrelevant." I smirk.

"For your information, that's only, like, the second bag I've bought since high school. I've evolved and mostly prefer baked desserts and pastries now." Her pink nose twitches before she turns away.

"I don't believe you for a second."

She scoffs, but her eyes shine with mischief.

"You used to walk out of the candy store carrying a stuffed bag of peach rings in both hands, fisting them like a drunk with two fifths of whiskey."

"You're right, okay? It's my *secret* addiction." Her laugh mixes with the crash of waves in the distance, heard above the howling winds and soft music coming from Nathan's as we approach.

At the window, we order two "Frankfurters," a boring old plain one for her and a chili cheese dog for me, loaded with condiments just the way I like. Madi takes one look at my finished product and exaggerates a gagging sound, which makes me puff out my chest and carry my tray with pride.

"You can't be serious about that." She points at my food like I sprinkled cockroaches on top of it.

"Oh, but I am," I deadpan as we sit at a picnic table under a red-and-yellow umbrella. I make a show of lifting the sloppy chili dog to my mouth for an obscenely large bite, making mustard run down my chin, and I lose some chunks of relish too.

"Hot," she jokes.

"You're telling me you wouldn't kill to lick this off me right now?" I jut my chin out and point to the mess covering it.

Her nostrils flare like she's considering doing just that. "No," she squeaks. "I have standards."

I lean forward and whisper, "Not what you said when you let me lick chocolate syrup and brownies from your belly button."

She raises her sunglasses to the top of her head and narrows her gaze at me. Clearly amused with a twinkle of revenge in her eyes, she takes her plain hot dog between her delicate fingers and turns sideways as she puts the end in her mouth. Then she closes her eyes and lets out a sensual moan that should only be heard in private.

I almost choke on my own bite and squirm on the wooden bench.

"So good," she says in a breathy voice that almost convinces me to order plain hot dogs from now on.

"You're giving that kid a real tantalizing show." I notice an employee sweeping nearby, but his broom isn't even grazing the ground.

He's too hypnotized by Madi's little performance.

Innocently, she nods and waves at him, and the boy, who can't be older than seventeen, quickly dips his head.

"If I would've known this would bring out the immature side of you, I wouldn't have suggested hot dogs," I say sarcastically.

As our laughter subsides, she sets her food down and folds her hands between her and the tray on the table. "Why did you want to get Nathan's, anyway?"

"Aside from wanting to watch you eat a hot dog like a porn star?" I joke.

She smiles, but it quickly fades.

And I know she senses that I'm deflecting.

Which I am.

I finish chewing and swallow as I reach for a napkin held down by her tote bag so they won't fly away. Wiping my chin and hands, I answer honestly. "Dad, Cash, and I used to watch Nathan's Hot Dog Eating Contest every year growing up. I thought it would be fun to say I had one. Maybe it would be something for us to talk about at Thanksgiving."

My stomach churns, and it's not from the odd combination of greasy food I'm eating.

Madi and I haven't so much as mentioned my brother since my confession at the salon. I'd barely thought of him at all until Madi asked what I wanted to do today.

Immediately, I was taken back to a time when the Bowman guys were one happy and boisterous group. Memories of my dad grilling hot dogs every Fourth of July in honor of the contest surfaced like wildfire. My mom always groaned because she didn't like hot dogs, and she complained we never ate enough vegetables.

I still never eat them, although Madi has been attempting to rectify that by pushing salads on me.

Cash and I would tear up a plate of hot dogs each, then round up the fireworks we'd collected over the two weeks leading up to the Fourth. We'd get distracted temporarily when our friends would show up. After we'd chase each other around with water guns for a while, we'd remember to shoot the fireworks.

There was harmony and laughter.

It was the most fun we'd have all year—even better than Christmas.

Being here at the actual Nathan's is like coming to the mecca, and it makes me miss my family.

The one we used to be, anyway.

"Can I ask you something?" Madi asks, peeking over at me, her sunglasses still nestled on top of her head.

I wolf down the last of my hot dog like it'll take the memories with it, but no such luck. Especially with the way Madi peers at me. I know she's going to delve into it, and I'm going to have to share more than vague details of what we used to be like. Once I swallow, I wipe my hands and brace myself. "Sure."

She takes a sip of water and swipes her hair out of her face. "What happened between you, Cash, and your dad?"

"You know what Cash did." I give her a tight-lipped smile, not willing to repeat it. Not when it's the reason Madi and I stopped talking to each other.

She gives me a small, pitiful smile, which makes me tense. "That might've started it, but what happened since then? And how does your dad fit into this?" She waves her hands. "I mean, you don't have to tell me, but we've been getting to know each other again, and they're part of you, even if they're not in your life much anymore."

I grind my teeth, hating the last line she spoke, because it's true. Although I talk with my mom here and there and get the occasional text from my dad, we're not close. Not even a little.

Cash has wedged a gap between us. My parents insist on making excuses for his bad behavior and refuse to accept him for who he is like I have.

I haven't actually spoken to my brother in a couple years, and the last thing I said to him wasn't kind in the slightest, although he deserved it.

"Cash played college football," I start, and she nods. She knows as much, but I think it's safe to say she doesn't know how that story ended since we went our separate ways right before the incident. "Dad was always so proud of him. I was too. It was one of the things I respected about him, because after playing football myself in high school, I knew it was much tougher to play at a higher level."

Madi squeezes my hand in hers.

"Cash was injured during a game. He was tackled to the ground, and he fell on his knee. Couldn't play anymore, and without the game, he, uh… Cash changed." I glimpse her sympathetic frown and swallow the edge in my voice. "I was already living in LA, so I didn't experience the worst of his wrath and destruction firsthand, but Mom would tell me all about it once he moved back home to recover."

"What happened?"

"He became a different person. I'd already lost some respect for him after what he said about you, but over the year or so after his injury, I didn't recognize him anymore.

He drank a lot, even though he wasn't supposed to with the painkillers he was taking. He lashed out at the people trying to help him." I take a deep breath for the final confession. "Then his longtime girlfriend left him after she found out he'd gotten another girl pregnant."

A tiny gasp escapes Madi as she covers her mouth with both hands.

I push my tray to the side, urging the food I just consumed to stay down. It's difficult since what I'm saying makes me want to throw it back up. "Cash married her, and they have a son named Peter. He's a loan officer at a bank now, and Dad applauds him like he set some world record or cured cancer, when all he did was hurt people. Mom's the same. It's like she forgot all about the shitty things she used to complain to me about." I let out a humorless laugh. "That's the Bowman family for you. Ever the optimists."

"I'm really sorry," she offers.

I fold my arms on the table, having gained momentum and courage to continue. "I ignored his shortcomings too. At first, anyway, because he was my big brother. My friend. But one night, I just… I don't know. I lost it."

"What do you mean?"

"I was visiting him at his house, and he snapped at Peter. The kid was just playing and wanted me to play with him too, but Cash yelled at him until he cried." I turn my attention to the view around us, frowning. "After Peter ran up to his room and slammed the door, I told Cash I couldn't pretend anymore, and I told him exactly how big of an asshole he is, not just toward his own family but to all of us. We haven't spoken since."

She stands and rounds the table to slide onto the bench

next to me. She leans her head on my shoulder, and we watch the waves in the distance, the air thick with salt and promise.

I rest my chin on her head, and her hair tickles me there as we stay like this for a few minutes, lost in the memories. We don't need words or any other gestures, content to be in each other's company—something I'll never get tired of.

But then I feel something like a tap on my other shoulder.

I look up expecting to find a person, but all that greets me is white-and-black goop dripping down my jacket. "A bird fucking shit on me."

"What?" She jumps off the bench like it's on her, and I'm about to clarify it isn't when there's another tap on my head.

"Fuck!"

Beyond Madi, there's a gasp from a woman and a girl walking along the boardwalk.

"Sorry," I call out with a wave while I choke down more vomit.

Grimacing, Madi looks me up and down like she's afraid to tell me I'm naked in public or something. "How bad is it?" I ask, peeking at her through one eye and clenching my jaw.

She backs away, bumping her heel on the picnic table next to us. "Ouch!"

I rush toward her, but she waves me off. "That bad?"

She bites her lip, and I can tell she's enjoying this. Her face is as red as a strawberry from trying to hold her laughter inside. "Hang on," she sputters.

Snickering under her breath, she hurriedly grabs napkins from the table and shoves them at me, then retreats toward the counter for more.

I'm wiping my forehead when the woman and girl who gasped at my outburst appear in front of me. The young one seems to be around fifteen years old, and she's blushing harder than a teenager meeting her celebrity crush.

Oh, wait...

"You're Ian Brock, right?" she asks, her voice high-pitched and squeaky.

"I am." I give her the best grin I can manage, considering I have bird shit still dripping down my shoulder. At least my head is somewhat cleaned, but I'm going to need several showers before I feel that way again. "And what's your name?"

"I'm Lindsey," she whispers in awe.

Madison returns with napkins and starts to wipe at the mess on my jacket, but she stops when she notices we have company. "Hi there."

"We're so sorry to interrupt your lunch, but my granddaughter is such a huge fan." The older woman smiles. "Of course, she's only seen you in the more age-appropriate movies."

This makes me laugh, and I almost forget about my gross situation. "Good call," I offer, and now I'm the one flushed, thinking over each curse word I uttered. Then of course, there was the scene where I stripped half-naked in front of the camera.

Dear God. Definitely not appropriate for this woman's granddaughter.

"It's so great to meet you both," Madison gushes. "Do you want a picture with Ian? I can take it."

"Oh my gosh." Lindsey stills. "Seriously? Can I?" Wide-eyed, she turns to her grandmother for permission, and the woman nudges her toward me, her shoulders shaking with laughter.

"Get in here." I wave for Lindsey to join me, and I throw

a thumbs-up while Madi snaps the picture, smiling behind the camera phone. "Get in for one too, Grandma," I call out to Lindsey's grandmother, who practically races toward us.

As we part ways, I hear Lindsey's hushed whisper. "Ew. What is this white goop on my hand?"

Madi pulls my arm to head in the opposite direction from them. "Hurry before they realize they just got your secondhand bird shit on them."

Hysterical, we rush off toward the subway like we've just committed a crime. Even though it's still early afternoon with plenty of daylight left and I have literal crap smeared on my jacket, this has been one of the best days of my life.

All thanks to the woman next to me.

EIGHTEEN

Ian

"That'll cost you one hamburger," an elderly man rasps toward a woman, who rolls her eyes and continues pushing their cart ahead of him.

Madi giggles into my shoulder. "What do you think they're talking about?" she whispers, watching after the older couple as they head toward the pet section.

I study the man's corduroy jacket, loose jeans, and shoes with thick insoles giving him an inch in height. The woman's wispy gray hair is pulled low in a bun, and her wrinkles suggest years of laughter with the guy.

"If I had to guess, I'd say she wants to buy another toy for their pet—probably a cat—but he knows they have too many already. They're the kind of people who spoil their cat."

Madi rushes to the front of our cart, her eyes wide with ideas. "Or she asked him to put his socks in the laundry hamper instead of tossing them on the couch to be found later."

I narrow my gaze at her, reading between the lines of her complaint—it's me. I do the sock thing. I've received more than a few scoldings over it already, but I always know the best way to make it up to her.

In the end, we both win.

"Why would she owe *him*, then? If that's how we're going to play it, what do you owe me?" I ask.

"Nothing," she hisses, her lips curling. She glances back toward the old couple just before they disappear down an aisle. "I think she asked him to eat his vegetables, and he was bargaining with her like someone else I know."

"I don't have any recollection of such events," I joke, my pitch raised with innocence as we pass a section of produce, where the cool air that keeps it fresh drifts over us.

"You tried to make a deal with me yesterday for a trade-off. For each floret of broccoli you ate, I had to lose a piece of clothing like we were playing strip poker: healthy foods edition."

"You're the one who's trying to be all healthy with your granola and shit, Miss *Floret*." I use quotations around the last word. I haven't heard it since my grandmother used it once when I was a kid.

I thought she'd made the word up and never recalled it until now.

"That's what they're called." Madi points a long finger at me. "It doesn't mean I'm even remotely a health nut, because I'm not, but you, Ian, have worse eating habits than a homeless dog. How you keep those abs tight is a cruel mystery."

"Checking out my abs, huh?" I wink, stopping the cart to let the old couple from before by.

As they pass us to head in the opposite direction, their

cart barely missing ours in the narrow aisle, the man points to a couple of blankets on the bottom shelf. "You said we needed one of those for the living room. Let's get one."

"Jerry, those are for cats and dogs."

As they keep shuffling their full cart toward the registers, he snickers. "Perfect. You're the cat and I'm the dog."

She shakes her head as Madi and I watch them disappear again.

"Ah, geriatric love," she muses, tilting her head to the side.

"That sounds like a cheesy movie for the elderly. I mean, I'd watch it, but I'd need a lot of alcohol," I tease.

She rolls her eyes much like the woman before. "No," she draws out, and her voice turns wistful when she says, "I'm talking about the kind of love that ages, filling an ocean with memories and affection. The kind that grows as you do after the initial novelty of a relationship wears off, but there's magic in the fact that you choose each other over and over again. The kind of love that is better for your health than any medicine because you know you've spent the better part of your life with your person."

I wrap my arm around her, splaying my fingers at the small of her back, and my chest suddenly swells. Right here in the middle of a grocery store next to my mortal enemies of greens and carrots, I'm overcome with emotion.

Since I laid eyes on Madi again, I've known that she's the kind of person to grow old with and to love the way she just described.

It's a feeling that's only grown stronger and more intense every day and night we spend together.

"I—*shit*," I hiss as a cart rams into my heel.

From behind me, a woman's voice rings out. "Joshua! I

told you to stay put." She wrangles the young boy's arm and glances at me and Madi, wearing an apologetic frown. "I'm so sorry. Are you all right?"

We nod and wave them off. "Of course. No harm done."

She sighs, then turns her stern glare toward the boy, who's already moved on to terrorizing the pile of apples spilling out of a barrel onto a table. "Joshua!" she whisper-screams.

"So, broccoli?" Madi asks, sneaking her hand into mine.

I exhale, studying the evil food that someone a zillion years ago convinced the world is edible. "Okay, but that'll cost you one hamburger."

Her laugh is soft with a hint of appreciation. "We have an inside joke now, don't we?"

"Even better than the space-time continuum one. We used to have many." I grab a head of broccoli, not bothering to inspect it for mold or whatever the hell Madi usually checks it for.

"Feels good." She grabs my hand again as we stroll through the market for more groceries.

"It feels damn good," I say and kiss the back of her hand.

As we finish loading our cart and check out, I'm content. Even shopping for groceries with Madi is fun. I don't need adventures like Coney Island every day to enjoy being with her. She somehow manages to give color to the dull and mundane.

And I almost told her I loved her.

Right in the middle of the damn store.

The words were on the tip of my tongue like they stood on the edge of a cliff, no parachute or anything. They were ready to take the leap and fly, nonetheless.

I would've meant the confession too, and I have no doubt

she feels the same. Maybe she wouldn't have said it back in the moment, but I know in my gut that she does.

This thing between us is real. Even more so than it was when we were teenagers.

I float into my trailer on set the next morning to prepare for an interview. I've just finished a bottle of water when my phone rings. Keith's name flashes across the screen, and I check the time to ensure I won't be late. With ten minutes to spare, I slide my thumb over the bar and answer. "Hey. I don't have a lot of time, but—"

"You have that interview with Pauline this morning, right?" Keith's voice is low and professional, so he must be at home, thank Christ. His office personality makes me dizzy sometimes. "I'll be quick. Just calling to give you some good news, buddy."

The underlying layer of excitement in his voice makes me stand a little taller. "What's going on?"

There's shuffling on his end like he's making sure his kids are asleep, which they probably are. With the time difference between us, it's extra early for them.

"I'll call you later to celebrate, but I wanted to give you a heads-up as soon as possible. Jay wants you to read for a role in the new *Time and Space* movie, and there are talks of a second *Ghost Predators* too. I told you it'd be a hit, didn't I?"

I hum, and my heart suddenly pounds in my ears.

"And how would you feel about being a guest on a new talk show? It would just be one segment. I don't have the name of it right in front of me, but I can text you the details when I get to my office. Oh! I can't believe I almost forgot to tell you. Kara wants you to read for a new rom-com she's working on. It's not definite, but I said I'd float the idea by you. Sounds like a moneymaker, but I know you might want to go in a different direction with your brand from now on. We can talk about it when you get back."

My stomach rolls as I try to keep up with what he's saying—movies and shows and… what?

Normally, I at least finish filming one movie before other opportunities and offers stream in. I'm not usually the kind of guy casting directors seek midmovie.

What is happening?

"I know it's a lot. I feel like I haven't talked to you in ages, but I guess that's what happens when we're on opposite sides of the country with a major time difference working against us. But that's what you pay me for. To keep up with everyone's grabby hands. Because I told you, man, everyone's going to want a piece of you as soon as they see you in action."

"You did say it." I laugh, but it sounds far away.

This is the dream, right? It's always been the plan since Keith and I started working together. Make movies. Be a star. Make more movies. Become a bigger star.

Maybe even write a screenplay myself one day.

Live and die in LA with other famous people I'd call my friends and enemies. Maybe I'd even have what those teen dramedies call *frenemies*.

There's a knock on my door, and I jerk my head toward it, letting Keith's voice fade.

"I need to go," I mumble into the speaker.

"Of course. Like I said, I'll call you later."

I nod, even though he can't see me, then click off before tossing my phone onto the couch behind me.

When I open the door, a shorter woman stands on the bottom step, and I blink a few times, bringing her in and out of focus.

"Mr. Brock!" She tosses her hair out of her face and smiles. "We're ready if you are."

I peer down and realize I'm not wearing shoes. "Almost."

After ducking back inside, I scan the confined space for them and take a minute to breathe.

This is the dream, I repeat to myself over and over again. *The fucking dream.*

But I can't help the flashes of Madi flicking through my mind.

Baking in her kitchen, my shirt hanging off one of her shoulders.

Sunday mornings in bed.

Grocery shopping and sharing special moments in the produce section.

Keith's innocent comment about being in different time zones makes me stop with my hand on the doorknob, my heart racing.

Madi and I will be on opposite sides of the country when filming is over.

What does that mean for us?

NINETEEN

Madison

Oh my God times three.

Ian and I shook his fucking trailer that time.

He went out with the cast last night, and I had to catch up at the salon, so we didn't see each other. But he texted me to meet him on the base an hour early today.

And he surprised me with a quickie.

Although that's not the right word. What he did in there was own and worship and ravish me. The way he gripped my hips while he drove into me was animalistic and vigorous.

It's been like that with him lately—more intense and passionate than before. Even when we're not having sex, he's more affectionate, holding my hand more tightly and wrapping me in his arms any chance he gets.

While waiting for coffee last week, he pulled me into his embrace, my back against his front. Resting his chin on my shoulder, he asked if I prefer to be hot or cold. At first, I thought he meant how I prefer my coffee, so I answered both, but then he clarified that he'd meant physically.

I was about to answer but was interrupted when our names were called to pick up our order.

Something about his tone had been off, though, as if there was more to the question. I didn't have time to mull it over because we got calls and messages regarding a change in the shooting schedule.

We've been so busy that sometimes I wonder how we're still sane.

Then there are days like today…

I peek out of his door for any foot traffic like I do the paparazzi at the salon. Now I understand the stress Ian goes through—a fraction of it, anyway—and it is not ideal, to say the least.

Once the coast is clear, I step out. Flushed and satisfied, I swipe my hair across my damp forehead and straighten my sweater over my high-rise jeans.

"Wait for me." Ian hops down to reach me and playfully swats my ass.

Gasping, I lean into him when he puts his arm around me, inhaling his cologne and absorbing it into my senses. He smells like sex and aftershave.

What a lethal combination.

All around the world, women's libidos are quaking, and panties are melting like snow on a sunny winter day in New York because of him.

My ovaries never stood a chance, did they?

And I'm the lucky one who gets to call Ian mine.

"I made up for last night, right?" he whispers, placing a kiss to my temple.

"Definitely. Not that you had anything to make up for. You had a thing, and I had to work," I rationalize, but it's true.

I much rather would've spent the night curled up beside him than going through the schedule, balancing the register, and trying to keep my eyes open.

"But I missed you."

I kiss him on the lips and murmur against them, "I missed you too."

"You two make me swoon." Searcy appears next to us, a fresh cup of coffee in her hand as she falls into step with Ian and me.

"What do I have to do to make you give up that cup?" Ian asks her, wiggling his eyebrows.

Her whimsical expression slides off as she cuts her eyes at him. "Find me a boyfriend who looks at me like you do her, and I'll consider it."

"Only consider? Ouch." His steps falter, causing him to fall behind as Searcy and I giggle.

In the makeup trailer, it's business as usual, except Ian steals a kiss or two and insists on running his knuckles against my arm, tickling and turning me on—it's a very confusing and heated combination.

"Do you care about me?" I whisper so only Ian can hear while I check him over.

Whiskey pools and swirls in his eyes, mixing with the darker brown of his irises as his gaze becomes hooded. "Of course."

"Then you'll stay still and keep your hands to yourself while I do my job." I smile, trying to loosen the sudden tension in his posture. "Otherwise, you're going to end up with too much orange, and that's just not a good color on you."

"I look good in everything." He winks, and some of his usual charm shines through.

But it doesn't put me at ease.

There's a nagging lump in my throat that only grows bigger throughout the day.

When the special effects makeup team steps in to take over and I leave, the lump nearly chokes me.

After I gather my things, I subtly wave goodbye to Ian, and he smiles widely back from his spot next to Annalisa. It helps, but something still feels off.

It's not just because I'm walking through a literal war zone—the set for today. Garbage litters the ground by knocked-over dumpsters, smoke clouds the air, and a couple smashed cars are parked to the side, ready for their debut.

But it blurs as I make my way out of here.

My mind races with overwhelming thoughts that crawl their way to the forefront while I rush to the salon.

As soon as I walk in, the smell of hairspray and other products fills my senses. There's sweet aroma as well, and Sofia points to a dozen roses sitting in a vase on the front counter. "Hey, boss lady. Those came for you. I didn't read the card, I swear."

She averts her gaze and pretends to sweep, but she's not even paying attention to the pile of hair she's scattering.

"And I totally believe you," I deadpan, then take one big whiff of the heavenly floral smell. Hoisting my tote higher onto my shoulder, I snatch the card and head back to my office, greeting the customers along the way like a friendly neighborhood tourist.

Although I still spend a lot of my time at the salon, it's nothing like I used to. Before Ian's movie, I was always the first one here and the last to leave. I'd log in more hours than a bodybuilder at the gym.

But when I throw my apron on and tie it around my back, my rattled nerves quiet, and the world feels calmer.

It's where I love to be most.

I frown at my reflection in the mirror by my desk— the one I keep to touch-up my hair and makeup before I head back out into the lion's den. But now, I'm not smiling because…

Is this where I *still* love to be the most?

Being with Ian might be sliding into its place, along with doing film makeup, but what does that mean?

As if he hears me, my phone vibrates with a new text from him.

> **Ian:** Let's do dinner tomorrow night. There's something I want to talk to you about.v

I'm well aware of the adage that "we need to talk" is a bad omen, but this is Ian. Less than eight hours ago, we were doing it in his trailer for the hundredth time, and he rattled into me like a jackhammer as if he was trying to nail me to the wall.

His text doesn't mean anything other than wanting to go out for a romantic night.

I pick up the card I grabbed from the flowers and read "Thinking of you" scrolled across it in ink, along with Ian's name. It's in his messy handwriting, which means he ordered these in person.

At this point, I would've clutched my chest with a dreamy sigh even if he'd written "Pepperoni is a vegetable," but the simple line is adorable.

He's thoughtful, and all he wants for tomorrow night is a lovely dinner.

It has nothing to do with the fact that we only have three more days of shooting left.

"So, how's that *fake* boyfriend of yours working out for you?" Bree asks, her tone full of accusation.

"You're never going to let me live that down, are you?" I sigh into the phone, clutching it tighter to my ear as I stroll down the sidewalk toward my apartment, the evening settled upon me after another day's work.

Shit, I might as well change my name to Madison Everly Works-A-Lot.

That, or Madison Everly Has-Sex-A-Lot.

Because those are the only two things I ever do anymore—work on the set or at my salon if I'm not having sex with Ian or eating baked goods off his abs. According to him, it's our daily doses of diet and exercise, and I don't have the willpower to tell him otherwise.

Instead, I pull every ninja move in my wheelhouse to sneak some greens into his meals as often as I'm around.

I may or may not have stashed a few bags of broccoli and kale in his refrigerator the last time I was at his hotel suite, and after he discovered them, he texted me a picture of him holding up a floret.

He was shirtless in the image, so I called it a win-win.

"I'll let up on the guilt trips as soon as I'm invited to date night," she throws back.

"It was a double date with Carter and Tessa almost a month ago. You and Erin were also invited but decided you didn't want to be fifth and sixth wheels," I remind her.

"Those were Erin's words. I was happy to attend as fifth wheel, had Miss Goody-Goody not lured me away with naked strippers and candy."

"I don't think that makes her a goody-goody."

"No, but making sure I flossed afterward does."

I giggle as I recall how my two friends spent that night watching *Magic Mike* while eating sugary treats. I did not know about the special guest appearance of floss, though.

"You missed margarita night this week," another voice sounds from Bree's end as I unlock the door to my building. "And we missed you!"

"Erin?" I take a guess.

"Yes, Erin's here because we're going over a very important lesson," Bree says, then whispers, "Isn't that right?" I assume it's for Erin's benefit.

"Uh-oh. What did she do now?" I ask the pair warily.

There's a heavy sigh, then, "I went out with a guy."

I wait for more from Erin, but nothing follows. "Is that the whole story?" I press as I enter my apartment and lock the door behind me.

"Tell her the rest," Bree demands, her tone amused yet sympathetic.

Exhaling, Erin's confession rushes out of her and through the speaker in one breath. "I went on a second date with a guy Bree had already warned me was bad news, but I didn't listen, and when he invited me up to his apartment at the end of the date, I accepted, only to find he lives with his ex-girlfriend and a snake."

From the sound of disgust in her voice, it's hard to tell which one she's more put off by—the ex or the reptile.

"I *hate* snakes." I can practically feel Erin shuddering as she answers my silent question.

"So, basically, instead of trying to teach her to sniff out the signs herself—because she always has an excuse to overlook them since she's too nice—I've moved on to teaching her to just trust me when I say, *he's no good*." Bree emphasizes the last part, and I imagine she's staring pointedly at our best friend.

"Sounds like a party." I snort as I reach into my refrigerator for a beer. "Sorry I missed margarita night. I've been crazed going to and from the set. And then there's the salon. I at least let Cheryl go and replaced her, so Sofia is extra happy and hasn't wanted to do harm to any cars, thankfully. The new guy is also full time and really helpful. He even knows the difference between black and red hair dye, so there's that," I ramble sarcastically. "With all the business my new famous relationship is bringing to the salon, I have almost zero energy left."

"For anything but sex, you mean." Bree snickers.

I hear a smack, followed by an *ow*.

"What Bree is trying to say is, we're very happy for you," Erin cuts in. "Do you two love birds have a plan for when Ian goes back to LA? Or are you going with him? I don't know what the rules are for your position with the team."

Instantly, I tense, freezing with the bottle halfway to my lips.

"Mads?"

"You still there?"

"Yes." I set the beer down and clear my throat, trying to keep my voice light. "I'm not going with them to continue working on the set. It was just temporary."

"And Ian?"

"I mean, there's no need for a detailed flow chart or anything of how we'll make it work. It's a fun relationship.

One we knew would come to a head once he's finished filming in New York."

"But this isn't the end, right?" Erin asks. Ever the positivity queen.

"No," I cough out around the ever-present lump in my throat. What is the freaking deal with that today?

"So you'll see each other," Erin says, like it's as simple as that.

"We're actually having dinner tomorrow night. He wants to talk, and it's probably about LA." I try to keep my tone even and unaffected, but it's too soon to tell if it worked.

When I get silence from their end, I know I have my answer.

"I'm freaking out, okay?" I give in, slouching against the counter and feeling the weight of it all on my shoulders. "Not about dinner but about what we're going to do. And I think he is too, because he's been different the last couple of weeks."

"How so? Is it Annalisa drama again? Because I can take care of that for you. I told you I would." Bree's voice—and offer—are comforting.

Although I'd never ask her to get involved or spread any gossip that Annalisa kicks puppies, or whatever idea Bree has this time, it's nice to know I have people in my life who have my back no matter what.

"It's not her. At least, I don't think it is." I swipe my beer from the counter and sit on the couch.

"It's not," Erin reaffirms. "She's been lying low and giving you guys your space, right?"

"Yes. But maybe that should worry me." I sip my drink and lap up the citrusy aftertaste with fervor, but it does nothing to ease my racing mind. "You should've seen the way she clung to him when we first met. She was practically peeing on him to claim him."

"But Ian didn't want her."

"He did at one point." I sit up as my mind races.

I mean, he did date Annalisa right before he and I reconnected. Who's to say it's really over between them? Maybe I was just a rebound.

Oh, God…

"Wait." I wave my hands in front of my face, getting a drop of beer on my jeans. "We're way off topic. It has nothing to do with her or any other woman. It's the opposite. Ian's been more loving and doting than ever. He's sweet and even sent me flowers to the salon earlier today."

"Excuse me, but I'm failing to see the problem here," Bree doles out.

I roll my eyes. "It's not a problem, but there's something else to it. I don't know. He's just been a little off, like he's overcompensating for something."

"Good thing you're having dinner, then. You can ask him," Erin urges.

"Or it's a good opportunity to call him out for any shit he might be trying to pull with any skanks."

A laugh breaks loose from my throat. "You two are like the freaking angel and devil on my shoulders. Where's Tessa when you need a tiebreaker?" I muse.

"Tessa's off in wedding planning bliss, so you're stuck with us."

"Lucky me, and I mean that," I tell them.

Beeping sounds on their end, interrupting us. "Our homemade kale chips are ready," Erin announces, clapping.

"That better be code for homemade pizza or french fries,

because I burned the last bag of kale you brought me for a reason," Bree warns, making me laugh.

These two could not be more opposite. Yet, they make it work.

"Good luck, Erin. I'll check in with you later to make sure you're still alive," I joke, knowing good and well Erin was serious about what's in the oven.

I hear mumbling before they click off, and I'm left with silence.

With that, my beer, and my jumbled thoughts, anyway.

Although the girls made me laugh and temporarily distracted me, I still have Ian and our impending distance to deal with.

It didn't work for us in the past, so who's to say we can make it work now?

We might be older and wiser, but that just means we have more to lose. He has a life in LA. A house. Friends. A career.

And I have the same here in New York.

Tomorrow's dinner can't come soon enough.

TWENTY

Madison

"**Y**our ass has never looked better than it did earlier," Ian says, leaning over the table to make sure our neighbors don't hear. "I mean, when you bent over for a brush from your bag and I caught a glimpse of your purple thong? I almost yelled *that's a wrap* myself and hauled you back to my trailer."

"And taken that announcement away from Richard? He never would've forgiven you," I tease.

"Would've been worth it." He smirks, rubbing his thumb over the top of my hand.

His hair falls loosely over his forehead, very unlike the way it was slicked back earlier for a scene. It's slightly longer than it was when I gave him a haircut at the salon—the turning point for us. I wouldn't mind a repeat one bit, either.

My nose twitches as I fight a blush. "This restaurant is way too fancy for that kind of talk."

"If you think the number of forks next to my plate is going to stop me from dirty talking to my woman, then you don't know me very well."

My heart skips a beat, but it's not because of the promise of dirty talk or the hope it gives me that he'll slide his hand up my dress by the time dessert comes out.

It's because he called me his woman.

That's a good sign that we have a future and are on the same page, right?

"Good evening." Our server appears at the end of our table like a limber dancer—quiet and graceful. He barely wrinkles his crisp white shirt when he points to the lone menu between Ian and me and asks, "Do you have any questions regarding the wine menu?"

"Oh." I blink at it. "You know, we got to talking and haven't decided yet. I'm so sorry."

"Take your time. I'll be back with a couple of waters and bread to get you started." He scurries away, his legs moving at warp speed, but the rest of his body remains stiff.

"I need to know where he learned to walk," Ian says as we both stare after him. "It'll come in handy if I ever need to play an uptight dude. Or a surgeon."

I giggle, and we continue back and forth, again forgetting about the wine menu. But when the server returns with water, we take a chance and point at a red wine at random just so we don't have to ask him to wait another minute.

Once he's gone, leaving us to talk in hushed tones over the low buzz of the restaurant, Ian takes my hand in his. "It'll be a fun surprise," he says, referring to the wine we just picked.

"I hope it's a good one, since you ordered an entire bottle."

"Tell you what. If you don't like this wine, I'll owe you one hamburger."

I stare pointedly, but I can't help my smile—and it's not just from our inside joke.

It's because I'm at a nice restaurant where the food is sure to be delectable, albeit in tiny portions. The plants in this place are lush and tall, rising high up the cream-colored wall. Outside, instead of a flimsy awning like ones from cheap pizza places, this restaurant boasts a ceramic tile covering, inviting its guests into another world. Pictures of the Tuscan countryside are scattered around us, making it even more romantic.

The company is romantic too.

"Here we are." Our server holds a bottle from the bottom, his hands strong and experienced as he pours us each a glass. "Enjoy."

Once we thank him, I bring the glass up under my nose for a whiff, and Ian does the same. We watch each other like we're playing the blinking game, waiting to see who takes the first sip.

"The true test," Ian says, lifting the rim to his lips.

"Let's do it."

I sip only a few drops, mulling the oaky taste over on my tongue. "My knowledge of wine doesn't extend beyond good or bad, dry or sweet, but this wine is damn good."

He kisses my hand, then gives it back to me to grab a piece of bread.

I follow his lead, and we settle into the evening, blending in with the other patrons as the clock ticks.

He doesn't mention what it is he wanted to talk about. Instead, we address everything from the movie to the salon to our friends.

He tells me more about Keith and one of his clients—Rhett something. At this point, it almost feels like I know them, even though we've never met in person, and it's comforting to be part of Ian's LA life like this.

But right after the server brings our entrees, our bubble bursts.

And not because of the food.

The single bite I take of my risotto is divine, and I'm certain they used black magic to cook this.

No, the food is great. It's the woman who comes to a stop next to us that leaves a sour taste in my mouth before she even utters a word.

"Annalisa, hey." Ian places his fork next to his plate and furrows his brows. "What're you doing here?"

"I could ask you the same. This is my little spot of heaven, but I can't get mad at you for bringing Madison here to experience how amazing it is. I know you loved it too when I brought you." She gives him a small smile, and if this food wasn't so good, I'd set my own silverware down too.

Instead, I stuff a big forkful into my mouth and give her a tight-lipped smile around the creamy bite.

Shifting in his seat, Ian laughs, but it's a nervous one.

"I'm so glad I ran into you, though." Annalisa leans her hip on the side of our table, her black satin dress a stark contrast to our white tablecloth. "I haven't had a chance to congratulate you since we've been so busy on the set, but I heard the big news about your upcoming projects."

Okay, now I drop my fork, and it lands with a loud clink against my plate.

"Projects? What projects?" I ask, focusing on Ian.

"You haven't told her?" She playfully nudges him, her

fingers barely grazing his shoulder like she purposely missed. Turning to me, she gushes, "This guy has quite the lineup of auditions when we get back to LA. Richard calls him a star, and he's not kidding. I mean, he's done some big things already, but these projects are going to launch his career into Clooney status."

Did it suddenly get hot in here, or what?

It's hard to swallow, and I almost choke trying to.

As I take a sip of wine, Ian waves her off. "I don't know about all that," he says absentmindedly. "They're not sure things, but I appreciate the optimism."

"Of course. I've probably become too much of a cheerleader after hanging out with Patrick so much these last few weeks."

"Oh, you and Patrick, huh?" Ian asks, briefly looking at her before his attention falls back on me.

"We're just friends. He's very sweet, though, isn't he?" She glances up and waves. "Speak of the devil."

Dressed in a gray suit and navy blue tie, Patrick strides into the restaurant like he owns the place and gives us a head nod.

"Will you excuse me?" I wipe the corners of my mouth with my napkin and stand. "I'm going to run to the ladies' room."

I don't wait for an answer or stop when Ian says my name.

Instead, I rush to the quiet asylum of the restroom, enclosed in a beautiful exposed brick wall. I'd stop to admire it, but I'm too busy trying to keep myself from hyperventilating.

So what if my boyfriend didn't tell me about some exciting career moves he's got in the works? No big deal. That's probably what he wanted to talk to me about tonight.

He wanted to make it special and talk to me about his future and possibly where and how I fit into it.

There.

It's fine.

I inhale and exhale with measured breaths, then splash a little water to each of my flaming cheeks.

When I meet my gaze in the mirror, though, my stomach recoils as one last thought punches me in the gut.

Annalisa already knew about his big projects. Ian's ex-girlfriend knew things I didn't, and my throat fucking burns—it's a hard pill to swallow.

With forced movements, I dab at my cheeks with a paper towel and run my fingers through my hair, bringing it over both shoulders to the front. The ends tickle my cleavage, down which a trail of freckles is sprinkled. Ian's part-time job has been running his fingers down that dusting of spots between my breasts, which he's dubbed "the Valley" after the one in LA.

Shimmying my fitted dress farther down over my tights, I exit the bathroom and zigzag between tables until I get to my own.

Ian sits alone, his hair sticking up on one side like he's run his hand through it a hundred times since I excused myself.

"Where are your friends?" I ask, jolting him. Clearly, he didn't hear me approach.

"They sat down to eat. I've already paid the check and thought we could go back to your place to talk." It's more of a plea than a demand. His mouth hangs open, and he leans forward, his chest so far over the table he could spill his wine with one more breath.

I toy with the boxed-up food, shifting my weight to my other foot. "I've lost my appetite, anyway."

The bag of our food rustles as I pick it up, and Ian places his fingertips at the small of my back to lead me out.

He's hesitant, though, like he's afraid to touch me.

And I hate it.

Ian has never had any fear of touching me. Just the opposite, actually. Every time we're together, he seems to make it a mission to touch me in any place he might not have explored before.

Now, his fingertips hardly graze the material covering me, and when he helps me with my coat, he holds it high and stands with more than a foot between us, sliding it on me like a bag over a ticking bomb.

Sighing, I don't wait for him to put his own jacket on. Instead, I race out into the chilly night. It's still spring, and we have plenty of these nights ahead of us before summer brings in the heat. When that happens, we'll be fighting for breath in the humidity and begging for chilly nights again.

Isn't that how it goes? We always want what we can't have.

Ian eventually catches up to me, his breath releasing in little puffs of air as he matches my stride.

We're silent the entire way to my apartment, and when we finally get there and close the door behind us, I let out a heavy exhale. It doesn't make me feel as good as it does when I do yoga, though.

"You don't have to explain anything." I shake myself out of my coat. "I was just surprised Annalisa knew more about what you have going on than your own girlfriend, but it makes sense."

"What's that supposed to mean?" He visibly tenses.

I spin around to face him, and the smile that spreads across my lips is sad. "She's in your world, Ian. As an actress, she gets you more than I ever will. She'll go back to LA with you. You'll probably do more movies together. You two will have your own inside jokes, and I'll be here, on the other side of the world, in more ways than one." My chest heaves as I unleash all my suffocating worries, but instead of offering relief, I just feel worse. "God, I know how that sounded, and I'm not jealous of her in the way you might think. I know there's nothing romantic going on between you two, but the fact remains that you and I lead two different lives."

He closes the distance between us and grips my arms, holding me in place. "What if we could have one?" Hope flashes across his otherwise dark expression.

"What do you mean?"

"After you left the set yesterday, I talked to Sarah, and she'd be happy to recommend you to other teams. To help you with a career in LA. She said you have plenty of talent. Well, what she actually said was that you're way better than the original makeup artist she'd hired and that she'd done us a favor by moving to Ohio. Anyway, she can call all the right people to get you started out there." By the end, his words are rushed and frantic, as is my heart rate.

I blink at him. "Are you serious?"

"Yes." He eases into a smile, rubbing his thumbs up and down my biceps. "Madi, I want you to come with me. That's what I—"

"I mean, you seriously talked to Sarah about me without asking me first?" I jerk out of his hold. "How could you do that? I'm going to look like such an ass when I tell her I won't be coming."

"I'm sorry." He runs both hands through his hair. "I didn't mean to overstep. I was just trying to figure this out."

I glare. "You went behind my back to make a very important decision on your own."

"Wait." He teeters onto his heel, stepping back and putting even more distance between us. "You don't want to do it—that's it? You don't even want to take a few days to think about it?"

"Ian, this is a big ask. It's not just accepting a job. It's moving across the country."

"You were the one telling me how happy you are working on the set. How you've been searching for something outside the salon for months and that this is the perfect thing. So, why not continue doing it? Bonus—we'll be in the same place." He holds his hands out like this solves all our problems.

And it makes my frustration level shoot higher, reminding me of the times Ian tried to reach a new high score on the hammer game at the fair when we were younger. When he swung harder, he'd get higher and higher on the scale, but in this case, he's about to run out of room.

"You're acting like that's the only option. I mean, what about my salon? I just close the doors and call it quits?" I jut my hip out, and my bottom lip trembles.

"Well, no. What if you promote Sofia to manager? She can run the place while you're away."

"So I'll be coming back, then? Like I'm just going on vacation?" I toss back.

"No. That's not what I'm trying to say—fuck."

"That's much better. *Fuck* is a lot more accurate too."

"At least I'm trying to make this work between us. Or am I the only one who even wants that?" He paces, then stops when I don't immediately answer and stares expectantly at me.

"What you're trying to do is make this work for *you*," I whisper, and he tenses, one foot on my rug while the other remains on the scratched linoleum floor. I've obviously struck a nerve and trapped him between two places.

One is in a parallel universe where we don't have to make this decision at all.

But this isn't his movie—this is real life.

And the sacrifice he's so flippantly asking me for is huge. Bigger than proposing we move in together or adopt a pet, even.

He's suggesting I give up everything.

I risk a peek up at him, and when I take in his sullen frown, my chest sinks. "You're asking me to be the one who leaves my life behind, but I don't hear you offering anything up. You could just as easily move here."

"I would, and I already talked to Keith about what that would look like."

My ears perk up. He's thought about this a lot, hasn't he?

He's planned out so much about where we go from here, and it gives me hope. But a heads-up would've been nice.

"When I talked to him about splitting my time between here and LA, Keith agreed I could if I get these next few roles so I could afford two places." His shoulders slump forward. "But right now, I need to be in LA. That's where the action is. In the future, I could be more flexible, but I can't leave yet."

I clutch my stomach. "I worked hard for my salon and my life here, Ian. I'm not ready to give it up."

"I know, and I didn't mean to belittle it. I'm so fucking proud of you, Madi." He wraps me in his strong and warm embrace, but I'm not comforted by it as I usually am.

"I'm not done." I squeeze my eyes closed and pull away from him, my frustration still climbing. "Acting fell into your lap when you had nothing else to do. You didn't fight for it like I did for my business. I shouldn't be the one to give up everything to chase you across the country."

His jaw tics, and he doesn't say anything for a long time. His frown is as droopy as I feel—it's certainly not one they teach in acting school. "Acting wasn't in my ten-year plan as a teenager, but it became my passion. Just like us."

As I shift my weight to my other foot, the floor creaks beneath me like it's about to cave.

And I'm afraid it might.

With the direction this conversation is going, I don't feel steady like I did yesterday when Ian and I were on solid ground.

We were happy.

And now, my world is imploding.

"I didn't seek you out, but that doesn't mean I don't—"

My jaw drops as I search his expression. "What?"

"That I don't love you." He sighs. "Because I do. I'm in love with you. I mean, only you could make being stuck in a hair salon bearable, let alone fun."

I laugh, but it's shaky as tears fall down my cheeks.

"I love you for that and for so many things." He steps up to me, using his fingers to wipe my cheeks clean. "There are so many times that I wish we were back in that salon. Just the two of us. No one else. No decisions to be made. Only champagne to celebrate."

"Me too," I whisper, leaning my face into his cupped palm. "What do we do now? How do we decide this?"

He chews on his bottom lip as his jaw tightens, and I know I'm not going to like his answer.

Not even a little bit.

"I think we already did." He nods, his frown deeper and more grim than before, but he tries to smile through it.

It appears painful, like this goodbye.

Because that's what this is.

Suddenly, I'm eighteen again and losing him for a second time, but unlike the first breakup, I'm part of the goodbye. I don't have to wake up and wonder where he went.

Instead, I'll have the excruciating image of his back as he walks away.

"Ian…" More tears fall, and I lose my voice to the lump in my throat.

"Bye, Madi." He turns on his heel and heads for the door.

When his hand reaches the doorknob, I lunge forward. "Wait, Ian. I have to tell you something."

He glances over his shoulder but doesn't unclench his hold from the door.

"You know I lo—"

"Don't." He hangs his head. "Don't say it. Just… I can't…"

I don't know how long we stare at each other before I will myself to cling to the rage inside me instead of the sadness.

"Fine," I choke, mustering enough energy to steel myself as I take large strides toward him. "Give up and go. You're good at leaving, anyway, but at least you had the decency to say goodbye this time."

"How long have you had that locked and loaded?" he shoots back, and it only fuels me.

"It was easier to get over it when I thought you'd changed, but it turns out, I was wrong." I sidestep him and yank the door open for him to walk through it.

With heavy steps, he shuffles out, whispering, "This isn't how I wanted this to happen."

I slump against the frame. "Guess we can't always have everything we want."

Once I close the door with a resounding click behind him, I furiously swipe at my cheeks, and the weight of exhaustion from the last several weeks finally gets to me. It's nothing compared to the last hour, though.

Ian's gone.

I'll see him on the set tomorrow, and that's it. He'll go back to his corner of the country, and I'll stay here, paralyzed with memories of him.

With fear that I'll never see him again unless it's on the big screen.

I never thought I'd say this, but watching him leave this time was much worse than when he disappeared without a goodbye.

"Shit, shit, shit," I mumble as I continue wiping at the tears, unable to keep up with how quickly they're falling.

I don't even have the energy to fish my phone from my coat pocket to call any of the girls. Instead, I slink onto the couch and hug my knees to my chest as I give up on trying to stop the tears from rolling.

TWENTY-ONE

Ian

"**Y**ou got it!" Keith slams both palms on his desk and jumps up like there's a trampoline under his chair. "You fucking nailed that audition, man, and they loved you. The part is yours."

I grip the armrest of the chair on the other side of his desk, my focus on the windows behind him. I wish I could say I'm sitting in silence because the view is distractingly breathtaking, but there's nothing special about the dirty white office building blocking the expanse of mountains in the distance.

Instead, I'm quiet because the only person I want to celebrate with is Madi.

The one person I can't call.

"What the hell are you doing, you son of a bitch? Get in here and give me some fucking love!" Keith rushes around his desk, arms open.

"Right." I stand and give him a pat on the back.

"We should go out and celebrate. How does Kay's sound?"

I stuff my hands into my jeans pocket. "Isn't that a jewelry store?"

"What? No." He waves his hand. "I mean, it is, but that's not where we're going, obviously. I like you, Ian, but not like that." He laughs at himself, and he's the only one.

"Drinks will be a hoot, huh?" I mutter under my breath as I follow him out.

"Afterward, we need to get you laid," he says over his shoulder, and his receptionist turns toward us. "I'm taking Ian out and will be back in a jiffy."

She nods and waves at us both, her gaze lingering a bit too long on me as it normally does. Even when my resume included only one soup commercial, she was infatuated with me. Now that I have a few movies under my longhorn belt buckle, her adoring eyes have just grown wider.

Before filming in New York, I thought about asking her out too, but Keith warned me against it. Said another client of his had gone out with her and returned with scratches down his arms like he'd been attacked by a cat.

To this day, Keith has no idea what happened, and I was never too eager to find out for myself, either.

In any case, just thinking about another woman—even one like the receptionist where there's no future—makes me want to vomit. Anyone other than Madi would be a major disappointment, and it wouldn't have anything to do with them at all.

It's been two weeks since I last saw her.

Longer since I last held and kissed her.

Fuck, if I would've known how that dinner would go, I

would've spent more time holding and making love to her while I had the chance because seeing her the day after our fight was torture.

We barely spoke to each other. When she hardly even flicked her gaze toward me, I wanted to march over there and shake her until she agreed to come out here to LA with me.

But it wouldn't have been right. It wasn't right to ask Sarah about her, and it wasn't fair to ask Madi to uproot her entire life on a whim after we'd really only been dating for a month. It doesn't matter that we've known each other longer.

The reality is—I was insane and desperate and out of my mind in love with her.

She was going to say it too. Before I stopped her, anyway. It was obvious, but I couldn't let her. I couldn't hear the fucking words from her perfect lips because they likely would've made me quit my damn job to stay in New York, where it snows and rains more than the sun shines.

I might be lonely at times here in LA, but this is where my life is. This is where I feel like I need to be right now, and I can't shake that feeling enough to give it all up.

"I don't know how you survived up in New York so long without this sunshine." Keith cuts into my thoughts like he's reading them. *What the hell?* "And no beaches. Fucking Christ, I wouldn't have lasted. I've gone up there twice for work and thought I'd drive a pencil through my eye before I stayed up there another fucking hour."

"It wasn't so bad."

As I step out of his Porsche, the salty sea breeze skates over my cheeks, very unlike the sharp cold air of New York nights. The sun is high in the sky, and the waves crash against the cliffs, on top of which, Malibu is nestled.

"You're only saying that because you had better things to do." He tips his sunglasses down, giving me a sly grin. "You had a woman keeping you too busy to notice the horrors of that city."

"Thanks for that."

"Come on." He slaps me on the back and nudges me toward what the likes of Annalisa might call chic with its patio and glass all around the boxy building. "Let's get a drink in you so you can start forgetting."

"That's what you said to me two weeks ago."

"And it hasn't been working."

"Maybe I should go home." I finagle my way out of his clutches. "I'm not great company right now."

He holds his hands up. "One drink. We'll toast to your continued success, and then I'll drive you home without any other protests, I swear."

"Okay. One drink," I relent and follow him down the pathway toward the hostess stand.

As we're shown to a table out on the patio, I notice a few people glance over, recognition flashing, but I also see a TV news anchor in one corner and a sports team owner at another table. Somehow, I'm relieved not to be the most famous person here.

It is Malibu, after all. If there's one thing I can count on beyond expensive drinks and seafood, it's rubbing shoulders with other celebrities.

But I imagine if I had Madi instead of Keith next to me, people here wouldn't know who the famous one between us was.

She'd put any Hollywood star to shame with her stunning smile and infectious laugh.

"I'll take a Scotch, neat, and my friend here would like a whiskey. Make it a double, please." Keith nods to our server, then clasps his hands on the table in front of him while I lose myself in the view.

Madi would love it here.

She's never been, but she'd fit in, for sure. Her pale skin can't take much sunshine, but there's plenty of things to do around here other than be outside. We could've explored them all.

Fuck.

I need to get her out of my head.

"Cheers." Keith and I clink our glasses and start with a sip.

Although mine is more of a gulp.

True to his word, Keith and I toast to my new role, and we keep the conversation light, mostly discussing my future parts. After we finish the single drink, he drives me home.

I scan the dark house as we sit in the driveway for a beat. "Thank you for this afternoon, even if I wasn't the best company." I let my head fall back against the headrest and sigh.

"You were fine." He rests his elbow on his door. "I just wish there was more I could do for you, buddy."

I nod, confused by his oddly serious statement. He didn't even use cuss words, and we're not within two hundred yards of his kids. Actually, he's been kind and considerate and nice all afternoon.

Who is this guy?

I can't decide if I like it or hate it, but I'm leaning toward the latter. At least when Keith is being vulgar and emotionless, I know to roll my eyes and take his "wisdom" with a grain of salt, but this version of him only puts me on edge.

Am I that pathetic right now that I broke Keith?

"There is one thing I can tell you, though. It'll get better. Always does." He shrugs, and I get out of the car before he starts quoting the Bible or some shit.

Not that it would be wrong to do so. In truth, I'd take all the divine intervention I could at the moment. But it would be highly unlike him. He once told me the only time he'd ever come near a Bible was when he bought one in college to impress a girl.

Except he never even cracked the spine, and eventually, he lost it, along with his interest in the girl.

I stand by my front door and wave at Keith's retreating car down my drive.

There's plenty of daylight left, but I don't feel like basking in it, no matter what kind of big role I've landed. No beach or tiki bar will replace the pain in my chest.

If I could at least talk to Madi…

Fuck, then what? We talk once or twice a week and never get over each other, then wait until I can move out east?

That could take years.

I kick my front door to open it as if my hands are just too heavy at my sides, and I step inside, going straight to the fridge for a turkey sandwich. If Madi were here, she'd make some crack about how I just left a perfectly good restaurant, but I wasn't hungry then.

I'm not hungry now, but I scarf it down, nonetheless, as I sit next to a pile of laundry on my couch.

The TV is turned on, but instead of watching it, I grab my phone and scroll through until I reach Madi's name, fighting the urge to click on it.

How long will this need for her consume me?

I'm in major damn trouble.

———

*I*t's after dark when a knock on the door jolts me out of my trance.

I'm upset, but I need to be careful before I become a recluse, or worse—a meditator. I heard Madi's friend Erin talk about meditating once a day and getting lost in the tranquil silence of her mind and world—her words.

I remember thinking it sounded like torture. I much rather enjoy people and the chaos of being among them, but I did just spend the last half hour since Keith dropped me off without looking up at the TV. I don't think I even heard it.

Fuck, am I good at meditating now? Who am I?

When did I last go for a jog? Or cook myself anything worthwhile? I'm no chef, but my mother sent me out of the house with at least a few easy recipes to survive on.

She'd be so disappointed in me right now.

There's another knock, and I reach for the remote to turn the TV up for some background noise.

Then I yank the door open, and as soon as it's wide enough to fit herself through, Annalisa jumps into my embrace, rambling on about some article. "I came as soon as I saw it. Are you okay? I mean, I had hoped you two would survive, but how can people like us find love? Is it even possible? Believe me when I say, I wish things had turned out differently for you two."

"Whoa, whoa, whoa." I peel her arms off me, but it takes more of a full-body effort to push her off. She's very strong for such a small person. "What're you talking about?"

"You and the makeup artist." Annalisa waltzes past me and into my living room. "It's all over the internet about how you two broke up. At first, it was just a small media outlet that reported it. They only gave you one tiny paragraph—a few sentences, really—but then it snowballed from there, worse than when those vultures thought Patrick and I were dating. Can you imagine if that were true? We slept together once, and it was, like, barely mind-blowing. But that's the media these days. They don't care if the shit they say is true." She stops and peers up at me as if it just occurs to her that this is my house. "Wait, it is true, right? You're not with her anymore?"

She says *her* and *the makeup artist* like she's suddenly forgotten Madi's name, but I know that's bullshit. Annalisa's just playing one of her mind games. The one where she belittles anyone in her way.

But why? That's what I can't figure out.

When she opens her mouth again, I hold my hand up to stop her. "It's true. Madi and I are no longer together. I thought you knew that." I scratch the back of my head and plop onto the recliner since the laundry is taking up most of the couch.

"Me? How could I know? I mean, when we were on set the last couple of days in New York, I thought there might've been a chance you two had called things off, but I didn't want to assume. People say I assume a lot, but they don't understand that I tend to be right most of the time." She takes a seat, crosses one leg over the other, and leans on the mountain of wrinkly clothes, her blouse drooping with the movement. "Just like you know I was right about you two in the first place. Come on, be honest. You and Madi were faking the whole thing, at least in the beginning, right?" She laughs like my relationship was a joke.

It might've started out as a lie, but it turned into so much more.

"I thought it did, anyway," I mumble, lost in my own head.

I'm so dazed with the conversation I'm having with myself that I don't realize when Annalisa gets up. Is she coming toward me?

Before I comprehend what's happening, Annalisa launches herself on top of me, nuzzling her face into my neck. "I missed you so much. Isn't it so much hotter now that we've been with other people, had our fun, and are back with each other? We were meant to be from the start, and I'm so relieved you finally feel the same."

I shake my head, trying to get her hands off me, but she's got me trapped and is going on a rant. I've never heard her talk so damn much at such a quick pace. It has to be a record of some sort. "Annalisa, this isn't—"

She places her fingers over my mouth. "Don't speak. Our bodies will do more than enough talking." She winks, and the sandwich I had earlier makes its way up my stomach.

After some wrestling that she mistakes for foreplay, I finally grasp both her wrists and pin her beneath me onto the floor. "For fuck's sake!" I yell.

This gets her attention, and the mischievous smile transforms into a frown faster than she snaps for room temperature water.

And I lose it.

"I don't want to be with you, Annalisa, and I'm sorry." I curse under my breath. "Actually, I'm not sorry. I'm not sorry we keep having to do this. I'm not the fucking bad guy, no matter what you or anyone else might think. I don't want you. I did several months ago, but you weren't it for me then. You're not it for me now. You should really listen to the people who tell you not to assume, but it's more than that. You need to stop throwing yourself at me, because I'm in love with someone else. But even if it weren't for Madi, you and I were never right for each other. It's time you accept it."

My head is pounding by the end of my own rant as I slide off her and lie on my back on the floor next to her.

"Jesus," I mutter.

I finally told her exactly what I think.

No more running away from confrontation or joking my way out of a difficult conversation, at least for now.

It's too soon to tell if I'm turning over a new leaf or if I've just had enough of Annalisa's advances, but as my chest expands with more ease, I'd like to think this is the first step toward something bigger.

It's a long time before either of us cuts through the tension. I just wish she were yelling at me instead of what she's doing now.

Which is crying.

Quiet sniffles sound next to me, and in my periphery, I can tell her shoulders are shaking.

"Jesus," I repeat and lean up onto my elbows.

"You're totally right," she sputters. "I do this to myself. I go after the wrong guys because they're easier to deal with than someone who really wants to be with me. I don't have a clue how to be with someone I love who loves me back."

"What're you talking about?" This woman is giving me fucking whiplash.

She lets out a shaky breath and blubbers, "Patrick. He really likes me. He writes me the sweetest letters like we're in the medieval era. I keep telling him I throw them away, but I've kept them all. I reread them every day, but I can't tell him."

Annalisa and Patrick are in love?

I did not see that coming, more so because I saw Patrick with a gamer, librarian, or a girl he met at a coffee shop who's working on her knitting. Not someone like Annalisa. I don't think she's ever even picked up a book, unless she was trying to hide from the paparazzi behind it.

Damn, I really don't know Patrick at all, do I? The guy surprises me more than if a dolphin were to say my name.

"Come on," I say, exhaling as I stand and motion for her to do the same.

"No."

"Get up," I press.

She makes an incoherent sound, and I lean down to take matters into my own hands and pull her up. I lead her toward the couch and shove the mound of clothes off to make room, then sit us both down.

"What's the problem exactly?" I ask her gently.

She swipes at her smudged mascara and licks her lips. "He's a nice guy, you know? One you settle down with. And am I ready for that? Am I even capable of such a thing?"

"You never saw yourself getting married?"

"No." She cringes. "I didn't used to, anyway."

I smile as understanding dawns. "But Patrick changed that for you."

"Yes," she gives in, throwing her arms in the air like it pisses her off that he's done such a thing. "Can you believe that? Me and Patrick—isn't that against human nature or something? Won't the planet implode if two people like us get together?"

I chuckle, rubbing my hands down my face. This visit is going better than I thought. Or worse. Maybe a little of both?

I don't even know which way is fucking up anymore.

"It's not funny. I'm being totally serious. It defies the basic laws of chemistry."

I search her wide-eyed gaze. "I know, but maybe—and please hear me out—are you maybe scared?"

After a tense moment of silence, she sinks into the back of the couch.

I stand and pace in front of her, running my finger along my bottom lip. I swear if I concentrate hard enough, I can still feel Madi's lips on mine. "Love is scary, Annalisa. You're not the first person to run away from it, and you won't be the last." I search for the right words. For anything that will convince her, because no matter how crazy she can sometimes act with me, she's a person, and she deserves love.

We all do.

I pause by the mantle, above which my TV plays a sitcom rerun, and I reach deep inside when I say, "But why should you miss out on it? Is fear worth it? Or would you rather face love head-on and be happy with the person who feels the same for you?"

She doesn't answer me right away, and I spin to face her to make sure she didn't cry herself into a coma or something. I can never tell how far her dramatics expand.

But she's staring right back at me, tears in her eyes. "Wow," she breathes. "What script is that monologue from? I have got to watch that."

"What? No," I stutter. "It's me. They're my words, Annalisa. All me."

"Really?" She clutches her chest like I told her the secret of great skincare.

"Yes. Really," I confirm, trying my best to keep the offense out of my voice but probably failing.

"You're very good. How come you were never so romantic with me?"

"Seriously?"

"Right. We already addressed that." She nods, then fidgets with her fingers in her lap. "You really think I'd be good at the girlfriend thing?"

I smile, my shoulders deflating. "Only one way to find out."

She smiles back. "Okay, I'll do it. I'll tell him I love him too. Because I do. I love how excited he gets over his little video games. And every weird thing that comes out of his mouth. Or when he compares my vagina to different flowers. Or—"

"That's great. Just... great." I grimace, the graphic description like acid on a cut.

"I'm going to tell him right now." She jumps up from my couch, her tears already gone. Were they even real? She may be more confusing and fascinating than Patrick. "Before it's too late."

My eyes lift to hers.

"Come on." She waves a manicured finger in circles toward my face. "It's written all over this. You're in love with Madi, and you think it's too late to get her back."

"It is too late." I make my way toward the door, ready to show her out.

But she stops in the middle of the doorway. "If you really believe that, you wouldn't be so mopey."

"I'm not mopey. I'm perfectly happy." I exaggerate a smile. It's one I don't feel or believe, but that's beside the point.

"Sure." She shrugs. "I just think you should take your own advice."

"Which part? I said a lot of smart things today," I joke.

"Just let me know what I can do to help like you've helped me." She blows me a kiss and waves over her shoulder, the beep of her unlocking her car echoing between us.

The couple next door bursts out of their house, laughing like they've been drinking for hours.

Must be date night.

I don't know them well, but the few times we've spoken, they've mentioned their sacred date nights. They're the only times each month that they get to be a couple since they have a toddler and full-time jobs.

I give them a wave and head back inside, exhaling with a huge weight lifted off my shoulders now that Annalisa and I finally got our situation handled.

I've always despised confrontation, but this needed to be done.

And it went well, unlike the last one I had—the one with Madi.

I didn't expect it to hurt so fucking badly. She looked at me like we were doomed from the start. That the end was always inevitable.

And on some level, I knew. I was just grasping at straws when I talked to Sarah about Madi working out here, something I apologized for when we got back to LA. In true Sarah fashion, though, she waved me off like she had a million more important things to do.

Which she probably did.

But it still stung because the favor I'd asked of her was significant to me. Madi was—and is—important to me.

I want to talk to her. To call and check in. Given the circulating news of our broken relationship, it's the perfect chance for me to reach out.

I want to know how she's doing with it.

Thanks to me, she's been in the media quite a bit the last couple months, but she's handled it a lot better than some. I'm not surprised, though. The camera is Madi's friend, even if the journalist isn't. In any case, she never let anything get her down.

Is she still staying strong?

Sighing, I pick up a shirt from the pile of laundry to start putting it away, but it feels as heavy as a brick in my hold.

Talking to Madi will only make this breakup harder on us both. Especially since I'm no closer to getting over her than I was when I left.

I'm putty when it comes to her.

I just wish there was an easier way to make it work between us. One that doesn't involve monthly date nights, where the other twenty-nine days of the month are spent on two different coasts.

What kind of relationship would that be?

TWENTY-TWO

Madison

"You beat us here—again." Erin slings her purse onto the back of her red-and-yellow chair, a smile brighter than the decor of this place on her lips.

I hold up my full glass. "It's margarita night. Never again will I miss one."

"I'll cheers to that." She pours herself a glass from the pitcher Harvey brought the second he laid eyes on me earlier. He knows us well and even had a shot ready for me before my ass hit the seat.

After I take a sip, I glance around the room and beyond the arches separating each section, scanning for Tessa and Bree, but all I see are a few unfamiliar faces.

"You can, though," Erin says, eyeing me.

"What?"

There's a crash from the kitchen, drawing our attention to the area behind the bar. Harvey holds his hands up in reassurance that everything's under control, his tattooed arms strong and capable. Then he disappears into the kitchen.

"Missing margarita nights is okay." My friend places her hand on mine.

"What're you talking about? This is our weekly tradition, and I'm not giving it up. Even after Tessa gets married this fall, we will drag her ass out here every Thursday night until we die. I already made her promise." I smile into my glass, the tangy drink infiltrating my senses and burning my nostrils.

Erin laughs and removes her hand from mine to grab a chip. "That's not what I'm talking about."

I lick the salt from my lips, studying the dip in the white specks on the rim of my glass—I'm scared to look up.

"You missed margarita night because you were with Ian, and that's okay." She exhales. "All I'm trying to say is that it's okay to be happy, and Ian made you happy. No matter what Bree says, we want that for you. We were, anyway, before he broke your heart. *Again*. But it's not the end all, be all. There's still hope."

I nod, lost in thought. She said "happy" too many times to count, like she was sending me a subliminal message, and I fixate on it.

I am happy.

And I don't need to rely on a man. I have my friends and family and successful business.

I love my life here, margarita night included.

These girls are a large part of my life, and just the thought of leaving them makes me emotional. What would I do without them?

After a pause, I gaze up at her. "Don't you ever get tired of being so positive and hopeful? I mean, you go on so many dates, but only one percent ever end in sex. *Good* sex is even more rare. Yet, it doesn't stop you from trying. Why is that?"

"Believe me, there have been plenty of times I've said I'm done. That I'm never going on another date for as long as kale is green." She giggles, and the ends of her chestnut hair rustle over her trembling shoulders.

"What changes your mind then?" I ask, leaning forward as intrigue overshadows any self-pity I've been feeling for the last few weeks.

"I meet a guy." She waves her delicate fingers around like she's solving a math problem on an imaginary whiteboard. "It won't be just any guy, either. It's usually someone I connect with over coffee or a mutual dislike of how open the produce sections at grocery stores are. I mean, seriously, anyone can—and does—just walk up to the parsley and touch every single leaf on each bunch like it's a sample station."

"I'm assuming you've had that conversation recently, huh?" I tease.

"That's beside the point." She sighs. "What I'm trying to say is that they each spark a little curiosity in me. Just enough to make me want to find out if they're the real deal. They never are, but it doesn't mean it's not out there. Look at Tessa and Carter." She flashes her hesitant gaze toward me, and I know I'm not going to like what she says next. "Or you and Ian."

I gulp more of my drink, and the tequila makes my eyes water. "I'll give you Tess, but you're wrong about me. The real deal lasts, and Ian and I didn't."

"Not yet," Erin mumbles. Whether she meant for me to hear it is unclear, but I do.

And it doesn't give me hope.

It just makes me sadder.

"Can you two try long distance?" she asks as someone rushes next to me, practically leaving a puff of air behind them like a cartoon.

"Who?" Bree asks, shaking her damp hair out over the back of her seat. Guess it started raining since Erin and I first sat down, and I didn't even bring a raincoat or umbrella.

Last week, another chair at my salon broke, and yesterday, I was super excited to have a beer once I got home, only to find I was out.

The universe just keeps on giving, doesn't it?

"Ian and Mads," Erin explains, pointing to me as if Bree might've forgotten my name. "You guys talked about long distance, right? And he just shot it down?"

I hand Bree a napkin, knowing even before she pours herself a margarita that she's going to spill—it happens every week no matter how much practice she's had over the last couple of years.

We resume as seamlessly as we might in a choreographed routine, passing napkins and more salt since Bree likes hers that way on occasion. She says it matches her bitter personality and thoughts on love.

When Tessa arrives, she jumps right into it all without a hiccup. "You could totally do a long-distance relationship," she says around crunching on a chip. I'm not even sure how she heard Erin's last question, but it's all part of our dynamic.

We're that close.

"We didn't talk about it," I confess and scoot a salsa dish closer to me while moving another toward Tessa.

"Why not?" Erin squeaks while the other two stare curiously at me.

"What good would it have done either of us in the long run? Those kinds of relationships never last, so we nipped it in the bud." I pop a chip in my mouth with more enthusiasm than I'm feeling. "Besides, we've been through this before. It didn't work back then, and it's not going to work now for the same reason, which is funny since I never bought into the whole idea that history repeats itself." I rub my hands together, dusting chip residue off my fingers. "But here we are."

"Except you're not eighteen anymore," Tessa points out.

"She is acting like it, though." Bree lifts a thick eyebrow at me.

"I will not take this abuse," I tease, holding my hands up. "We've talked about Ian and dissected every detail about the whole mess already, then again when the media blasted it all over the internet. I've gone from angry to sad to freaking pissed, then to wiping my tears with chocolate chip cookies—"

"When the hell did that happen?" Tessa asks.

"And why did you ruin perfectly good cookies over an asshat like Ian?" Bree adds.

I choke on my laugh. These girls know how to make me smile through a sucky situation. "It was a figure of speech," I draw out. "All I'm saying is that we don't need to go down that road again. In fact, I prefer we don't."

Bree lifts her glass to the middle of the table. "To saving the cookies!"

I roll my eyes but clink, nonetheless.

After a short pause, Erin offers, "The principal at my school is finally retiring and leaving. For *good*."

Bree purses her lips like she's fighting a smile, then bites out, "I don't love the redirect in conversation, but that's fantastic news. You've been complaining about him since you started teaching there."

Tessa rubs my back and smiles in celebration with our two friends.

I lean into her, nudging her shoulder with my own in silent thanks.

"Right? He always left his pants zipper down and could never remember any of the kids. I mean, I know we have a lot of them, but my God, take an interest. The students basically live there for four years, and he can't learn their names?" Erin curses into her margarita, then knocks the rest of it back.

"What happened to being positive?" I bite the inside of my cheek.

"I usually am, but it disappears when I'm referring to Principal Garth," she says.

I give Erin a once-over to make sure this is the same girl who smiles through every obstacle in life. "We should've ordered the strawberry margarita to curb that sass tonight."

"Did I hear strawberry margarita?" Harvey appears next to our table, large hands on his hips. "What jerk are you four cursing tonight?"

Our table erupts into laughter.

"You know us too well." Tessa giggles.

"And I'd like to get to know these abs better." Bree waves her finger over his stomach.

I toss a balled-up napkin at her. "You better stop, or you'll scare him into leaving us." I look at Harvey. "Shonda's nice and all, but she likes to pour more sweet and sour than tequila sometimes."

"Plus, she's not as hot as you," Bree butts in. Did she hear anything I said?

"You ladies sure know how to flatter a guy." He touches his face. "I think I'm blushing. I don't know if that's ever happened before."

"Just wait until you get on stage for the bachelor auction this weekend. Women will faint left and right." Bree squeezes his bicep.

"Thank you for filling in at the last minute, by the way." Tessa holds her hands up in a prayer-like manner. "You saved us after Erin's accountant backed out."

"I'm happy to do it." Harvey waves her off.

Bree snorts, leaning back and crossing her arms. "Really? Because when I asked you earlier this week, you said you'd rather dunk your head in the ice box back there."

Oh, Harvey's done it now.

"Those weren't exactly my words," he defends, slowly backing away.

Tessa covers her mouth as she laughs. "Even so, we appreciate it, and I'll make sure Bree isn't allowed on the main floor so she can't bid on you."

"Whoa! I did not agree to that." She points between them, which makes Tessa laugh harder.

If Harvey wasn't blushing before, he definitely is now.

And this is also why we leave such a generous tip every Thursday night.

He's called back to the bar, waving to us over his shoulder, and our laughter subsides.

"So, do you know who the new principal will be?" Bree asks Erin, picking up right where we left off.

"Not yet. But I hope it's someone who knows how to wash their own coffee mugs instead of leaving them all over the teacher's lounge for the rest of us to clean up. Usually, that means me." Erin rolls her eyes, then lets out a long exhale. "I'm so sorry, guys. I have no idea what's gotten into me tonight. Maybe it's just end-of-year stress. I'm like this every May. In any case, I *am* feeling sassy tonight."

"That's what I'm here for." Harvey pops up again, wearing a grin that stretches across his sharp jaw as he sets a pitcher of strawberry margarita in the center. "Enjoy."

"Oh, you magnificent, beautiful man," Bree praises him. "Thank you. We will put it to good use."

"You always do." He winks and returns to the bar to continue filling orders. The place has livened up with more people since we first sat down.

And more come and go over the next couple of hours as we drink, talk, and laugh—the soundtrack to Thursday nights.

It's what I look forward to every week.

But I have to admit, Ian added a special kind of flavor to my days. His jokes and masculine smell and tongue.

His freaking tongue.

It was fun, and I loved every minute of it, even though it ended badly.

By the end of girls' night, my cheeks are sore from laughing, but I'm not distracted or buzzed enough to stop thinking about Ian.

Will this empty feeling ever go away?

"It doesn't get better," Tessa says to me, her voice low while Erin asks for more napkins from the bar and Bree is in the bathroom.

"What?"

"That void." She places her hand over her chest. "When I thought Carter and I were over, I felt like I was just going through the motions. I thought that's how I'd live the rest of my days, and the feeling got stronger the longer he and I were apart."

I sigh—she just described exactly what I'm going through. "What do I do about it?"

"I wish I had the answer, babe." She wraps her arm around my shoulder, pulling me close, and my chair scrapes across the floor as I scoot toward her.

"Hey! I want in too." Erin shuffles in and wraps her arms around both of us.

"Relax. I'm back. No need to pout." Bree's voice sounds from somewhere behind Tessa. "I wouldn't have gone to the bathroom had I known you'd miss me so much."

My giggle is muffled in this group hug, which only gets tighter. I assume Bree joins us, squeezing from the outside.

I'm sure the people at our surrounding table are staring, but it never stops us. Ian and I may not be together, but I'm the luckiest girl alive to have this group of friends—my family.

"I love you all," I say as we pull apart.

"And we love you too." Tessa nods around the table as we all take our seats. "Just know—we'd love you even if you were on the other side of the country too. You'd never lose us."

I freeze. "What do you mean?"

Bree tilts her head to the side and smiles. "Just that we're here for you. Whatever you decide."

I open my mouth to insist that I have decided. That Ian and I are over, but something stops me. Maybe it's the knowing looks they give me or the lively evening.

In any case, they give me more hope than I've felt in a while, although I don't know what it means.

TWENTY-THREE

Ian

"They want you to be a guest on a talk show," Keith says through the speaker of my phone. "I already told you that, right?"

"Yes, but I never agreed," I answer as I shut the refrigerator door.

"You'd do your twenty minutes or so, grab those exposure points by the balls, and get the fuck out of there."

"What exactly does that role look like?" I ask doubtfully.

What I really want to ask is—what's the catch?

The last time he gave me the same casual tone about a show that he's using now, I ended up playing a dog owner on and off camera. The trainer was belligerently drunk and couldn't tell his left shoe from the right, and he forgot the dog at the studio. I didn't mind one bit to take her home with me for the night, but the cops showed up the next day, accusing me of stealing, even though I was just trying to help.

I was the fucking hero in that story, but whatever.

Of course, I've done talk shows before that turned out to be great experiences, but a couple threw me for a loop. They're the ones I'm afraid of repeating, so I know better than to believe Keith right away.

"Let's put a pin in it and discuss the details at our next meeting." His office phone rings in the background about the same time as a knock sounds on my door. "Need to go, Ian. Talk soon."

"Bye." I click off and head toward the door, water in hand.

The show sounds harmless enough. If anything, it would be great to promote *Ghost Predators,* and more screen time is always a good idea to get my name out there.

But the fact that Keith didn't give me much to go on is making me cautious.

The second I open the door and see who's on the other side, standing in the flesh on my welcome mat, my jaw drops. All thoughts of the show fade, and I freeze.

What the hell is he doing here?

Staring into Cash's eyes, I quip, "I'm surprised you know where I live."

"Nice to see you too, little brother." He huffs as he brushes me aside and enters my home like it's his own. Whistling, he spins around in place, spreading his arms. "Hollywood's treating you well, I see. What kind of interest do you have on this place? Because my bank would—"

"Not *your* bank, Cash." I clear my throat and steel myself, still trying to wrap my head around the fact that he's here. "You're a loan officer at a bank that's not yours, no matter how you or Mom and Dad might act. It's not your business."

"Easy." He holds his hands up. "Fuck, I didn't come here for a fight."

I step down into the living room and finally take a good look at him. He's lost weight, and his cheeks are sunken in, which makes his eyes appear bigger. His clothes are baggy, like he hasn't gone shopping in a while, and his scruff is different too. He's normally clean-shaven and groomed, and I am too, although I'm ready for the end of filming so I can let my beard grow out again—much less maintenance.

"Why did you come, then?" I ask warily, more afraid of the answer than if the floor split open like in the show *La Brea*.

With Cash, I never know what to expect.

"So I could thank you in person for all the cards you send to Peter," he deadpans.

"All right." I nod toward the door. "You know your way out."

He sighs, scratching his head much in the same way I often do when I'm reluctant to give straight answers. "Norma and I are having problems. Counseling doesn't seem to help. In fact, it often makes things worse."

I furrow my brows.

"And Peter sees and hears everything, which he then repeats to anyone who will listen, including Mom and Dad. They all think everything's my fault, and you know what"— his posture relaxes like we're old friends falling into a regular conversation—"I'm sick of constantly defending myself. Norma's the one going out with her friends every weekend, leaving me alone with Peter like I know how to entertain him, and then I'm the one in trouble when Peter throws up because I gave him a peanut butter and jelly sandwich."

I cross my arms. "Peter's allergic to nuts, man. Even I know that, and I've only met the kid in person three times."

He stares pointedly at me.

"Don't look at me like that." I make a beeline for the whiskey in my cabinet, set out two glasses, and pour. "All I'm saying is, if you came here looking for sympathy, you won't be getting it from me, but I can offer you a glass of whiskey."

"I'll take that." He accepts a glass, swirls the liquid around, then takes a drink. After a pause, he points at me from around his glass. "There was a time when you would be on my side no matter what."

"That was *before*," I say evenly.

"Before my injury, it seemed everyone was on my side, and now that I can't play football, it's like no one gives a shit."

I set my glass down on the counter, but it's more like dropping it, given the loud thud that follows. "No. You were a jerk even before your injury, although it didn't help."

"What're you talking about?"

I laugh, but it holds no humor. "Are you serious?"

He puts his drink next to mine and clutches the edge of the counter, expecting an answer.

"Cash, don't you remember Madison? She was my girlfriend, and you wanted to date her. You hit on her, but she rejected you. Then, you got injured playing football, which sucked, but you used it as an excuse for us to forgive your shitty behavior. You cheated on Megan after being with her for two years, for Christ's sake, and you got Norma pregnant. I could go on, but I think my point is made—you've always been an asshole." My face heats as anger bubbles in my blood.

Did I seriously just say all that to him?

Cash stands back like I punched him, and even I'm

surprised by the things that just left my mouth, no matter how true and long overdue they are.

Damn, I've been on a roll since Annalisa stopped by here last week.

"You were always jealous of me," he spits.

I grind my teeth and build on the momentum coursing through me. "I was. Hell, I wanted to be you. I played the same sports you did, wore the same clothes as you, and planned to major in business administration like you. But I quickly realized how delusional I was." I down the rest of my drink and pour another.

He slides onto a barstool, his face falling.

"I know it's harsh, but Cash, you made everyone's life a living Hell for years. I'm not going to sugarcoat it." I lean my back against the opposite counter, my refilled glass clutched to my chest like it'll run away.

But I need it if I have any hopes of getting through this conversation.

"I'm sorry." He hangs his head, his own glass of amber liquid dangling in his hands. If he had a tail, it would be tucked between his legs right now.

"What?" I blink. Did I hear him correctly?

Did Cash Bowman actually apologize for his actions?

This has to be some kind of joke. It feels eerily similar to the time when we were kids and he told me our dog, Shadow, had rabies just so I'd be scared of him. And it worked. I was too terrified to even sleep, and Mom and Dad forced him to tell me the truth.

He's going to yell, "Gotcha," any minute now...

"I said I'm sorry, okay?" He lifts his gaze to meet mine. "And I fucking mean it."

I search his thinning face for any sign that he'll burst into laughter—or flames. Because that's what devils do, right?

His gaze doesn't waver, though. He doesn't even show a hint of a smile.

Fuck. I think I believe him.

"I know I'm an asshole, and that's part of the reason I'm here. I think…" He waves his hand in front of him like he's trying to stir up the right words.

"Yes?" I urge him.

"I think it started with you, so if I can just… fix this between us, maybe I can… I don't know. Maybe it would help." He shrugs, then tosses back his drink like a pro and stands for more.

"You're serious, aren't you?"

"I wouldn't have flown out here in the middle of the week, used up vacation days, and put up with a screaming toddler kicking my seat on the plane for three hours if I wasn't serious." He stares pointedly at me.

"Your visit and apology are huge steps of progress, but we still have a lot of work to do with that attitude stinking up the room," I fire back, adrenaline rushing through me and helping me keep my confidence to openly work through whatever this is with my brother.

Cash runs a large hand through his hair and squeezes his eyes closed.

"I don't even know where to begin." I shake my head.

He pauses to take a sip of his drink, then says, "You and I used to be close. We talked all the time. Hung out way past our bedtimes and laughed so hard, Dad used his Army voice on us."

I grin, thinking back to how twisted Dad's face would get

before his jaw would set and he'd unleash the stern tone he used while he was in the military.

"We were friends before you hated me."

"I don't hate you," I whisper. "I just don't respect you anymore."

"Same thing." He holds his drink up in salute and takes another sip.

It's not the same thing, but I can tell in his eyes, he believes it is.

"Fuck." I run a hand over my chin. "You're going to get me to forgive you, aren't you? Maybe even forget."

"That is the plan." He raises his eyebrows. "More importantly, you've already gotten me to apologize and spill my guts like a pussy. You've gotten me to forgive you too."

"Me? What the hell did I do to you?" I raise my voice.

But he doesn't flinch. He keeps his eyes on me as he says, "I thought this whole thing was your fault because you moved away. You couldn't get far enough away from me. I was like the piles of cattle shit on Uncle Gunther's ranch that we had to scoop up." He lifts, then drops his eyebrows. "Well, the piles *I* scooped up because you couldn't stop vomiting."

"I did clean the puke up every time, though," I point out with a laugh.

He quickly sobers, and it makes me wonder—does he ever laugh anymore? His smile stretches awkwardly across his face as if he's unfamiliar with the action.

And my chest sinks at the thought.

I may not have liked him before he walked through the door, but his visit—seeing him so vulnerable and apologetic— is giving me a new perspective.

Cash is a person. He's not the idol I used to see him as,

but a real person. One who makes mistakes and screws up. No matter what happens when he leaves here, he'll continue fucking up because he's still human.

I can relate.

I frown. "I'm sorry I jumped on the first chance to move away, especially without telling you until I'd signed my first lease."

But he shakes his head. "I wasn't available. According to the therapist, I'm not emotionally or physically available to the people who love me."

"At least you've learned something." I chuckle.

"Smartass," he mutters.

"What does Norma say?"

He takes a long sip, and I can tell where this is headed—not anywhere good. "That's part of the reason I'm here. I'm hoping you could help me with her because she agrees with the therapist."

"What makes you think I have any answers?"

"You and Madison. If you could get a girl to fall in love with you a second time, I figure you could help me do the same."

I blink at him. "I thought you didn't remember her."

"Of course I remember her. I just don't remember hitting on her, and I'm sorry I did." His gaze drops to his shoes as he rocks on his heels, the bottom of his pants bunching up at the ankles since his belt can barely do its job.

I nod, mulling over what Cash said about Madi falling in love with me a second time. She did, didn't she?

I've been asking myself a lot lately if she still loves me. If she thinks about me as often as I do her. If she wants me back, even though I can't promise we'll survive the distance.

But who am I kidding? A woman like her… she's bound to get snatched up by the likes of Chaz. If they have any sense, that is.

I stare at Cash, but I don't really see him as I tip my glass back, only to find it's empty. I set it to the side and cross my arms. "Well, we're not together anymore. I figured you would've seen it in the media. I assume that's how you knew about us in the first place, right?"

"Yes and no. Some of the girls at work are pretty obsessed with you and literally gush over every single fucking thing about you." He sticks his finger in his mouth and makes a gagging sound.

My jaw drops, but not because of what he said. It's still crazy to admit, but to be honest, that's nothing new.

What is new is that Cash actually sounded… jealous.

It can't be.

"Which reminds me," he continues. "I need you to sign a bunch of shit I can give them. Turns out, no one around me really enjoys my company, so I could use the brownie points. Especially since I took Janine's cake out of the fridge in the break room to make room for my lunch and forgot to put it back in, so it went bad."

"You sure know how to charm people," I say sarcastically.

"Shut up." He shakes his head, then levels me with his stare again. "I haven't heard them talking about your breakup, though."

I rub both hands down my face, squeezing my eyes closed. "It's a long story."

"I have plenty of time. Until Tuesday, in fact."

"We're going to need more whiskey."

"Amen to that."

Cash rides with me to the closest liquor store, fighting me over the radio station the entire way there. According to him, the only Texas thing about me is that I like country music, but that's the one quality he doesn't possess himself.

I'm not surprised we still bicker like that—after all, some things never change—but I do get confused when he doesn't fight me on the whiskey I buy. Instead, he just grabs the bottle from me and marches to the cashier, wallet in hand.

When we return to my house, he pours us both a glass and sits in my living room, as comfortable as ever.

And we talk.

My brother and I actually fucking talk. About Madison. Norma. Peter. We even reminisce about our old dog, Shadow. He only interrupts me three times all night to one-up me or because he doesn't like what I have to say, but I still call it progress.

By the time the sun sets, we're huddled around takeout boxes like they're a campfire and scraping the last of our dinner from the containers.

"I'm glad we did this." Cash points his plastic fork between the two of us.

I nod and swallow my last bite. "I'm glad you came out."

"It wasn't easy. I'm not good at the whole confrontation thing, but it's worth it."

I sink into my seat, my mind racing after hours of laughing and arguing. At one point, we were both on the verge of crying as if we were on *Oprah*.

But what he just said about confrontation makes my head spin in a whole different way.

"I'm not good at it, either," I whisper. "Never have been."

"It's easier to be a coward and run away." He tosses his

empty container onto the coffee table and sighs. "If I would've been honest with my ex about seeing Norma, no one would've gotten hurt, but it was easier to sneak behind her back, especially since she worked a lot. Instead, she followed me to Norma's one night, caught me kissing her, and bashed the headlights on Norma's car. Woke up the entire neighborhood. When I went home to get my stuff, she'd already tossed all my clothes into the firepit and lit it up." He hangs his head. "I deserved worse. Definitely don't deserve Norma."

"I'll drink to that." I hold my glass up, and we toast for the twentieth time.

"I just hope I can salvage our marriage."

"The first step is wanting to do so."

He lets out a huff. "You sound like my fucking therapist."

"That's what I was going for." I chuckle.

"I have to take a piss."

As he disappears down the hall, I close my eyes, and the same thought runs through my mind.

Not about the bathroom, but the other thing.

If Cash can swallow his fear and pride to confront me, I should be able to do the same, right? I could call Madi and apologize for being Ian, the cowardly dick, then tell her how I feel. I have her number, after all. All it would take are a few taps on my phone screen to dial her up and confess my love for her.

Maybe I could even video chat her, and she could flash me some skin. Perhaps even take off her top…

"Fuck," I mutter, jolting upright. I slap myself and barely feel the sting.

This is not good.

My eyelids suddenly grow heavy as I tilt the bottle back to find we've had plenty to drink tonight.

In fact, I'm drunk as hell right now.

It's the only reason I'm talking crazy about calling Madison. I can't just tell her I love her over the phone while she's so far away. Not after the way I left.

She was so damn pissed, and it's going to take a lot more than a few words to convince her to trust me again.

I shove the heels of my palms into my temples, groaning as Cash returns. I'm going to have a headache in the morning, but thankfully, I have nowhere to be anytime soon.

My phone buzzes, drawing my attention to where it sits on the coffee table. I grab it to find a message from Keith, explaining what the talk show is all about.

And it hits me.

The perfect idea.

"What're you staring at me like that for?" Cash lifts a brow. "Are you about to ask me to stay here? Because that would actually be a huge help since this trip was last minute, and I didn't book a hotel."

I roll my eyes. "Sure. Stay here as long as you'd like, but that's not what I'm thinking about."

"Care to explain, then? Don't leave me hanging on the edge of my seat."

"I'm drunk, but I can still smell your sarcasm." I glare at him, but he just shrugs, his own eyelids fluttering like he's trying to fucking wink at me.

Ignoring his slurred smartassery, I give Keith a call.

The moment he answers, I talk over any pleasantries he tries to offer. "I need a huge favor, and as my most favorite agent in the world, please say yes."

"Are you drunk?" he whispers, or at least I think he does. It could just be the booze muffling my hearing.

"A little, but I'm still serious." I blow out a breath in an attempt to clear my mind, not that it helps. "I need a huge favor."

TWENTY-FOUR

Madison

"You're up, chica." Sofia pops into my office, her thumb hooked over her shoulder.

I check the time on my laptop and jump up. "Shit. Is Mrs. Frita ready? Please tell me she's not pissed that it's five minutes past her appointment time. I was paying bills and totally lost track of time—why are you looking at me like that?" I skirt around the desk and grab my apron from its hook beside the door.

"I already did Mrs. Frita since her appointment was actually an hour ago." She leans on the doorframe. "I'm talking about you."

"You hate doing her hair," I whisper, just in case a customer is back here to use the restroom. I don't want them to overhear us gossiping. "And what about me?"

"Come." Sofia disappears, and I race after her, my fingers struggling to tie my apron as my mind sifts through every appointment we had scheduled for today. Mrs. Frita was my last one, so if Sofia already took care of her, I'm done for the day.

Not that I had much to do.

Personally, I've been surprisingly slow the last couple of weeks, although our schedule has been booked up as usual.

Tonight, we've had a bunch of girls come in to get their hair done for their high school graduation, but Sofia and the new guy took care of them while I supervised. They didn't even need me to do that, though.

Which has been a relief for me, I must say.

It's given me the opportunity to do things like stay on top of our bills, change the lightbulbs in the salon, and go to yoga class with Erin. On top of that, my own fridge has been stocked with more than just beer since I've had plenty of time to grocery shop.

Bree and Tessa gasped when I told them, and I couldn't blame them. My fridge is never stocked.

Things in my life are going rather—dare I say it—well. Better than well. Fantastic, even.

On the outside, anyway.

Each time I check my phone, I keep expecting there to be a text or missed call from Ian, but there's nothing. Only silence.

And it stings every time.

I don't know why I keep doing that, but apparently, I just *love* to torture myself.

I like to be pissed at Ian too, which is what ends up happening. It's easier that way, although it doesn't fix anything. Instead, I just keep driving myself crazy with questions like, why the hell hasn't he called? Does he seriously not care about me?

He hasn't even drunk called or texted, and the more silence he gives me, the madder I get at him.

The media doesn't help. Every time I find an online picture of him outside a café in LA, I waste precious time trying to find out who he's with—if anyone.

It's an unhealthy cycle I've developed.

"Sit." Sofia stops at a swiveling chair and points.

Understanding finally dawns—it's me. I'm the one who needs my hair done. The last trim I had was several months ago, and I won't even get started on the color.

"Are all of your appointments finished?" I glance around as Yuri, the new hire, curls the front of a young girl's hair, laying each tuft with care.

"Of course, boss lady. What do you think? That I'm a slacker?" She tsks, and there's a twinkle in her eye as she pats the back of the chair again for me to sit.

"Fine. A touch-up wouldn't hurt."

"Are you kidding? We need a whole facelift over here." Sofia holds the end of my hair up for me to see. "Why do you hate your hair and want to see it die?"

I note the split ends, and immediately, my cheeks flame. "Oh my God. Have I seriously been walking around like this in public?" I cringe, snatching my hair from her to inspect it more closely.

And I wish I hadn't, because when I see the damage up close, I am officially horrified.

The ends of my hair are more jagged than the edge of a chainsaw.

"I tried to tell you weeks ago." Sofia unfolds a cape and throws it over me. "But you've been too lovesick over a certain movie star to notice anything other than your phone."

I narrow my eyes at her in the mirror.

But she carries on like I didn't just try to warn her—I'm losing my touch. "He hasn't called, huh?"

"No," I mumble. "But thanks for bringing it up during my pampering session."

"Oh, this is not pampering. This is hardcore damage control." She grabs the scissors from in front of me, then shuffles back to her position. "You were on the internet in front of millions with this hair. I'm embarrassed for you."

"Maybe this should be a silent session," I suggest.

She continues without another word.

Once I'm two inches of hair lighter, I break the silence myself. I'm too curious. "So, you did Mrs. Frita's hair earlier?"

"Uh-huh."

"And she didn't complain?"

"Of course she complained. She always does. Today, the problem was that the AC was too high."

"At least it didn't have anything to do with her hair for once."

She smiles and checks her work in the mirror, fluffing both sides of my hair over my shoulders.

I study her expression. What am I missing?

"And you didn't complain, either?" I ask.

"Of course I complained. Silently." She shrugs, then proceeds to stand in front of me to trim a few strands to even them. "But as it turns out, she has a lot in common with my abuela. They're both cranky old women who love the same soap opera. They just want to get out every now and then. They like when someone listens to them too."

I stare at her like I'm seeing her for the first time.

"Now"—she slides the scissors back into their place by the mirror and gives me jazz hands—"your roots."

I nod as she gets to work, still considering what she said. This is the girl who's called Mrs. Frita names I can't repeat to my mother, and what? They're best friends now?

"I love it," the girl behind us squeals and hugs Yuri. "Thank you so much."

"You're going to be the cutest one walking across that stage tonight," he gushes.

When they walk arm in arm to the counter to check out like they're the best of friends, Sofia mutters to me, "Can you guess how many girls he's said that to this afternoon?"

I giggle into my hand, then straighten up. "Well, it's working, because everyone loves him."

"Meh."

I shake my head, and as I do, I catch a glimpse of the smiling girl at the front. She's graduating tonight, and I can't help but think of my own high school graduation.

It was the last time I saw Ian before he popped back up as my fake boyfriend.

We had our whole lives in front of us back then. We could've gone anywhere and become anything, but we chose our paths.

And they didn't involve each other.

"You should call him," Sofia says as Yuri grabs a bottle of Windex and cleans the mirror behind us.

"You definitely should," he says over his shoulder.

I smile. "Not you too."

"Even Mrs. Frita thinks so," Sofia casually says, using a brush to color my roots. "She said so earlier, and I didn't even bring it up myself."

I groan, and if she wasn't putting chemicals in my hair, I'd bury my face underneath this cape too.

"Why haven't you called him?" Yuri asks, leaning his hip against the mirror.

"He's the one who left. He's the one who should call," I state.

The truth is, I was so angry with him for disappearing when we were teenagers. For ignoring my calls and texts until I was too furious to keep trying.

Which didn't take long.

I'm not the most patient person as it is, but when he wrote me off like that, I was so hurt.

I'm starting to think that's why I haven't reached out to him now because… what if he ignores me again?

After the time we spent together, I couldn't take it if he did.

My heart would break even worse.

That, or I might fly out there just to trash his place, then strangle him like I originally wanted to when I saw him again.

Either way, I'd be screwed.

"You shouldn't have let him leave in the first place," Sofia says.

"He was in the middle of filming a movie. What was I supposed to do? Tie him to a chair in my apartment?"

"That's what I would've done," she jokes as she sets the color down.

The pair work together to put foil in my hair, and we move on to talking about how hot Ian is.

They don't have to remind me.

I've sunk so low as to repeatedly watch Ian's shirtless scene in that romantic comedy on Netflix. I've even debated on putting the screenshot of that scene as the background on my phone. But then I decided against it since it's humiliating enough that I took the screenshot to begin with.

Sofia is almost done styling my hair when the front door opens. Over her shoulder, she calls out, "We'll be right with you."

From this angle, I can't see who it is, but I get a whiff of perfume that smells heavenly—and expensive.

"All set." Sofia smiles and undoes the clasp of the cape at the back of my neck.

I tilt my head from side to side. "Much better. Thank you," I say to both her and Yuri. I'm about to offer my help to clean up, but I catch sight of the woman at the front counter and freeze.

Sofia gasps next to me, and I follow the direction of her gaze—she's seeing the same person I am.

Annalisa Hughes.

The actress slides her hair over one shoulder and lifts her large sunglasses onto her head as I approach, holding my chin up. "What can I help you with?"

"I'm actually here to help *you*." She intertwines her fingers on top of my counter, her pink nails long and shimmering.

I cross my arms over my chest. "What're you even doing in New York? Aren't you supposed to be filming or doing whatever actresses do in Hollywood?"

"Yes, but my beauty line is having a big anniversary party. I'm only here for the night and had to stop by." She glances over my shoulder, and I turn back too, where I find Sofia staring at us, her left eye twitching. "Can we go upstairs to talk in private?"

"Upstairs?"

"Yes. Isn't that where you live?"

"No," I answer, furrowing my brows.

"Oh, thank God. I saw a window busted right above us,

but I didn't want to judge. I hear I do that a lot, but I also was wondering if maybe this salon is two floors. This space is kind of small, otherwise." She waves her hand around, and her head moves from side to side as she checks out my business. "But we all start somewhere. That's not even why I'm here, though. What was I saying?"

"You were not judging," I deadpan.

"Right," she continues, her tone still high pitched and unaware. "I'm here to get you and Ian back together." She puts both index fingers together in front of her. "He's miserable without you, so much so that we needed fourteen takes for a scene the other day that should've taken about fourteen seconds total. He totally botched his lines. And I'm pretty sure Richard would've fired him were we not so close to the end of filming, but you didn't hear that from me."

"Of course, but—"

"So, anyway, I spoke with Ian last week. Well, I hit on Ian, but he rejected me. Which is fine—"

"No, actually, none of that is *fine*." I grind my molars, tensing all over.

"Did I hear correctly?" Sofia appears next to me, her voice low and threatening. "Do I need to get the tire iron?" she mutters to me while keeping a narrow gaze on Annalisa. "I don't care if her hair is perfect or that her skin is sparkling. No one messes with you, boss lady."

Annalisa laughs. "Oh, you're adorable, but I'm with Patrick now. Ian made me realize we're perfect together, so I owe him. Which is why I'm in this part of New York today." She does a little shake like she's slinging off water and exhales.

I grimace.

"I want you to come back to LA on my jet with me in the

morning." Annalisa flashes us a wide grin more fit for the red carpet than in my world and "this part of New York."

Sofia's jaw drops, as does my own.

"We'll leave at seven a.m. sharp, and the jet is fully stocked for breakfast. We have mimosas too, obviously, and there's plenty of space for all your things. I only brought four suitcases with me this time," she says more proudly than if she would've fed a whole third world country.

But I'm still stunned in silence.

Does she really think I'm going to up and leave to fly on a fancy jet out to LA? Then what? I find Ian, finally confess my love for him, and live happily ever after?

She can't be serious.

Annalisa snaps her fingers. "I'll send a car to pick you up as well. What's your address? And I'll say it again, I'm glad it's not upstairs."

"The apartments upstairs were renovated last year," Sofia cuts in. "The window was just busted yesterday when some stupid kids were playing baseball on the basketball courts across the street, so calm down, lady."

"That's, um, a relief, then," Annalisa says, but it sounds more like a question, as if she's unsure if it's actually a good enough explanation. "Oh!" She holds her finger up, then digs into the tote bag hanging on her shoulder to retrieve clear pink products that match the color of her nails. As she sets them on the counter in a row, she points to the shelves against the wall and says, "Here are some samples from my line. When you see how much you love them, feel free to talk to my people to stock the salon. They'll give you a great deal. Friends and family and all that." She exaggerates a wink. "So, what do you say?"

I purse my lips, still at a loss for words, and not just because Annalisa threw so much at me. "Did Ian put you up to this?"

"No." Her eyes widen. "This is totally a surprise. How fun and awesome would it be if you just showed up and get back together with him, and he would have me to thank? Because I do feel really shitty about coming onto him like I did."

I scowl.

She holds her hands up. "And I owe you an apology too, even though you two aren't technically together. But I am sorry."

I roll my eyes. "Look, it's... sweet that you came down here to try and help, but Ian obviously doesn't want me to surprise him. We haven't spoken since he left, so it's clear to me that it's over." I pick up a lipstick that she set on the counter, secretly excited to try it.

I do love her products...

"But thank you for stopping by." I hold up the lipstick. "And thanks for these."

She frowns, making no indication that she'll leave now.

Sofia has grown quiet next to me too, and I know she's dying to get her hands on the hairspray Annalisa placed next to the lipstick. If there's one thing Sofia loves more than her heels and tire irons—she's a complicated woman—it's hairspray.

"Now's the time for backup." I blink at Sofia, but she only shrugs. "What're you waiting for?"

"I think she's right," Sofia says, and Yuri appears on the other side of her, nodding in agreement.

"You will get a free flight out to LA, more than enough mimosas, and a chance to hang out with me. What do you have to lose?" Annalisa flashes another giant smile. Doesn't that hurt her face?

"I'll think about it. How's that?" I offer, and it's the best I've got.

I need her out of my damn salon immediately before I do something I regret and actually accept her invitation.

Annalisa claps. "I'll take that as a win!"

She grabs a business card from its holder, and as she scribbles across the back of it and two other cards, there's a sting in my chest from the thought of having a chance to see Ian and not taking it.

Should I?

"Here you go." Annalisa whips her hair up like she's at the beach and hands out a card to each of us. To me, she says, "That's my number for you to text to let me know you'll come." When Sofia and Yuri accept theirs, she tilts her head. "And these are just my autographs for a couple of fans."

As she turns on her heel, we all stare at her retreating back, dumbfounded.

"I didn't say I was a fan," Sofia says when the door is closed and snatches the hairspray. "But I do love her line. I smelled this at the mall last month, and it's better than flowers or any perfume. We need to stock it."

"I'll add that to the list of things to think about." I give them both a tight-lipped smile and move toward my office.

Hurried footsteps sound behind me. "You don't seriously have to think about it, do you?" Sofia asks. "*Annalisa Hughes* is offering you a once-in-a-lifetime chance. It's like a Cinderella story."

"If I was Cinderella in this scenario, Ian would be the one coming after me. Not his ex-girlfriend doing his bidding behind his back," I throw over my shoulder as I reach my office.

"What if he really did send her? I got the impression

she was lying about that part, and I know how to tell when people are lying. My mother grew up in Puerto Rico, and it was an important skill she passed on to my brother and me." Sofia hooks her thumb toward the door that Annalisa just disappeared through. "That girl was lying. Ian totally sent her."

"I don't—" I'm cut off by my ringing phone, and when I see the area code on my screen, my back stiffens.

"Is it him?" Yuri tilts his head over Sofia's shoulder.

"No, but it's an LA number."

"Answer it," Sofia hisses.

I bite my lip as I use my thumb to swipe across the screen.

"Madison?" A deep voice sounds, but it's not Ian's. "Is that you? You there?"

Sofia and Yuri stare at me expectantly, so I shake my head to clarify it's not Ian and answer the guy on the other end of my phone. "Yes, it's Madison. Who is this?"

"It's Keith, Ian's agent."

And my back stiffens further.

"I'm so glad I caught you. I have a huge proposition for you, if you have a minute." His tone is light but still businesslike, which is how I remember him from the times Ian had him on speakerphone.

But I don't think I like where this is going. First Annalisa, and now Keith? Is Ian seriously having everyone speak on his behalf instead of just having the balls to call me himself?

"I'm not sure I can help you, Keith."

"Hear me out." There's a pause before he says, "Please."

I sigh and tell him to go for it.

As I listen, I'm starting to think Sofia was right. That Ian has orchestrated this whole thing, including Annalisa's request. It's too much of a coincidence.

Keith settles into more of a rigid tone, and I imagine it's the one he uses when negotiating contracts with and for his clients.

It feels like he's doing the same for Ian now, but even so, by the end of his intriguing spiel, I'm almost compelled to accept.

"What do you say? Will you come?" Keith asks.

"Listen, I appreciate the offer, but I have a business to run. I can't just lock the door and fly out there on a whim. Even if I wanted to, it's not feasible." I blow out a frustrated breath.

"Hey, I totally get it, but I would not be asking if I didn't feel that you were the best person for the job."

"Now you're just laying it on thick," I tease, but in reality, I am flattered.

"Put it on speaker." Sofia and Yuri appear at my doorway again, gesturing toward the phone.

"What?"

She points to my phone, stepping inside and urging me to do as she says.

"Hang on, Keith." I pull the phone from my ear, turn the speaker on, and set it down on the desk.

"Whoever this is, she'll do it," Sofia calls out, resting her elbows next to my laptop.

"No!" I counter. "I can't leave the salon."

"You did it before, and we were fine," Sofia whispers, and even though her voice is softer, it doesn't lose any of its stern edge. "And that was before Yuri got here, which was a miracle in itself that we survived. With him here, we'll be more than fine."

"Keith, I'll have to call you back," I say into the speaker, glaring at my employees.

"I'll be waiting," he says, but ironically, he doesn't wait for me to click off. He does it himself before I can even blink.

I rub both hands down my face, and my rigid eyelashes coated with mascara scrape against my palms. I need to wash my face. Freshen up. Get a full night's rest.

It sounds much better than the pressure of this decision.

"You have to go," Yuri urges.

"You two don't even know what he asked." I drop my hands on the desk and laugh.

"Okay, what did he ask?" Sofia crosses her arms, and the office is suddenly tense.

They're ganging up on me—*great*.

"That was Ian's agent, and he wants me to come out to LA to work for one of his VIP clients. He wouldn't say who it was exactly, only that he's a big deal. Said that I did such good work on the set of *Ghost Predators* that this guy wants me to be his personal makeup artist. Pfft, can you believe that?" I roll my eyes and sway in my office chair.

"Holy shit. Are you blushing?" Sofia asks, and Yuri snickers.

"Is it flattering? Of course, but it has Ian written all over it. For all I know, he put Keith up to this just to get me to come out there. I mean, it's too ridiculous to be legitimate." I shake my head, still in disbelief that I'm actually wanted in LA for something like this. "It can't be real," I insist, although my heart keeps fluttering.

Sofia and Yuri exchange a look I can't decipher, but before I have the chance to say something, Sofia speaks first. "You want to go, whether it's for this new gig or for Ian or for both. And you have a private fancy flight leaving first thing in the morning to take you. What's really holding you back, Mads?"

I avert my gaze away from them, glancing instead to the doorway that leads to the rest of the salon. The longer I stare, the stronger I feel the sting of tears in the backs of my eyes.

"If this is a real opportunity to do makeup out there, what will happen to this place? I've put so much into this salon. It feels like I'd be giving it up if I get on that plane tomorrow, and not just for a few weeks, but for good." I gulp, and the lump in my throat hurts. "What if I'm not ready for that?"

Sofia comes around to rub my shoulder, and Yuri halfway sits on the edge of my desk, one foot planted on the floor.

The air in the room shifts as this decision brings me to a fork in the road, but this isn't like the time I decided to dye my hair blonde one summer to try it out.

This is the rest of my life.

It's hard not to think that Ian might've had something to do with this, even though I specifically told him I didn't want to move out to LA just to be with him.

But I can't deny how good it felt to get a call from someone like Keith, who represents clients ranging from child stars on Disney to superheroes and FBI agents on the big screen.

And if I'm being honest, I miss working on the set. The makeup trailer had become part of my life. Searcy and I had a good routine going, and each time I entered, it felt like the sun rising to a new day. When the actors would arrive and we'd chitchat about the night before or what new restaurants they tried in the city, it felt like our own little community, and I loved it.

Keith's call lit that same fire in me that Carter's did over three months ago.

But what do I do with that flame—throw some lighter fluid or a bucket of water on it?

"You don't have to make a solid decision right this minute about the future," Yuri says, cutting into my thoughts. "You can go tomorrow, see what happens in LA, and come back with a decision. Maybe even a permanent boyfriend."

"And Yuri and I will run the salon. We'll keep the other two in check too," Sofia adds.

"I can't ask you to do that."

"You're not. We're offering, and if you're smart—which you are—you'll accept our help and go be happy." Sofia gives me a nudge and tilts my chin toward her. "It's time, chica. You've been moping around here ever since the movie star left, and I just can't take it anymore."

Wincing, I squeeze her hand in mine.

"Besides," she draws out and glances back at Yuri. "We've been handling most of the appointments lately, anyway. I even did Mrs. Frita today, so you know I can deal with anything that comes our way."

"It's true," Yuri cuts in. "I witnessed a rare event today when this one was actually laughing with Mrs. Frita."

I smile as my gaze bounces between them. "Are you two serious? Because Keith said it would be a month. I might be able to fly back for a weekend, but in the chance I can't..."

"Then the salon will still be here when you get back." Sofia shrugs. "We've got your back, always."

"I don't deserve you two." I pull them in for a group hug as something blooms in my chest.

Hope.

I'm optimistic, and it's not because I've been hanging around Erin too much these days.

With this newfound energy, I call Keith back to tell him the news, and he answers on the first ring like the phone is glued to his hand.

Which it probably is.

"Is that a yes?" Keith asks.

"Yes," I confirm, and across from me, Sofia and Yuri silently celebrate, giving me a thumbs-up and quietly clapping.

"Fantastic. We'll see you tomorrow, then."

"Wait." I bite my lip. "You're positive Ian has nothing to do with this, right? I'm not going to fly across the country just to find out this was all a big prank, am I?"

He chuckles. "You don't know me very well, but there is one thing I can tell you—I don't fuck around when it comes to my job or clients. I might be an asshole on occasion, and my wife might often get upset because I constantly leave empty glasses lying around the house, but I don't mess with people's personal or professional lives."

I let go of the breath I've been holding since I dialed his number. "That's a relief."

"Do you need travel arrangements to be made? I can transfer you to my receptionist," he offers.

"Oh, umm…" As if I needed more proof that this group of Californians isn't all working together, Keith knocks the doubt right out of me. "I have a flight, actually."

"See you in LA. Oh, and don't forget your sunscreen."

Just like before, he abruptly clicks off, and I type out a text to Annalisa to save me a spot on the plane tomorrow.

Looking up at my two friends, I squeal, "We're doing this!"

Sofia and Yuri both high-five me, jumping up and down, but it's short-lived.

Sofia holds her hands out. "Is this a good time to ask for a raise since I'm covering the salon for the foreseeable future? Because mama has her eye on a new purse."

I let out a laugh. "Okay, let's talk logistics."

She claps again and settles into the seat on the other side of the desk.

And the more details we finalize, the more excited and confident I am about this decision.

TWENTY-FIVE

Madison

"*H*ow big was the jet? And how many mimosas did you have? If you tell me you only had two, we're going to have to reconsider our friendship," Bree rants as I unlock the door to my hotel room.

"I only had one, actually," I confess as the door clicks shut behind me.

She gasps. "That's even worse."

"Calm down. It was only seven in the morning when we left, and I didn't get any sleep last night. More than one mimosa would've put me in a coma, and you know it. Although, a coma would've been better than listening to Annalisa list the sex positions she and Patrick haven't tried yet." I sling my tote onto the white bedspread and sit on the edge, my feet planted on the floor. "There were very few, by the way."

"I'll give you that, but it's the only pass you're allowed this month."

"How very generous of you," I deadpan.

"I still can't freaking believe you're talking about these people like it's no big deal. You're living my dream life, and I hate you."

"You love me," I tease.

"I do, but I'm still mad as hell that my first boyfriend sells T-shirts out of his van, while yours went off to own Hollywood." She huffs. "Shit, I have to go here in a minute. I'm getting stuff ready for the auction tonight."

"You're going to bid on every bachelor, aren't you?"

"That was the original plan—I mean, what else have I been saving up for?" she asks sarcastically. "But Tessa called this morning and asked me to fill in for her behind the scenes since she's not feeling well. And Ava just texted me to come to the venue early to help her with setup since her assistant is running behind. I swear, event planning is so stressful. I'm glad I'm just a volunteer. Otherwise, I'd be screaming at everyone within a one-mile radius."

I giggle.

"I'm serious."

"And that's why it was a nervous giggle." I pick some lint off my leggings. "Speaking of event planning, though, we need to discuss Tessa's bachelorette party soon. September will be here before we know it, and we have to throw our girl a kickass farewell to the single life."

"Yes!" she draws out. "I have so many inappropriate ideas. I can't wait."

"I'm not surprised," I chirp.

"And just think, whatever we don't use or do for Tessa's, I'll save for yours."

My laugh gets caught in my throat. "That's not... There's no need for..."

GEORGIA COFFMAN

"*Please*. You're in LA. You might not be there to work with Ian, but you'll surely see him. He'll realize how much he misses you, fall head over heels for a *third* time, and beg you to stay with him, which you will because you love him too. It's a fucking fairy tale, Mads."

"Then why do you sound so angry about it?" I ask.

"Because I will be the only person in our group who will die alone while you're all with rich and famous people. Do me a favor, will you? Will you at least DoorDash me food every once in a while, please?"

"You'll find someone. We all will. Tessa has paved the way," I reassure her as I suppress the fluttering in my stomach from the thought of seeing Ian again.

Even though I'm mad at him for leaving.

For not calling.

No texts or any indication that he still knows I exist.

But when I got off the plane earlier and breathed in the California heat, I felt close to him. This is his home.

To be honest, I half-expected him to be waiting for me on the runway. I was disappointed to only find Patrick and an unfamiliar guy, who drove me to my hotel. But I still have this inkling that I'm here for him.

Somehow.

"Mads? Are you there?" Bree interrupts my thoughts. "Did you hear me?"

I clear my throat. "Yes. Totally. The one is out there."

"Um. Sure. But I said I need to go."

"Oh. Okay." I nod at myself in the mirror. "Bye!"

"Let me know every single detail of your trip, okay? Don't forget about me!"

With that, she ends the call, and I'm left smiling like a

moron. Is there something in the air out here?

I tug at my hair to work out the tangled mess, then rub under my eyes. I look high, and I haven't even gotten to sightsee yet. I just got more sun this morning than I have all year.

When I stand, I shake my hips to loosen up after a long morning of traveling and retrieve my suitcase, which Annalisa thought was a joke. Evidently, she's seen light packers on TV but didn't think they existed in real life.

Here I was concerned I overpacked, but she wasn't kidding about bringing four suitcases, a carry-on, and a small leather backpack that seemed to be more for aesthetic purposes than function. She even arrived thirty minutes early to take pictures for her Instagram, in which she's angled just enough to feature the backpack like it was an ad.

Come to think of it, it might've been.

Once we were on board, she spent an hour showing me each photo and explaining why every single one was her favorite.

I snort as I fish out my shampoo, ready for a shower. No matter how fancy the jet was, it was still a plane, and traveling makes me feel like I have a layer of grime over me.

Annalisa, on the other hand, somehow stepped off looking better than when she got on.

It's weird to admit, but the woman is actually growing on me. It's surreal enough to have spent the morning with Annalisa Hughes and her people, but to say we might even be friends?

Now that's just crazy.

Before I hop in the shower, I send a quick text to Tessa to check in since Bree mentioned she's not feeling well. She responds immediately, wishing me luck on my new adventure, then sends another to demand I let her know every detail any chance I get, just like Bree.

Smiling, I duck under the hot water in the stand-up shower, letting the steam soothe my skin and clear my mind.

I need to get my head out of the clouds and into Hollywood.

Sofia and Yuri stayed late with me last night to draw up plans for my absence. Before I left, I connected the salon phone to an app on my cell just in case they need help answering calls, which I can do in my spare time. It's a small gesture, but I want to do anything I can to make the transition easier.

Although I still have my doubts and concerns about leaving, my team eased them, and by the time we parted ways, we were laughing.

It could've been because of the late hour and we were delirious, but in any case, I felt light and happy.

I have everyone's blessing. The people I love support me no matter what happens, and it gives me so much peace.

As I finish scrubbing my body clean, I can't help but imagine Ian's hands on me, his fingers gliding over my slippery skin as he hums in appreciation like he often did.

"Stop," I mutter and remind myself that I'm livid with him.

He doesn't get to keep taking up precious space in my mind and heart anymore. Even if we are on the same turf.

Nothing's changed between us.

My phone rings on the bathroom counter, and I curse under my breath, quickly rinsing the rest of the way off. I don't get to it in time, though, so I carry on, taking my time to dry myself.

But it rings again.

I lunge for the phone, water dripping from my hair and down my back. "Hello?"

"I hope I didn't catch you at a bad time, but I'm in a bind and hoping you can help."

I pull the phone back to read the name across my screen since I was in too much of a rush to do it before I answered.

It's Keith.

"What's going on?" I ask, hurrying into the next room for my clothes. I guess I won't be turning on Lady Gaga and getting ready in peace.

"The makeup artist for my client had an emergency with her dog and is spending the afternoon at the vet's office, so she won't be able to come into the studio today. Can you fill in?"

"Um…" I scan the bed and locate my tote, which holds my own makeup. "Sure."

"We'll need you there by one."

I check my watch. "Plenty of time. Just text me the address."

"Will do."

Given our past interactions, I know he's already ended the call even before I check, so I toss my phone onto the bed, grab my outfit and makeup, and skip into the bathroom to get ready, heart racing.

Does this industry always move so quickly?

One minute I'm in New York, and the next, I'm jet-setting off to LA with an A-list actress and getting called to fill in on another set before I've even unpacked.

There's definitely an appealing thrill about it.

I just hope I can stop thinking about Ian long enough to keep up.

Istudy my phone to ensure I'm at the right lot and studio, but this all looks much different than the base in New York.

Searching left to right gives me whiplash, and when someone taps me on the shoulder from behind, I jump.

"Madison?" A tall man in a suit, the top two buttons of his shirt open, sticks his hand out for me to shake.

I hoist my tote bag up higher onto my shoulder and grip his hand. "Yes. Hi."

"I'm Keith." He smiles.

"Oh, thank God. What a relief." I let a soft laugh loose. "Can you point me in the right direction? Because I'm pretty sure I'm lost."

"You aren't, though." He points to an unmarked door next to us and nudges me toward it. "You just need to go through there, and a production assistant will show you to your dressing room."

"To your client's dressing room, you mean," I correct him.

"No, I mean *yours*." He raises his eyebrows, and his smile turns mischievous.

"What?" I furrow my brows, more confused than I was to find out Annalisa had already made my hotel arrangements before I even had the mental capacity to remember to do it myself.

"Your dressing room," he says matter-of-factly. "You're going to be on the show tonight."

I glance around for someone to pop out with confetti and a sign that says, *Kidding!*

LA moves quickly, indeed, but what Keith is saying is on a whole other level.

He sidesteps me, rubbing his chin. "I know I told you I needed you to fill in for a makeup artist, but I don't. I actually need you to be *on* the show."

"But wait… I don't do that sort of thing." My mouth falls open. "I barely have enough experience to be part of the behind-the-scenes team. You can't put me on camera," I say, my words rushing out in a panic. "Besides, you told me you wouldn't lie to me. You said that. You said you wouldn't joke around about needing me out here. I had to leave my salon to—"

"Whoa, whoa." He grips both of my shoulders. "I did not lie to you about that part. My client, Rhett Stevens, really does need a makeup artist for his new movie, but the favor I asked you for today was for a different client. You just didn't ask me which one."

It's obvious that he's talking about Ian.

I fold my arms over my chest, the strap of my bag squeezing my shoulder. "Was this *his* idea?"

Keith steps back, and it gives me more room to breathe, although I'm going to need more than that if I'm supposed to get on a freaking show in front of the world with my ex.

"He did ask me to put this together," Keith confesses, his words slow like he's choosing them wisely.

"*This* being what exactly?"

He shifts on his feet. "Just today."

"So he had nothing to do with Rhett?" I ask as I try to think back over my research into the child star, who's evidently transitioning into young adult films.

I'd heard of the name when Keith mentioned it this morning. I didn't have a ton of time to look into Rhett, but I never did find a connection between him and Ian other than having the same agent.

But I have to hear it from the agent himself.

Keith sighs as he spreads his jacket and places both hands on his hips. "Ian mentioned you to Rhett at a party, but you came up in conversation. Ian did not know that Rhett needed a makeup artist."

"That motherfucker," I mutter.

"I'm telling you the truth—Ian didn't know," Keith reassures me, but I still have a knot in my stomach, especially since my life has been turned upside down and sideways in the last twelve hours.

This conversation isn't helping.

If he didn't look so apologetic and sincere, I would be stomping out of here in a rage so fierce, LA itself would ask me to leave.

But Keith is just the messenger. And lackey, apparently, as he's doing Ian's dirty work.

"Okay," I mutter slowly. "Say I believe you. What's Ian's angle with today? Why am I getting ambushed?"

The door flings open, and a young woman bursts through it, her eyes wide and frantic. "You're Madison Taylor, right?" she asks.

"I am."

"Oh, good." She taps her earpiece and says, "I found her."

I open my mouth to try and ask for a minute to think, but she grabs my arm and pulls me inside so quickly, my hair is almost caught in the door as it shuts.

"We're on our way to hair and makeup," she says into her earpiece, then gives me a once-over. "She has a cute outfit on, but you may want to see for yourself."

"Thanks," I mumble as the doors along the hallway blur.

I'm thrust into a chair, and the bright lights around the mirror in front of me are blinding.

A man pulls and tugs on my hair until it's freed of its holder. I went for a Serena van der Woodsen low but textured ponytail, which I was proud of, but the man obviously does not appreciate it, given his grimace.

I'm quickly distracted by a woman matching my skin tone to a foundation before smearing the right one across my cheeks.

For one, it's an odd feeling being on this side of the chair.

And two, while they get to work on me and make me look better than I ever have in my life, I quietly devise a plan.

I don't know what awaits me out there, but Ian Brock is going to pay for all the shit he's put me through, once and for all.

TWENTY-SIX

Ian

"Lights, camera… exes?" Lynn, the host of *The Lynn Anderson Show*, practices what I assume is her opening line for our segment as she paces, her heels softly clicking to their own beat in front of the couch. It's perched on a stage facing an ungodly amount of filming equipment.

When I arrived for my first taste of this industry, I thought each set was just a storage space for equipment.

I had no idea they actually used most of it each time they recorded.

It's still daunting. I feel like all the lights and cameras are staring at me while I wait for my ex to either think this is super romantic, or strangle me once and for all.

I wipe my sweaty palms down my jeans and adjust my sports coat. My team and I went for a casual but trendy look, but I barely comprehended anything they said or asked.

All I could think about was the fact that Madi was going to be here soon.

Keith talked to her and confirmed she's here, and I've been a giant ball of nerves ever since I heard. She's in the same building, and I'm on stage, watching the regular host of the show rehearse and call out for a new bottle of water.

Her team and network were thrilled I'd not only accepted their invitation to be on the show tonight, but also that I had a proposition of my own. It's crazy how much these people care about my love life, but it works out in my favor this time.

"You're nervous." Lynn lays her pieces of paper on the couch and uncaps her water for a sip, her attention on me. Unlike me, she's as chill as an ice cube, and I'm suddenly jealous of her.

I've been on TV and the big screen before, but this is so much different.

This is my life... and Madi's.

I let out what sounds to be a mix between a laugh and exhale. "How could you tell?"

"You're sweating more than I do during spin, and it's making me anxious. Need a Xanax, perhaps?" she offers, her tone serious. Is that how she's always so relaxed? And is that how she went from being a briefcase showgirl on *Deal or No Deal* to the host of her own show?

"No, no. I just need this not to backfire." I take a seat across from the couch in a chair that looks more comfortable than it really is, which doesn't help my nerves or my posture.

"Terribly hard on the ass, isn't it?" Lynn asks, pointing to the chair.

"You read my mind yet again." I put both hands on my knees, and my foot bounces as Lynn gets back to muttering her opening lines, waving her hand around like she's conducting an orchestra.

This all seemed like a solid plan a few days ago. Even Cash was impressed and is sticking around to see how it plays out. It's also part of his new goal to be more supportive.

And honestly—I never thought I'd say this—it's nice knowing he'll be here soon, right after he's back from getting coffee. Said he was up early today for a run along the beach, which is a new habit he's formed since his arrival.

I declined his offer to bring me a cup since I'm bouncing off the walls as it is.

"We're all set, man." Keith claps me on the back, and Cash comes down the steps between the rows of seats that will soon be occupied by the live audience. "You ready?"

"This is a good idea, right?" I ask for the hundredth time. "I was drunk when I first came to you, but when I sobered up, it still seemed like a good idea. Am I insane?"

"Dear God, don't fucking ask me that again." He grips the back of his neck. "Even if I'd changed my mind since you asked me this morning, it would be too late to stop it now. You're literally on the show, and she's here to join you. So, good idea or not, this shitshow is happening."

"You do think it's a bad idea, then," I whisper.

"Is he asking again if he should be doing this?" Cash interrupts, chuckling.

"Yes. Please deal with him. I can't take it anymore." Keith curses under his breath as his phone in his hand lights up. "Oh, shit. Actually, I'd rather stay here with him than answer this."

"Aw," I coo sarcastically. "I knew I was your favorite."

"Fuck off." He puts the phone to his ear. "Hey there.

How's my favorite client?" he says loudly enough for me to hear as he disappears behind the collection of cameras.

Cash steps in front of me in the same spot Keith was just standing and sips from his coffee cup. The gulp that follows is louder than if he were in my shoes, nervous as shit. "It's going to work out, little brother."

"You sound awfully confident. A lot more so for a guy going through his own relationship trouble." I stare pointedly at him. "Have you even spoken to your wife since you left?"

"No one likes a smartass." He lifts the cup to his mouth for another sip, but I have an inkling that he's hiding behind it. "I'm giving her the space she asked for." He lowers the cup and sighs. "And I'm a chickenshit, okay? But I will call her today."

I remain quiet, but smile.

Baby steps.

We've gotten updates on Peter from Mom, who's been babysitting him more in Cash's absence. All the pictures she's sent has made me realize the kid is going to be a teenager before we know it, and I need to visit him more often before he completely grows up and forgets me.

More people appear, crowding the studio with their presence and buzzing chatter.

Ah, the sound of televised magic on the horizon.

Before the stage is cleared, I grab my brother's arm. "Thank you for everything. I won't go as far as to say I couldn't do this without you, but I am glad you're here."

"I'm never going to live down my asshole days, am I?"

"Not as long as you keep using the word *amongst* in every sentence."

"What's wrong with that?"

"It's a pretentious and douchey word." I laugh, and he waves me off, then follows instructions to join the audience.

I'm ushered off the stage with the other two guests of the evening. I'm the last one, so I know I need to get comfortable, but how? I'm a nervous damn wreck.

It's dark back here, and I can't stop myself from searching for sinful red hair.

But I come up empty.

I guess they're holding her to make a big entrance as well.

"Fuck, fuck, fuck," I mumble, and one of the production assistants turns his head, looking questioningly at me.

"I'm sorry—did you need anything?" He practically leaps toward me with the ambitious energy of an eager protégé.

"No, just talking to myself." I nod. "Don't worry. It's normal."

His smile is forced, as if he thinks it would hurt my feelings to tell me I'm weird. It wouldn't. After all, I got through high school where kids called me IBS, so this interaction is hardly embarrassing.

I sit in my designated chair as a makeup artist checks me to ensure I don't need any touch-ups. She's not as lively as Madi, and her touch isn't as gentle.

But I cut her some slack since I'm heavily biased.

Once she's satisfied, she leaves me with a parting smile, and it's not long before the studio fills with murmurs from the live audience taking their spots.

I open and close my fists as blood rushes to my ears while the other two guests—a singer and one model—do their segments.

I don't even comprehend what they say or laugh about, and before I know it, it's my turn.

This is it.

I'm putting my heart on the line in front of hundreds of thousands of viewers across the country—no big deal.

A few minutes later, the audience cheers as the cameras make a half-circle in front and above them for the beginning of the episode. Afterward, Lynn's voice booms across the studio with the opening line she repeated moments ago.

"Lights, camera… exes?" She folds her hands in her lap and crosses her feet at the ankles. There's a short applause before Lynn continues. "We have an extra special guest on tonight's show, and I can't wait to dive into his upcoming movie, his favorite kind of animal, and his relationship history with you all." She smiles, glancing around the audience and shifting in her seat. "So let's just jump right in. How does that sound?"

Another round of applause erupts, and it gets me on my feet, as ready as I'll ever be for my introduction.

"He's stolen the hearts of women everywhere, and he's made men want to take their fitness game more seriously because, hello abs! Am I right?" She tosses her hair over her shoulder. Lynn's a real natural on camera, that's for sure. "On top of that, you will see him next summer on the big screen in the upcoming sci-fi action film, *Ghost Predators*. Join me in welcoming Ian Brock!"

I lunge onto the stage and out of my comfort zone, thrusting myself into the spotlight—literally. Large pictures of me flash across the backdrop of the stage, ranging from premiere candids and headshots.

They're distracting, as are the bright lights, and I fight my urge to squint. They're so blinding, I can't even make out the audience, but I hear their applause. A few people in the front row gasp too as I walk to my seat, smiling and waving at them.

Lynn stands, holding her arms wide open for a quick embrace to greet me.

"Howdy," I tell her and nod again toward the spectators, raising my hand like I'm tipping a hat. Keith mentioned that greeting has become part of my brand and that I should keep doing it, but honestly, I probably couldn't stop if I tried.

It's part of *me*.

Once we settle onto our seats, facing each other, Lynn folds her hands again in her lap. "Thank you so much for being here tonight, Ian. This is definitely a treat for our viewers, as you can see and hear."

"I'm happy to be here. Thanks for having me." I nod, and my foot immediately starts bouncing, so I set my ankle over my other knee and wrap my hand around it.

"You have made quite the impression on Hollywood the last couple of years. How does that feel?"

We did a mock interview before the cameras started rolling, but I pretend it's the first I'm hearing it. I want to sound authentic, after all. "It's been exciting. Auditions are a thrill, and cast parties are a lot wilder than I expected, that's for sure."

"I bet everyone is asking this at home, so I'm going to help them out. What is the wildest thing that happened at one of those parties?"

"Let's see." I scratch my chin, thankful this was not a question she previously asked so this is a very real reaction. "We've broken into karaoke on the way out of a restaurant before, which was fun. Not for anyone listening, but it was for us."

Lynn waves me off. "I'm sure there's nothing you can't do."

"The stray cats crying in the alleys were better than me," I joke and hold a finger up. "Oh! But the actual craziest thing was a party I attended last year. There was a baby shark in a small saltwater tank at one of our producer's rentals. It was insane, but it made me want one." I chuckle.

"To be a fly on the wall at one of those parties." Lynn turns her attention toward the audience, holding her arms up. "Only a fly, though, because I don't think I could handle attending myself!"

I laugh along with her as she turns to the camera and says, "When we come back, we're going to dig into Ian's romantic life and see what his future looks like."

"And cut." The director scoots back on his swiveling stool, and the room buzzes with low whispers during the commercial break.

A woman brings both Lynn and me a bottle of water. Once she swallows her sip, she leans over and pats my knee. "Nice job so far. You're much better than the guy who was on last night. Some reality TV star. The asshole sneezed more than my Aunt Muriel during spring in Georgia."

I make a non-committal sound, distracted by the chaos in my head.

A few seconds and beads of sweat later, the director waves to count us down from the break.

When we're rolling again, Lynn is the first to speak, and she asks me about the movie. We talk about the writing and direction, and she asks about filming in New York too.

Which she uses as a segue into her next series of questions.

"Now, I have to ask about your romantic past. You are currently single, right?"

I give a tight-lipped smile toward the audience. "Yes."

"How does your busy filming schedule affect your love life?" Lynn asks, her voice filled with seemingly genuine concern.

Yeah, she's damn good.

I clear my throat and drop my foot onto the floor next to the other. "It's difficult. If I was a one-night-stand type of guy, my inconsistent schedule would be great, but I love being in a serious relationship. It's just hard for me to maintain one."

"A man like you is so hard to find." Lynn clutches her chest and frowns. "Is your schedule why you and your last girlfriend broke up?"

The lump in my throat forms more quickly and suddenly than a tall wave in the ocean.

Even with the little practice we had, this is harder than I thought.

Fuck.

"Partly," I answer.

"Tell us about her. She was your makeup artist while you filmed *Ghost Predators* in New York this spring, right?"

"Yes." I shift in my seat and lick my dry lips. "She was actually my high school sweetheart before that. We broke up the day of graduation and hadn't spoken until we showed up to the set."

A collective *aww* from the audience fills the space, and it eases the tension in my shoulders.

"That must've been a shock," Lynn observes.

"It was, but after some initial hostility and getting stuck in her hair salon, we picked up right where we left off."

"Sounds like an interesting story that we'll need to hear later." She winks. "So, what happened?"

"The same thing that happened the first time," I say,

sinking into my confession like I do this seat. The more I talk, the more I forget about the studio full of strangers or that I'm ninety-five percent positive Madi herself is listening.

I just speak from the heart. That's the entire reason I wanted to do this show, right?

"We live on different sides of the country, and I asked her to come out here with me. To drop everything and be with me." I laugh, but it lacks humor. "It was unfair, and I hope she knows how sorry I am. I'm sorry for a lot of things, especially for being too chicken to figure out a solution that worked for both of us. I gave up too easily, which is what I did back then too."

"Ian, I never would've expected such honesty from a guy like you."

"The new and improved Ian Brock," I tease, but I don't feel it.

She gives me a small smile, pauses for dramatic effect, then asks, "Would you like a chance to tell her how you feel?"

I knew this was coming.

This is a talk show where most of our chat has been rehearsed, but now that we've come to the reality of this moment, I'm taken by surprise.

I suck in a deep breath.

Here we go.

"Definitely," I confirm on an exhale.

She does a mini fist bump and angles herself toward the camera again. "More surprises when we come back after the break."

I exhale as the murmurs pick back up like the previous break. "This is why I often get so angry at commercials. They interrupt every *gasp* moment."

Lynn shrugs. "Part of the job."

I chuckle to myself and peer over my shoulder behind the stage. Where is she?

After a few minutes and several gulps of my water, we return to the show, and Lynn addresses the crowd. "Welcome back. What do you think? Are you ready for this next surprise?"

An echo of positive responses bursts from the crowd.

I grab hold of both armrests, preparing myself because rehearsals did nothing to curb this mixture of overwhelming emotions for me.

Madi is about to strut onto the stage like it belongs to her.

If she's still here, that is.

"Let's welcome Ian's ex, Madison Taylor, out here!" Lynn calls out.

I feel her presence before she comes into view. She's a force of nature more powerful than the heavy-duty fan we used while filming the finale of *Ghost Predators*.

When she stands in front of me, her lips pursed and eyes ablaze, I'm dumbfounded.

Completely fucking speechless.

I haven't seen her in over a month, and now that she's standing right in front of me looking sexy as hell, all I want to do is get down on my knees and beg for her forgiveness, then haul her back to my dressing room for some *alone* time.

But I can't tell from her expression if she'd give me the former and want the latter.

Impulsively, I jump out of my seat before she can take hers next to Lynn and pull Madi into my arms.

Lynn hugged me when I first came out, so it's normal, right? For me to hug my ex-girlfriend—the same woman I tricked into being my fake girlfriend at one point, then tricked again into being here today?

I'm definitely getting kicked in the nuts by the end of this.

She freezes in my arms, and instead of doing the smart thing and letting go, I hold on tighter. "What the fuck are you doing?" she hisses in the crook of my neck.

"I missed you," I whisper back.

Silently and subtly, she shoves me away, her back to the crowd, and I return to my seat, my nerves firing faster than a number on speed dial.

I'm suddenly glad I'm doing this. Although she looks anything but thrilled, it brought her here, and it's made me realize I'll do anything to be with her again, even if it means seeing her once every few weeks.

Madi would be worth it.

"Madison, we are all so excited you could join us tonight." Lynn grips her forearm and watches me out of the corner of her eye.

The only response Madi offers is a hum and forced smile.

"Did you hear what Ian had to say?"

The entire room falls deadly silent. Or it fades away. It's hard to tell since all I can see is the woman sitting across from me.

All I can hear is the beating of my heart in my ears.

All I can taste is her sweet mouth.

Madi's lips are light pink tonight, and her puff-sleeved dress has a low neckline that draws my attention to her cleavage, down to the cinched waist, until I settle on her lean legs, one crossed over the other in poised and graceful perfection.

I can't stop staring at her.

At Lynn's question, Madi lifts her head, her hair flowing in soft waves over both shoulders so effortlessly. There's a new shine to it that wasn't there the last time I saw her too.

She nods again, holding Lynn's gaze. "I did," she says, her voice hoarse.

"And what did you think?" Lynn maintains her composure, and I do too.

But I'm so close to cracking.

The sweat beading down my back is no longer because of the hot lights, but because of Madi.

How could I have let her go… again?

She doesn't immediately answer Lynn's question, and it feels like an eternity while we wait. I'm sure it takes her a few seconds because she's silently wishing she wasn't here.

She's obviously pissed.

I put her on the spot.

Shit. What was I even thinking?

This is the worst idea I've—

"I don't think anything about it," Madi says, then turns her steely stare toward me. "He didn't say anything I haven't heard before."

There's a low hum across the crowd, and I think I even hear a faint snicker from backstage.

"Can you elaborate?" Lynn asks, crossing her legs as she settles in for what will probably be her best episode of the year.

"Sure." Madi shrugs, her confident gaze bouncing between Lynn and me.

This is not going to go well…

"Ian and I broke up over a month ago, and the media had a field day over it, of course, which I expected. But they dragged me through the mud pretty hard and made fun of my cheekbones—an odd choice, if you ask me. In any case, Ian"—she points to me like she wishes she could be jabbing that finger into my chest—"didn't have the gall to call and check if I'm a wreck." She purses her lips and shakes her shoulders, obviously flustered. "I didn't mean to rhyme, but the point is that he disappeared on me yet again." She takes a deep breath, then finishes me off. "Ian Brock is as handsome as he is a coward. That pretty face just doesn't stick around, nor does he tell you if he misses you after he's long gone."

Her aforementioned cheeks are now a deep shade of red that is more from anger than humiliation.

She's not holding back, but then again, what did I expect?

I've ambushed her, and this is Madison Taylor. She wouldn't be herself if she didn't strut out here and speak her mind.

"Tell us how you really feel." Lynn's eyebrows lift into her hairline as she looks from me to the audience and back to Madi, a shocked expression covering her features.

We purposely didn't rehearse this part since we wanted this to be a totally genuine conversation, but I'm regretting agreeing to this.

"I would, but I know there's only so much time for this episode," Madi clips.

"Ian, what do you—"

"In my defense," I blurt, "I didn't see everything the media put out there, or I would've contacted each outlet myself. In fact, when I get home, I'll make a list and call them each individually. I'll do it." I spread my arms.

"What a fantastic waste of time," Madi throws back.

"I don't see you offering anything useful," I snap, and Lynn sits back in her seat like she's joining the spectators.

"Here's something—why don't you grow a pair?"

I lean forward, my frustration building, one word at a

time. "You didn't seem to mind *my pair* the entire time we were together."

I barely hear the gasp from those around us.

My blood is boiling.

To make matters worse, Madi's chest heaves with each breath she takes, and the tops of her breasts rise and fall, teasing and distracting me.

Scoffing, Madi holds her finger up, but I cut her off. "You want me to tell you what *I* think?" I pull my jacket off—the heat on this stage paired with the tension is too much. "You were just as scared as I was. You didn't want to take the leap with me because you thought I'd leave just like the first time. You were sitting around waiting for it, and when I did bring up the conversation of us, you literally opened the door and shoved me out of it instead of fighting for what we have."

"*Had.*" Her thin lips tighten, and heat pricks my skin. "What we had."

I'm moments away from turning the furniture upside down. She's as infuriating as ever.

Lynn interjects, "I am loving the raw emotions that are being spilled right now, and I'm sure you all do as well. Let's find out if this argument ends in what appears to be a *third* chance, or will these two call it quits once and for all?"

When the camera cuts out, Lynn dabs at her forehead with the back of her hand, her eyes bright and full of delight—the complete opposite of Madi and me. "Phew. You two are on fire." She cups her hand over her mic, leans forward, and whispers, "God, I imagine you two would be going at it on this couch if we weren't filming. Are you sure you're broken up?"

"Yes," Madi asserts, her eyes boring into mine as her nostrils flare.

"Can I talk to you in private for a second?" I nod to the side for Madi.

"Why?" She clasps her fingers over her knee, pushing her damn breasts together and making my mouth water. "You wanted me here for a very public conversation. Why should we speak in private now? There's plenty more to say on camera."

"Good, good." Lynn points at her. "Hold on to that rage. This is going to be so great for the viewers."

I blow out a rough exhale and fold my sleeves up my forearms, then adjust the collar around my neck to stop myself from feeling like I'm suffocating.

This is not going as planned. I'm getting my ass fucking handed to me on national television, and all I can think about is grabbing hold of Madi and showing her how much I've missed her.

And kissing her until she knows how much I love her.

We just have to get through this show in one piece first.

TWENTY-SEVEN

Madison

He wanted a war on camera, so that's what I'm giving him.

What the hell was he thinking by blindsiding me with this show in the first place?

This is so much worse than talking to Sarah about a job for me without asking me first.

Worse than when he told Annalisa—and the world—that we were together before we were actually a couple.

This might be even worse than the worm he threw in my hair.

I'm so angry, and my thoughts are jumbled more than the lottery balls in the big spinning machine they're drawn from.

Lynn fluffs her hair, and part of me wants to yank her extensions right out for laughing and making money over my disaster of a love life.

But I can't blame her, can I?

All the blame is saved for the man sitting across from me.

The one who's brooding and sexy in his pale blue shirt tucked into his snug jeans.

Ian's hair is tousled and free, and his golden tan is deeper now that he's back in his element. Right where he always wanted to be.

It all only pisses me off further to the point where my lips are twisted, and I'm taking it out on the couch. I'm about to rip a hole in the armrest with my fingernail from anxiously scratching at it.

How dare he suggest that I'm the one who was scared? It's such bullshit.

"We're back to either throw a bucket of water on the heated tension between this Hollywood celebrity and his ex... Or should we add fuel to the flame?" Lynn smoothly opens the show back up in her clever little way. "Madison, before the break, Ian threw some pretty heavy stuff your way."

"Yes, he sure is chatty after several weeks of silence, which I find especially interesting," I say, uncaring that there might've been a specific question she wanted to ask. Why stop now when I'm on such a roll? "And it's also *interesting* that he's trying to blame this on me when I'm the one who's been open with him instead of playing games." I wave around the studio. "This being one of many."

Ian clenches his jaw, and I know I'm about to win this thing.

Not that there are any winners besides Lynn and the network, no matter what ending awaits Ian and me.

"What other games do you mean?" Lynn asks, rubbing her hands together. Her eyes flash bright and curious, and I know it's because she's struck gold.

This just gets better and better, doesn't it?

"Do you want to tell her, or should I?" I watch Ian as his jaw tics, and guilt consumes his eyes, unlike the fury in them from before when I refused to speak to him in private.

What good would it have done, anyway? Even if he wanted to apologize and offer me a way off the show, it wouldn't have changed the mess he created the moment he stepped in front of the cameras and talked about us.

I'm just finishing what he started.

Never mind the ache in my stomach.

But instead of squirming like I thought, Ian softens his disdain and eases his grim frown into a real smile. "The first time I kissed Madi in front of cameras, we weren't actually together as we led everyone to believe. She was simply helping me put on a show for a different ex, who was still hung up on me."

I tense, glancing around for everyone's reaction.

"Before you ask if that ex would be hurt over this revelation, Lynn, she probably would be, but I already apologized to her directly for my actions. I even helped her patch things up with her new boyfriend." His grin widens the more he talks. "That same ex is the one who convinced Madi to be in LA today because, even though she's here for a job—one she originally told me she didn't want, by the way—she's really here because she missed me, too. And because she knows I was right when I told her she'd enjoy herself out here. She's just too stubborn and proud to admit it."

If I was smug before, I'm definitely not now.

Why is his confession not at all satisfying?

It was supposed to be. I hoped it would be this aha moment for everyone, who would then boo him off stage and draw devil's horns on all of Ian's headshots.

Instead, the show carries on in a lively fashion.

Well, not for me, actually.

Lynn jumps in. "That is a lot of information to process. How do you respond to this, Madison?"

Ian's accusation replays in my head, and it's hard to breathe as I blink back sudden tears. How do I respond, indeed? That he's right?

That I'm the one who was scared?

Ian comes in and out of focus as the tears become stronger, filling my eyes to the brim and threatening to spill in front of millions of eyeballs.

I don't know how long I'm quiet until I finally manage, "You want to know how I respond? Here it is." I gulp, and these lights seem to disappear like I'm inside a tunnel.

Ian stands on the other side, giving me the strength to voice my thoughts and feelings.

The ones lying deep down underneath the layers of anger.

"You're right," I mutter, facing him. "My first instinct was to let you go because the alternative was too overwhelming, but it wasn't fair of you to plan our future without giving me a say."

Ian stands and crosses the small makeshift living room to kneel in front of me, gripping my hand in his.

His touch is so warm and comforting, it shatters the wall I came in here wearing. The wall that was protecting me from feeling the love I still have for this man.

Because of course, I still love him.

Can this day get any crazier?

"I'm sorry. I was just too afraid of losing you, and I overstepped." His voice is deep and gruff.

Next to us, Lynn scoots to the other end to give us more space.

"You were right about the job too," I whisper. "I was terrified of such a big life change and needed time to figure out what I wanted. When Keith called, I knew I was ready."

He kisses my hand, his whiskey eyes dancing. "I love you, Madi. I've loved you since I first saw you in the cafeteria that day."

In my periphery, I see Lynn's hands fly up to her mouth, and it feels like the audience beyond the cameras is holding its breath.

Join the club.

"I don't expect this to fix everything. In fact, I fully expect to apologize repeatedly and pay for this whole production until I die." He chuckles, and his comment earns a soft laugh from the rest of the room. A watery laugh even escapes me too. "This is going to be difficult, but I'm fully prepared for it all. I want the good and the bad. I want everything if it's with you."

My lip quivers, unable to work with the rest of my mouth to form words. They're lodged in my throat as my heart beats faster and faster.

Looking into Ian's eyes as he says all these things—in front of all these people, no less—makes me realize this is exactly why I came here.

I wanted to see him and tell him I want all the same things he does. I would've preferred to do it in private, but what the hell. This works too.

Deep down, I knew we weren't over, and my anger quickly fizzles into warmth.

Ian slides onto the couch with me, the muscles in his arms flexing as he squeezes my hand and lifts it up to his lips. After he places a hot kiss to my palm, he speaks in a low voice that

I'm not sure anyone else can hear. "Madi, you've known me as Ian Bowman and as Ian Brock, and you've fallen for me both times. What do you say to a third?"

I squint, trying to bring him into focus, but it's difficult with the bright lights above and around his head forming a halo.

Not as difficult as it is to fight this thing between us any longer, though, and besides, I don't want to fight it. It's been hard enough being without him the last few weeks, and I don't want to wait another second before I tell this man how I really feel.

It's not going to be easy, but the leap will be worth it.

I cup his cheek with my free hand, sliding it up his smooth jawline until I'm holding on to the back of his neck, his hair in my palm. "I'm sorry I was ever afraid of this. Of you. I…" I lick my lips as I fight through the lump in my throat. "I love you," I say on an exhale, immediately relieved that they're finally out into the universe—quite literally since we're still rolling.

At least, I think we are.

My eyes are now watering from trying too hard to focus through the lights.

I barely notice Ian's smile before his lips are molding to mine, his body halfway on top of me. I even arch my back around the armrest and pull him closer, deepening the kiss and unleashing the last few weeks of pent-up desire.

Somewhere behind him, I make out Lynn's blurry figure as she stands to face the camera. She sniffles as she says, "I think we can all agree that this was a successful reunion. One that actually made me tear up, and you all know how rare that is. I'm just glad it's from the beauty of love and not

GEORGIA COFFMAN

from the pepper spray like on last week's episode." There's a low rumble of laughter before she continues. "Ian Brock has had his fair share of happy endings on the screen, and we are thrilled to assist with his real-life happily ever after. Thank you all for joining us tonight, and tune in tomorrow for an all-new episode. Spoiler alert: there's a pet hamster involved."

"That's a wrap!"

I smile against Ian's mouth as the room fills with chaotic sounds and crew members moving equipment around us. From the stands, a few women yell variations of "I will always love you, Ian" and cheer for us.

He drops his forehead to my shoulder, and his grin stretches just above my breast, his breath heating my skin the longer I hold him like this.

"You two are free to get a room now," Lynn calls out as she strolls past us. If her tears were real before, there's no indication in her eyes or tone now.

But I don't care.

She helped Ian and me get back together. They should give her a raise because when I first arrived, I didn't think that would be possible.

I just needed the truth to smack me out of my furious trance.

And he dropped a lot of truths. Ones I refused to face until I saw him again.

"Come on," Ian's gruff voice against my neck sends vibrating ripples through my body.

"Where are we going?" I ask as he grabs hold of my hand and leads me through a jungle of people, some of whom almost trip trying to pave a path for us.

"Excuse me," Ian says to each of them as he holds my hand

304

high above our heads. "Coming through. Hot lady in tow."

I give apologetic nods and smiles to them until we emerge into a hallway, my lips still tingling with the taste of Ian.

"Ah!" I yelp as he yanks me into a dressing room, and his urgency further riles me up.

"I need you," he whispers against my mouth through a throaty groan. "Now."

Pressing his body into mine, he pushes me backward until my shoulder blades hit the smooth wooden door.

"Then take me," I murmur back, working his bottom lip between my teeth.

I yelp again as he whips us both around, landing by the mirror, which feels oddly similar to the station at my salon where we made out.

But this is different.

We're open and in love and determined to keep it that way.

Each touch feels that much hotter.

Every swipe of his tongue that much more delicious.

I moan into his mouth as Ian ruffles the hem of my dress up and wraps his fingers around my upper thigh, his grip firm and possessive.

I'm weak in the knees.

My core is on fire.

Our breathy pants echo around us.

All the tension from before when we were arguing on stage has transformed into lust and intensity.

"Take me, Ian," I demand again, hiking my leg up and around his hip.

He fists my hair and kisses me once again as he thrusts his hips forward, and the edge of the counter digs into my ass.

My back hits the mirror so hard I'm nervous it'll break.

But I don't care enough to stop.

I just want Ian.

"You're fucking mine, Madi." He leans down to lick between my breasts while he runs both hands up the outside of my thighs until he reaches my thong.

Gasping, I rake my fingers through his dark hair, need pooling between my legs.

Ian deeply inhales as he rises back up for a kiss. "I've missed you."

"I've missed you too," I whisper, and a weight lifts off my chest.

In a blink, he rips the panties off my body with feral power and slips his middle finger inside me.

Finally.

"Yes, yes." My mouth hangs open as he slowly relieves the pressure in my core.

I fumble with his belt, my hands trembling with urgency.

I crave him like I do water.

The mirror and products left in front of it all rattle as we continue making out like the teenagers we used to be, our kisses harsher and more feverish than ever before.

Then he angles my head to the side so he can nip at my neck while he continues working me.

My parted lips drag across the side of his face as I release his belt and undo the button and zipper of his pants, blindly feeling my way around the front of him.

My eyes are squeezed closed, loving the way he slides his finger in and out of my drenched heat, but when he presses his thumb to my clit, I almost fall slack against the mirror.

"Oh my God, that's good," I slur like I'm drunk.

By the time I free him of his pants, I'm riding his hand, rocking my hips into him and making the mirror thud to our rhythm.

Unapologetic.

Relentless.

"Come here," he growls, and in quick, excited movements, he pulls his finger out, hoists both my legs up, and carries me over to the couch.

We fall onto the cushions with a bounce, and his weight on top of me is exactly what I need.

That, and his boxers out of the way.

"Get these off," I pant in his ear and claw at him.

"Mr. Brock?" a voice sounds from outside, followed by a knock.

"In a minute," he calls out, rising up.

He stands over me, tall and unruly, and his face is red as if he's going to burst.

And I'm more than happy to relieve that pressure for him.

I lick my lips and take the opportunity to slide the boxers down his lean thighs, his hard dick springing out of them, glorious and thick.

I bite my lip as I lie back down, my hair flowing to the floor, and I bring him with me.

"Wait. A condom," he rasps.

I shake my head. "Ian, I need you *now*."

"I am clean…"

"And I've been on the pill for a while now."

He shifts onto his knees, pulls me up onto his lap by my ass to position himself right where I need him, and thrusts down into me.

I sharply inhale as Ian fills me, and this angle creates friction that makes my head spin.

"We have to hurry," he whispers, flicking his gaze toward the door.

I nod, my eyelids fluttering as he pulls out, then drives back in with ease, every inch of his cock sliding against my clit and making me gasp with pleasure.

"That's it, Madi." He spreads my ass cheeks and plunges deeper into me, the corners of his dress shirt grazing the insides of my thighs. The extra sensation is welcomed and perfect.

Ian continues driving down into me fast and hard and wild until I'm halfway off the couch, and my hand slaps the glass coffee table next to us.

He bites out a curse.

I cry his name.

Panting, his hips jerk forward, and his cock pulses inside me.

His name becomes a satisfied sigh on my lips. My hands roam up his damp back, and one of my legs falls onto the floor. "Shit," I breathe, dropping the rest of the way.

Ian's laugh rumbles out of him, and he falls to the floor with me.

I giggle next to him, wrapping my arms around his waist as the blissful fog consumes me. Exhaling, I snuggle into him and ignore the people walking up and down the hall outside. "Thank you for making me do this."

"Sex?" He clutches his chest. "Ouch. I thought you were into me."

I smack his pec, still smiling—it might as well be tattooed on me now. "That's going to cost you one hamburger," I tease.

"And I thought you owed *me* one. Call it even?"

I hum, pretending to think about it. "How about we call it a date?"

"I'll have to check my calendar, but I think I can make it work."

I huff. "Now you owe me two hamburgers."

Ian kisses my cheek, then nuzzles his nose in my mess of waves, his voice sober and serious when he says, "I'll get you as many as you want. Just as long as you stay with me."

Pulling back, I hold his gaze so he knows I'm not going anywhere. That I'm in this for the long run. He's all I want.

"Forever," I whisper.

I said before that Hollywood moves quickly, each minute bringing with it the unexpected and all the excitement a person could ever need in a lifetime.

It brought me back to Ian, the best surprise I could've imagined, and if this town was a person, I'd be kissing its feet for it.

But I'll settle for a ride into the sunset, the top down, wind in my hair, and my hand in Ian's.

EPILOGUE

Ian

One year later…

Lights flash faster than my racing heart rate, so I grip Madi's hand and ground myself in this moment.

This career.

This life.

As if in slow motion, we take steps together down the red carpet back out the way we came in, side by side and in love. People beyond the ropes on both sides of us stick their hands out, calling out questions and making comments I can't decipher.

Many of them yell for me.

It's crazy and deafening and overwhelming.

I couldn't have gotten through the night without Madi here. She's held my hand since we stepped out of the limo for our grand arrival to the premiere. She even whispered the dirty things she would do to me tonight as we walked down the infamous carpet on our way inside.

We're making our exit now from a successful exclusive viewing of *Ghost Predators*, the movie that brought my woman and me together last year.

To think, I owe the best thing that ever happened to me to ghosts and several different realms.

We stop next to Annalisa and Patrick, who pose for pictures with fans and answer questions from the media, while we do the same. Madi waves to the other side and smiles, blending in perfectly with the rest of the cast and their plus-ones.

She and I have taken Hollywood by storm over the last year. We were even called this year's power couple by various magazines and online blogs.

Behind the scenes, we're just average, though, joking with each other while we grocery shop, waging silly bets while we run together, and getting naked any chance we get.

We've been doing a lot of the latter lately, especially since she moved into my place in LA and made it ours.

Madi and I moved into our own apartment in New York a couple months ago too. We bought and decorated it together, although Madi made most of the decisions with the decor. I just lifted the furniture and moved frames as she wished.

I also hid a few of the paintings she bought as a little move-in prank, but I'd forgotten all about it by the time she found them a week later.

She got me back by turning the hot water off—that was a doozy.

I've resumed a steady schedule of filming as new roles have started coming in like hotcakes, and Madi and I split our time between LA and New York. Since working with Rhett out here, she fell in love with the city and being a makeup artist, so after a lot of consideration, she decided to promote

Sofia to manager and take a much bigger step back from the salon, although she still helps out with clients and the back-end work from time to time.

I wouldn't have supported that decision had this new California lifestyle not caused a glow in her whole being. Knowing that it wasn't based solely on me is a relief, and I'm happy that things have fallen into place for both of us in every way.

"Let's stop here for a quick picture." Madi places her hand on my chest, angling herself into me and flashing a smile for the cameras.

"I didn't realize you'd love being in front of the camera so much," I say out of the corner of my mouth as I grip her waist.

"It worked out so well the first time that I thought I'd keep it up." She sways for a second pose, and it warms my chest. "Besides, this is all part of dating you. What kind of girlfriend to a movie star would I be if I didn't stop and say cheese for a few pictures?"

"Cheese?"

She peers up at me and makes a half-circle motion with her finger in front of my mouth. "See? It works. *Cheese*." Her wide smile is infectious, and shit, do I love that she's into all this.

At first, I wasn't sure how she'd adjust, but she's been a real trooper being in the spotlight. Sometimes, she's better at it than I am.

As Madi and I make our way to the limo waiting for us, Annalisa and Patrick mumble vague sexual references I'm glad I don't get the details of. And I count myself a lucky son of a bitch for that, but mostly because of this life I get to lead.

I'm not sure how it happened, but I plan on holding on to it extremely tightly.

After we duck into the limo, Madi scoots to make room for me on the leather seat, and I close the door after me.

"That was so damn fun." She smiles, rubbing a finger below each of her eyes. "I'm still shaking from all the excitement. Just… *wow*."

"You and me both." I chuckle, pulling her into my side as the driver peels out of here through a throng of people.

Eventually, we manage to steer out onto the main road and continue on our way home. I slide my sweaty palm down my pant leg, my adrenaline still higher than is healthy. Madi angles her body toward me, and her eyes sparkle like the dress she's wearing.

A hot fucking dress that's been torturing me for the last few hours since I haven't been able to do anything about it.

Yet, anyway.

I have big plans for her later.

But first things first…

"I am so proud of you." She cups my cheek and kisses the other. "You were amazing. I mean, I don't even like sci-fi films, but this one blew me away."

"Hold on." I lean back. "You don't like sci-fi, and you're just now telling me?"

She throws her head back and laughs, the strap of her dress dangerously close to falling down her shaking shoulder. "I couldn't tell you!"

"So you chose the night of the premiere to do it. Wow. I need a minute." I hold my hand over my face to shield her from me, but I can't help my chuckle.

It's not like she could ever confess anything that would make me love her less.

"Deep breaths," she suggests sarcastically as her phone buzzes from the pocket in the door. "In the meantime…"

I peek over to find she's checking her phone, and the light illuminates the subtle way her lips move as she reads a new text. If I had to guess from the number of calls she got on the way to the theater tonight, I'd say it's Bree trying to get insider information.

Or, it's Erin and Tessa asking when we'll be in town next.

They miss us as much as we miss them. I may not have known them for as long as the girls have known each other, but they've become my family too. We can't go too long without our dose of their brand of quirky and love.

"Bree says we both looked amazing tonight and that my dress was made for me by angels." She pauses again, then clicks her phone off and shakes her head. "My super crude friend also made a comment about your ass that I cannot, in good conscience, repeat, although I don't disagree with her."

"Oh, yeah? Why don't you come over here and show me how you really feel?" I ask, wiggling my eyebrows.

"Are you saying what I think you're saying?"

"Sex in a limo, baby," I whisper, my voice husky.

She narrows her gaze and leans in, lightly touching her lips to mine before she melts into this kiss, her tongue drawing mine out to play. I run my hand up her bare arm until I reach the tiny strap holding her dress up and slide it down, which causes the material covering her breast to drag down, nearly exposing it.

So close.

Instead of leaving it to gravity to do its job, I take charge and dip my hand inside, cupping her breast and eliciting a moan from her.

We're both high on this night.

This crazy energy is in the air swirling around us like a tornado.

She scoots closer, her tongue never missing a beat from massaging mine as she reaches inside my jacket.

Her hand roams across my abs and stops.

When she pulls back, I see her lips are swollen, and the sparkling dress is disheveled. "What is that? And how have I not noticed it all night?" She opens one side of my jacket and points to the inside pocket.

"You didn't spend the last few hours with your hand in my jacket, no matter how many times I tried to get frisky in the theater, for old time's sake." I wink and force a swallow, tamping down my urge to prolong what we were about to do—sex in a limo, for fuck's sake.

She rolls her eyes, then presses, "Don't leave me guessing."

I take a few deep breaths and calm my heart rate.

It's no use, though.

Tonight has been yet another dream come true, and it was such a fucking thrill to experience it with Madi.

I'm at a place in my life where everything is damn near perfect.

I even have a good relationship with my brother and his family. We saw them for Christmas, during which I made my dad and Cash extremely jealous that I'd had a hot dog at Nathan's. They were more peeved about that than they were over the time I met the Dallas Cowboys quarterback.

We played Dirty Santa together, which got ruthless between the adults pretty quickly. Poor Peter had to play referee, which gave us a good laugh over the holiday dinner Norma and Madi helped my mother prepare.

That trip also gave me the chance to speak with Madi's father in private for his blessing.

Like I said—it's all nearly perfect.

More so than a man's life should be, and if this is all just a big illusion, I want to bring it home before I wake up.

Pulling out the chunky square box from my pocket, I give Madi a shy grin.

Once she lays eyes on it, they bounce from the box to me and back down to the box in my hand.

"Madi," I start, emotion lodged in my throat. "I've actually been carrying this around for a few days, trying to find the right time to give it to you, if you choose to accept."

She covers her mouth with both hands.

"I almost did it on the red carpet in front of everyone because I want the world to know you're mine, and I'm yours. But I think they get it after all of our public stunts." My chuckle is shaky. "So, doing this in private after this surreal night seems like the best idea." I lick my lips, my thoughts muddled.

Hell, I can memorize pages and pages of scripts, but I'm drawing a blank right now to remember the short speech I'd rehearsed to tell this woman how much she means to me.

"Yes," she says, nodding enthusiastically, but in the same breath, her eyes widen. "Oh, I'm sorry. You didn't even ask, and I totally jumped the gun. I just... I really love you." She grips my jacket lapels. "This is real, right? Not like the time you were on one knee in our bathroom, and I freaked because I thought you were proposing by the toilet."

I laugh, sputtering, "Damn. I forgot about that."

"I just wish that was the only time you faked me out." I feel her glare as I wipe the happy tears from my eyes and look at her.

My laughter subsides, and I take her hand in mine, my chest swelling. "This is real. My love for you is real. This life we have together is very real, and I want to take the next step." I pop the box open, revealing a diamond ring that, admittedly, Annalisa helped me pick out. She caught me browsing ring designs on my phone during the *Ghost Predators* promotional tours, and I'm glad she did because she has great taste. By the appreciative way Madi looks at it, I'd say we did good. "Will you marry me, Madi?"

"Yes, Ian." She grips the back of my neck, leaning her forehead against mine. "I love you so much, and I can't wait to spend the rest of my life with you. You've always been my person."

I kiss her as the limo slows and comes to a stop in front of our house. "Let's get inside and do all the things you promised," I whisper.

"You read my mind." She opens the door but stops with one foot out, leaning over to grab the champagne bottle from its spot in the ice bucket. Holding it up, she says, "We are celebrating, after all."

"Damn right."

"Oh!" She stops again, this time with both feet on the ground outside. "The ring. I didn't put it on."

"Right. Fuck." I fumble to open the box again, not having realized I closed it, and take out the ring.

My hand trembles as I slide the slender band onto her finger, and she gushes over its design, using words like teardrop cut, which I became extremely familiar with while shopping for it.

Once it's all the way on, I kiss her finger and lead her inside, calling out my thanks to the driver.

As we walk up to our door, she grabs my arm, halting for a third time. "We have to take a picture! I need to show the girls. And my parents. And your family too."

I pull my phone out and turn the camera toward us, the limo in the background next to the flowers Madi and I planted together.

I don't need to say *cheese*, either, since my wide smile is still intact. Madi holds her hand up to show off the engagement ring, and I snap a few. Some are of me looking at her, excited to tell everyone the news.

"Let's get inside now," I whisper in her hair and place a kiss to her temple, my body humming with anticipation.

I'm about to make love to my fiancée, and I can't wait another minute. It's already been too long since I last had her.

Which was yesterday, but still.

I throw the door open, and she skips through it, calling over her shoulder, "We have Lynn's show next week for our one-year anniversary segment of getting back together!" She spins around, clapping. "I get to show off this rock on national television."

"That's right." I kick the door closed behind us and wrap my arms around her waist, pressing her back to me as we both stare at the shining ring on her hand.

"We'll have such good news to report," she squeals, turning in my arms. "But right now, it's just you and me. We have some celebrating to do."

She gives me a quick kiss, then holds the bottle of champagne above her head as she rushes to the bedroom, her other hand working the dress off her shoulders.

And I chase after my soon-to-be wife.

THE END

Want more of Ian and Madison? Check out your **FREE BONUS EPILOGUE** here:

HTTP://BIT.LY/SWTMSBONUS

ALSO BY GEORGIA COFFMAN

Stuck with You Series
Stuck with the Billionaire
Stuck at Christmas
Stuck with the Movie Star
Stuck with a Date
Stuck with the Boss

The Heat Series
Falling for a Stranger
Falling for a Player
Falling for a Bachelor
Back for Me (A FREE Short Story)

KB World
Heartbeat

The Salvation Society
Unbreakable

ABCs of Love
Official

ACKNOWLEDGMENTS

*T*hank you so much for reading! I hope you enjoyed Ian and Madison's story. This little romcom gave me a heck of a time. I started writing it, then set it aside for a couple months because these characters were giving me such a hard time. But when I dove back in, they were loud and ready to shine. And I'm so glad I didn't give up on them! Because their story was so worth it, and I'm so happy to share their HEA with you. Thank you again for giving them a chance.

A special thanks to Kelly for your honest feedback and insight into the movie biz. I so appreciate your encouragement, and I'm grateful for your check-ins because this book was not easy to write. But your help along the way made such a huge difference. You're the best.

Amanda, aka the best editor ever, a huge thank you! Working with you has changed everything for me. Your feedback is so valuable, and I can't tell you how much working with you means to me.

To my girls in the KKSB---Chelle, Mae, Claire, and Julia—thank you for your unconditional and constant love and support. This author gig wouldn't be the same without you, and I'm eternally grateful for our friendship.

The two people I always thank are my mom and husband, my biggest cheerleaders. Thank you for your continued love, support, and encouragement.

To my husband, in particular, thank you for being there for me every step of the way. For being patient when I'm daydreaming about a new story and for giving me ideas when I'm stuck. I love that you talk through plot problems with me, and I love you, forever and always.

ABOUT THE AUTHOR

Georgia Coffman is an author of steamy contemporary romances and romantic comedies. She has a Master's in Professional Writing and loves the TV show *Friends*, as well as shopping. She and her husband enjoy working out and playing with their two pups. Georgia loves to connect on social media or through email, so feel free to reach out with any questions, your fave book recommendations, or even a funny joke!

Newsletter
www.georgiacoffman.com/newsletter

Website
www.georgiacoffman.com

Facebook
www.facebook.com/authorgeorgiacoffman

Instagram
www.instagram.com/authorgeorgiacoffman

Pinterest
https://www.pinterest.com/authorgeorgiacoffman

TikTok
www.tiktok.com/@authorgeorgiacoffman

BookBub
www.bookbub.com/authors/georgia-coffman

Amazon
amazon.com/author/georgiacoffman

Goodreads
http://bit.ly/georgiaonGR

Verve Romance
https://ververomance.com/app/authorgeorgiacoffman

Manufactured by Amazon.ca
Bolton, ON